THE ROLL OF
THE DRUMS

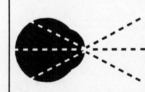

This Large Print Book carries the
Seal of Approval of N.A.V.H.

THE ROLL OF THE DRUMS

JAN DREXLER

THORNDIKE PRESS
A part of Gale, a Cengage Company

Thorndike Press, a part of Gale, a Cengage Company.

Thorndike Press® Large Print Christian Romance.
The text of this Large Print edition is unabridged.
Other aspects of the book may vary from the original edition.
Set in 16 pt. Plantin.

LIBRARY OF CONGRESS CIP DATA ON FILE.
CATALOGUING IN PUBLICATION FOR THIS BOOK
IS AVAILABLE FROM THE LIBRARY OF CONGRESS

ISBN-13: 978-1-4328-7195-6 (hardcover alk. paper)

Published in 2019 by arrangement with Revell Books, a division of Baker Publishing Group

Printed in Mexico
1 2 3 4 5 6 7 23 22 21 20 19

To my dear husband.
Thank you for your constant
encouragement.
Soli Deo Gloria

Thou hast turned for me my mourning into dancing: thou hast put off my sackcloth and girded me with gladness; to the end that my glory may sing praise to thee, and not be silent. O Lord my God, I will give thanks unto thee forever.

Psalm 30:11–12

1

"What would I do without you?" Ruby Weaver's sister, Elizabeth Kaufman, sighed as she sat on the edge of her bed.

"You'd probably sleep until noon." Ruby propped the door of the old cabin open as she took a deep breath of the morning air.

She stood in the doorway and threw her shoulders back, taking in the scene that stretched before her. Elizabeth's dingy cabin stood on a rise above the valley that had been home to the Weavers for more than fifty years. Weaver's Creek wound through *Daed*'s fields, sparkling in the morning light. The Berlin road made its way past the cabin before it ran along the slope down toward the creek and the farms beyond.

Ruby corrected herself. This was Reuben's cabin, not Elizabeth's. Once she had married Reuben, Elizabeth had given up everything that she could claim to be her own.

Her home, her name, even the clothes she wore belonged to the man who had gone off to fight for the South, leaving his wife and property behind. What was it about men that made some women lose all the sense the Good Lord had blessed them with?

She paused, the doorframe rough beneath her hand. She knew. She knew all too well.

Ruby leaned into the cabin and plucked her shawl off the peg by the door. Elizabeth still sat on her bed.

"I'm going to do chores." Ruby paused, watching Elizabeth yawn as she rubbed her face. "I'll bring the eggs in first thing, so you can start breakfast."

"I'll be ready for them." Elizabeth stretched. "I don't know how you can be so cheerful this early in the morning. Is the sun even up yet?"

"I still think you need to ask Daed or Samuel to put a window or two in this old place. Wouldn't the morning sunlight streaming in make everything more cheerful?"

Elizabeth shook her head. "You know I can't think about making any changes while Reuben is away. When he comes home, he's going to want to find everything just the way he left it."

10

Ruby settled her shawl around her shoulders without answering her sister. If Reuben came back from the war, Ruby doubted he would notice any changes that had taken place during his absence. He had left nearly a year ago and Elizabeth hadn't heard anything from him since that day.

When Ruby opened the door of the henhouse, the rooster strutted out ahead of his wives and flew to a fence post, ruffling his feathers in the chilly morning air. He crowed a few times, then hopped to the ground to grab his share of the cracked corn Ruby scattered for the chickens.

Last year when Reuben left to fight for the South in this terrible war, Ruby had volunteered to move in with her sister. At the time, it was to protect Elizabeth from having to put up with Ned Hamlin. Reuben had asked his friend to look in on Elizabeth and take care of her in his absence, but Ruby knew Ned and his ways. No woman was safe with him around. Two women, especially one who was experienced enough to see through his schemes, could keep him at bay, though.

Ruby closed her eyes. Had it been wrong of her to rejoice when Ned followed Reuben off to war? Had it been wrong of her to feel relieved when they got the news that

11

Ned had died in faraway Mississippi? She pulled in her bottom lip and bit it to keep her thoughts from running to the next thing, but it was too late. She couldn't pray that Reuben would meet a similar fate, but she could wish it, couldn't she? Glancing toward the cabin that squatted into the sloping ground like a gray toad, Ruby hoped Elizabeth didn't guess her thoughts. But perhaps Elizabeth had her own dark hopes concerning Reuben. In the past year, she had returned to acting like the little sister Ruby loved rather than the dim shadow she became whenever Reuben was present. Ruby feared the change wouldn't last once Reuben showed up again.

By the time Ruby returned to the cabin, Elizabeth was dressed and coaxing a fire to life in the smoking stove. Leaving the basket of eggs, she went to find the cow their brother Samuel had loaned to them. Without the milk and eggs, they would have had a hard time during the winter, even with *Mamm*'s canned goods to help stretch things. But the spring greens were already plentiful, and soon the garden would be giving them fresh vegetables. In a few weeks they could start picking berries along the creek bank and filling the root cellar with the summer's bounty. In spite of what the women in the church said, a woman didn't need a man around the house. For sure, sometimes it was handy for Samuel to stop by when they needed the garden plowed or the well cleaned out, but that didn't mean she and Elizabeth couldn't get by on their own.

When Ruby reached the cabin with the pail of milk, Elizabeth had the eggs cooked and a loaf of bread on the table. After their silent prayer, Elizabeth put her elbows on the table and leaned toward Ruby.

"Are you planning to go to Farmerstown today?"

Ruby dished half the pan of scrambled eggs onto her plate. "I wasn't planning to. I told Katie I'd stop by and help her with some sewing this morning. Why?"

"Harm Bontreger drove by while you were out milking the cow. He stopped and said he was on his way to the store if we needed anything."

"If Harm is making the trip, I don't see any reason why I would need to go." Ruby looked at her sister, suddenly suspicious. "What are you up to?"

Elizabeth moved the eggs around on her plate. "Nothing."

"You told him I was going to town, didn't you?"

"I said you might go to see if there is any mail for us."

Ruby laid her fork down on the table. "We've talked about this before. I don't want you trying to find a husband for me."

"Harm is a good man, and only a few years older than you are."

"Harm is a simpleton."

Elizabeth frowned. "You know Mamm doesn't like it when you talk like that."

"I only tell the truth."

"But you could tell the truth with . . ." Elizabeth took a sip of her coffee as she searched for the right words. "With gentleness and humility. Harm may not be the smartest man around, but he's very nice. And he likes you."

Ruby glared at her sister. "For the last time, I am not going to marry Harm Bontreger."

Elizabeth met her defiance. "Then who will you marry? He's the only unmarried man in the community that's close to your age, and you're not getting any younger."

Ruby ignored the stab. Her sister meant well. "If I never marry, it won't be the worst thing that could happen to me. Sometimes being alone is better than —" She broke off, realizing where her words were taking her.

14

Elizabeth's eyes brimmed with tears. "You're right," she said in a flat, quiet voice. "There aren't many things worse than marrying the wrong man."

Ruby grasped her hand across the table. "I'm sorry, Elizabeth. I wasn't thinking about what I was saying."

"I'm sorry too. I don't want to push you into anything, but I want you to be happy."

"I'm happy."

Elizabeth shook her head. "You're a lot of things, but you're not happy. You're hard. You seem to be trying to prove something to me, to the family, to yourself, and you don't have to. We love you the way you are."

Ruby laughed. "With my red hair sticking out all over the place? With my stubborn ways?"

"Even with all that." Elizabeth smiled. "You wouldn't be our Ruby without those things."

"Sometimes I wish I was more like you."

Elizabeth shook her head. "You don't want to be like me."

"You're kind and gentle. You would never call Harm a simpleton, no matter how much of one he is."

Ever since Elizabeth had been born, she had been the perfect Amish girl, exhibiting all the virtues Mamm tried in vain to instill in her red-haired daughter. Even the sad circumstances of her marriage had only made Elizabeth purer, as if she were gold being refined over a fire.

Ruby suppressed a sigh. "I don't know if the Good Lord intends for me to marry. Perhaps that is why he made me the way he did."

Elizabeth squeezed her hand. "Perhaps he has the perfect man for you, but you just haven't met him yet."

"Then he had better hurry. I'm getting too old to even be called an old maid. The children will start calling me Granny soon."

Now Elizabeth laughed, a sound so rare that it brought tears to Ruby's eyes. "No child would dare call you Granny! Auntie Rue, maybe, but never Granny!"

"How much farther, Daed?"

Gideon Fischer kept his eyes on his team's ears rather than answering his daughter immediately. At eight years old, Roseanna had taken on a burden much too heavy for her fragile shoulders, but hearing him admit that he wasn't sure where they were wouldn't help ease her mind. Clearing his throat, hoping a bit of cheer would be conveyed through his voice, he turned and smiled at the children.

"It can't be too far now." His smile faltered when he saw Lovinia lying on her cot in the back of the wagon, her face pale. If he didn't find a safe place for his family soon, his wife might not survive this illness. He forced the smile to return. "The folks at the store back there said that we'd find quite a few Amish families up ahead, along Weaver's Creek."

Three-year-old Ezra stepped over his sisters in the wagon bed to join Gideon on the seat. Grasping his son's trousers, Gideon helped him climb up. He smiled at six-year-old Sophia as Ezra's bare feet narrowly missed kicking her. She worried more than the others about her mother's illness. While Roseanna cared for the baby, Sophia had kept Ezra occupied on the long journey from Maryland. But her little face showed the strain of the last few months, with a pinching tension around her mouth that made her look much older than her years.

As Gideon urged the horses toward the crossroad ahead, he tucked Ezra close to his side. That must be the road the *Englisch* woman at the store in Farmerstown had spoken of. The ford through the wide, shallow creek was just as she had described, and the road on the other side would take them to their destination. After crossing the ford and making the turn onto the smaller road,

Gideon halted the exhausted horses.

"Just resting Samson and Delilah for a few minutes," Gideon told the children.

"Down?" Ezra asked, peering up at him.

At the same time, Sophia stood and plucked his sleeve. "There are flowers in the meadow, Daed. Can we pick some?"

Gideon wrapped the reins around the brake handle. "*Ja,* for sure. All of you should get out and run for a little. I'll stay with Mamm and the baby."

While the children ran through the meadow, Gideon sat next to Lovinia in the wagon bed, eight-month-old Daniel on his lap. His dear wife smiled at him and patted his arm.

"We're almost there?" Her voice was nearly a whisper.

When he clasped her hand, it was hot and dry. "I hope so. The woman who gave me the directions wasn't very clear about exactly where the Amish community is."

"Once we stop traveling . . ." She coughed, turning on her side as he supported her.

When the coughing spell ended, he finished her sentence. "We'll find a place to stay and good food to eat. And then you'll get better."

The children's laughter made Lovinia smile. "You'll make a new home for us,

18

husband."

He touched her cheek with the back of his hand. It was still hot. "We'll make a new home together, far from the war."

As Lovinia's eyes closed, Gideon stroked her cheek. How long could she go on like this, with every bit of her strength consumed by fever? Daniel fussed, rubbing his eyes. He was hungry again. They were all hungry.

Mein Herr . . .

Gideon faltered. The words wouldn't come. What could he pray that he hadn't already said?

During the weeks he had been held captive by the army, forced to transport their supplies in his wagon, he had worried about the family and the church he had left at home. Then when the company he had been with was defeated in their last battle and the few survivors taken captive by the opposing force, their commander had released him.

When he returned home, he found that his family had fared worse than he had imagined. While their neighbors had moved on, away from the constant presence of the armies and their insatiable appetites, Lovinia had stayed on the farm, unwilling to leave until she knew what had happened to him. But with only a few supplies over-

19

looked by the hungry soldiers, she had succumbed to worry and illness. By the time he had arrived home after six weeks away, there was nothing to hold them there, even if the scavenging soldiers had overlooked something they could survive on. All that was left was the worn-out team and his wagon.

Even his flock had scattered, leaving him a minister without a church. The young Amish community he had worked for ten years to help establish was gone.

Mein Herr . . .

Knowing that the army had intended to move north, into Pennsylvania, Gideon had loaded his family and a few possessions into the wagon and set out for the west. To the large Amish communities in Ohio. There, they would be safe. There, Lovinia could recover from this sickness. There, they could be a family again.

But would he . . . could he . . . fulfill his calling as a minister again? Would God use a broken man?

Gideon rocked Daniel in his arms until the baby fell asleep, and he laid him on the cot next to Lovinia. Roseanna and Sophia were bent over in the middle of the meadow along the road, looking at something on the ground. He climbed out of the wagon, careful not to wake Lovinia.

"Daed." Roseanna waved to him. "Look what we found!"

She held something in her hand. Something shiny and metal. Gideon broke into a jog.

"What do you have there?"

He tried to keep his voice light, but he could see what they had found. Buttons. Two round, brass buttons.

"Aren't they pretty?" Sophia held hers up to show him. The US eagle molded into the surface was clear enough for anyone to see.

"We found them here, on the ground," Roseanna said, crouching to push the blades of grass aside. "We found two. Do you think there might be more?"

Gideon stood, scanning the quiet crossroads. An army had been here once, and they could come again. His heart pounded in his ears. How long ago were they here? How long did they stay?

"I think you need to leave those here," he said, ignoring his daughters' disappointed faces. "Whoever lost them might come back to look for them."

"What are they?" Sophia asked.

"They are buttons," Roseanna said, then she held hers up to Gideon again. "Why is there a bird on the front?"

21

"It belongs to an army officer." Gideon pushed them back toward the wagon. "He'll be back to look for them, for sure. And it's time for us to move on."

Gideon picked Ezra up and glanced around again, knowing it was foolish to think an army might be close. Those buttons were soiled. They had been here for a long time, a year maybe.

But he still listened for the roll of drums.

Once they returned to the wagon, the horses had rested enough to continue. Gideon walked to relieve some of the wagon's weight, leading the team as the road sloped upward, away from the creek. They passed a lane leading to a house as they reached the crest of the slope, then Gideon stopped. In front of him, the valley spread out. The road they were on went down to meet the creek again, then followed it along the bottom of the valley. Beyond a wood, a large barn and farmhouse settled into the landscape on the far side of the creek. From there, the road swung to the right, away from the creek and past another farmhouse to disappear up the rise beyond.

Unbidden, a verse from the book of Matthew came to him: *"For I was hungry, and ye gave me meat; I was thirsty and ye gave me drink; I was a stranger, and ye took me in."*

Gideon bowed his head. Pride ate at him, rejecting that he and his family were in need. Refugees from the war they had left behind.

Mein Herr, you are teaching me humility. Once more. Help me to humble myself before you.

Gideon glanced behind them, still uneasy. The war couldn't follow them here. Ohio was a safe place.

"Is this where we're going, Daed?" Roseanna's voice called, laced with longing.

I was a stranger . . .

"I hope so, daughter." He climbed back on the wagon seat before driving down the slope to the creek.

As they passed another farm lane, one that disappeared into a stand of pine trees on the right, a young woman met them, striding down the lane with an unhurried gait that would fit better on a man. She wore a proper *kapp,* but no bonnet, and wild strands of red hair framed her face. Gideon's gaze met hers for a second, long enough to watch the coffee-brown eyes narrow and then shift to the wagon and the children watching her.

Gideon pulled the team to a halt, leaning on the brake handle. "We're trying to find the Weaver's Creek community —"

"You've found it!" The red-haired woman broke into his question as she halted and crossed her arms. He had spoken Englisch, unsure if he was in the Amish community yet, but she answered in Deitsch, his own language. "I'm Ruby Weaver, and my father's farm is across the stone bridge there."

A smile crept over her face as she looked back at the children and then at Gideon again. He blinked to keep himself from staring at her. So forward! Perhaps they shouldn't stop at Weaver's Creek but go farther into Holmes County instead. Perhaps the Good Lord might lead him to a more conservative community where the women acted more like women than men.

Then he glanced at Lovinia, asleep with Ezra and Daniel napping on either side of her cot, her raspy breath audible in the afternoon quiet. She couldn't travel any farther. They had to stop here, at least until Lovinia was better.

"Is there a place we could stay?" Gideon looked back at the young woman. "My wife is very ill."

"Ja, for sure. If you drive on to the house, we can ask my father where he thinks would be best."

"Daed, can she ride with us?" Roseanna didn't stop staring at the stranger. "She

24

doesn't have to walk if we're going the same way, does she?"

"*Ach, ne.*" The woman's laugh bubbled, a sound Gideon hadn't heard an adult utter in more months than he could count. The girls grinned. "I'll run on ahead and tell Mamm you're coming. She'll want to make sure you have a good supper."

Ruby Weaver ran toward the stone bridge as Gideon stared after her. When she had said she would run on ahead, he thought she had been using a figure of speech. But ne, she ran as if she were Roseanna's age rather than a grown woman. Roseanna and Sophia stood in the wagon bed, their heads on either side of him.

"I like her laugh," Sophia said.

"What do you think, Roseanna?" Gideon waited for his oldest daughter's answer.

Roseanna glanced down at Lovinia, then back at him. "I think she could make Mamm feel better just by smiling at her."

Gideon caught Roseanna's narrow chin in his hand and stroked her cheek with his thumb, thinking of the way the red-haired woman's presence had brightened the afternoon, even with her forward ways. "I think you're right, daughter. Shall we go meet the rest of the Weavers?"

Both girls nodded as Gideon started the

horses down the gentle slope. The road followed the creek at the bottom of the valley, then went to the right while Gideon turned the horses into the farm lane on the left and across the stone bridge.

Ruby had disappeared into the large white farmhouse ahead of them, and as Gideon pulled the team to a halt by the porch, an older man stepped out.

"Welcome, stranger. Welcome." He tied the horses to the hitching rail. "I'm Abraham Weaver. My wife, Lydia, is inside. She'll have a meal ready for you soon, but she's already pouring glasses of fresh buttermilk for the children."

"You don't have to —"

"For sure, we don't have to, but I can't stop Lydia when it comes to spoiling little ones." He lifted Sophia to the ground, then reached for Roseanna. "Ruby is making up the bed in Jonas's room." He peered over the side of the wagon where Lovinia and the boys slept. "We'll put your wife there and Lydia will take good care of her."

Gideon jumped from the wagon seat. "I'm Gideon Fischer, and my wife is Lovinia. I'm afraid she is quite ill. The trip has been hard on her."

Abraham glanced into the wagon again, his face grim. Gideon knew what he saw.

No supplies. A sick woman. Poverty.

"Where have you come from?" Abraham asked, turning his gaze back to Gideon.

"From Maryland, just south of the Mason-Dixon line."

"Did you see anything of the war?"

"That is why we left our home. The armies ravaged our farms, scattered the families of our community, and left us with nothing." Gideon swallowed, pushing past the pride. "We need refuge. Just until we can get back on our feet. Then I can pay you back."

" 'I was a stranger and ye took me in.' " Abraham smiled. "The Good Book only asks us to give, not to expect repayment. We have a place in our home for all of you, and you will stay with us as long as you need to. Perhaps you will find a new home for your family here in Weaver's Creek."

Gideon pulled his girls close as he glanced around the Weaver farm. "Perhaps we will."

"Do you live here too?" the oldest girl asked Ruby later that afternoon.

What was her name? Roseanna. That was it. "I live up the hill with my sister."

Ruby laid plates on the table for their supper while the two girls watched her.

"Sisters are little girls, not grown-ups."

That statement came from Sophia. Her

hair was so blonde it was nearly white, and the straight, fine wisps escaped her braids, making her look like a dandelion puff.

"Hush, Sophia." Roseanna frowned at her sister. "When we're grown up, we'll still be sisters."

Ruby hid a smile as she continued setting the table. Mamm took a pan of cornbread out of the oven. Ruby glanced at the big pot of ham and beans simmering on the stove and the apple cobbler she had made for dessert.

When Mamm had seen the Fischer family coming, she must have started planning the meal she could serve them. Otherwise, how could she have readied a supper like this so quickly? Only Mamm could be so well prepared.

Roseanna followed Ruby as she circled the table. "Who is your sister?"

"I have three sisters. Rachel and Miriam are married and live with their families several miles from here. Elizabeth is my younger sister, and we live together in her house."

"Do you have children?"

Ruby shook her head as she placed the last knife on the table. "I'm not married."

"Why not?"

If Mamm was listening to the girls' questions, she gave no sign.

"I'm just not."

Sophia tugged on Ruby's skirt. "You could marry our daed, then you could be our sister."

"That isn't how it works." Roseanna frowned at Sophia. "If she married our daed, then she would be our mamm."

Ruby couldn't keep back her laughter anymore. "That will never happen." She led the girls into the sitting room and sat on a footstool. "If I get married, it will be to a man who isn't married already."

Leaning against Ruby's knee, Sophia grinned up at her, showing an empty space where she had recently lost a tooth. "When I grow up, I'm going to marry Ezra."

Roseanna gave a loud, practiced sigh. "You can't marry Ezra."

"Why not?" Sophia's eyebrows rose in surprise. "He isn't married."

Ruby smothered a smile as Roseanna sighed again.

"Because he's our brother, and just a little boy. You have to marry a man, like Daed."

Ruby leaned back, bracing her hands on the edge of the stool behind her. She was glad for the silly turn the girls' conversation had taken, because she didn't have an answer to their questions. Contrary to what

Mamm was fond of saying, God didn't have a man for every woman.

"Tell me about your journey," Ruby said. It was time to change the subject. "Have you been traveling for a long time?"

"Forever and ever." Sophia ran her finger across Ruby's knee, feeling the fabric of her apron.

"It hasn't been that long," Roseanna said, correcting her sister again. "But it's been a long time. We had to sleep under the wagon."

What kind of father would make his children sleep on the ground? "Were you warm enough?"

"For sure we were." Roseanna smiled. "Daed slept with us and wrapped us in his big coat. We never got cold once."

Ruby pressed her lips together, mentally chiding herself for judging the children's father before she knew all the facts.

"Mamm and Daniel slept in the wagon." Sophia pressed closer, looking up at Ruby. "She coughs a lot."

"How long has your mother been ill?"

Roseanna looked away. "She got sick while Daed was away. She couldn't get out of bed, or even talk to us."

Ruby glanced at Mamm again. This time she was listening to Roseanna.

"Who took care of you?" Mamm asked, looking into the room from the kitchen.

"Roseanna did," Sophia said. "She even changed Daniel's diaper."

Mamm frowned. "The neighbors didn't help you?"

Roseanna shook her head. "They all moved away. But then Daed came home and Mamm felt better."

Ruby and Mamm exchanged glances. This family had suffered a lot before they reached Weaver's Creek.

Mamm smiled at the girls. "We're glad you're here now. And supper is almost ready. Would you go out and call Abraham and Ezra to come in? They went to look at the animals in the barn."

As the girls went out the kitchen door, Mamm pulled Ruby aside. "Their father has been upstairs with his wife and the baby in Jonas's room ever since they arrived. He needs to come eat with us, but he may not want to leave her alone. Will you offer to sit with her while he has his supper?"

"For sure, I will." She paused. "Don't you wonder what happened to the family? Why did their father leave them?"

Mamm shook her head. "I don't know, but we'll wait for him to tell us in his own time. We won't pester him or the children

31

with questions."

"You're right, but I hope he tells us their story soon."

Mamm tapped her finger on the end of Ruby's nose. "Your curiosity will get you in trouble one day."

"There's nothing wrong with being curious." Ruby started for the stairway. "I learn a lot of things that I'd never know otherwise."

She ran up the familiar stairs. To her right was the room she had shared with her sisters, and tonight the Fischer children would sleep in it. How long would they need to stay here? Ruby shrugged her shoulders. Mamm would insist that they stay until the mother had recovered from her illness, at least.

She turned left to go to Jonas's room but paused in the doorway. The man, Gideon, sat with his back to the door in a chair at the side of the bed, his head bowed in his hands. The baby sat on the floor at his feet, mouthing a string of wooden beads. The little one grinned when he saw her, drool soaking the front of his shift. The mother seemed to be asleep.

Clearing her throat, Ruby spoke softly. "Supper is ready. Mamm says you should come down and eat with the family. I can stay with your wife."

The face Gideon turned toward her was haggard and gray with exhaustion, but only for an instant. As soon as he saw her, his expression changed to the confident man she had first seen on the road. Ruby took a step back, feeling like she had intruded into his private moment of pain.

"Ja, for sure. The children . . ." His gaze dropped to Daniel, still chewing on his wooden beads. "I'm sorry . . . I just left them downstairs . . . Are they all right?"

Ruby smiled, determined to keep her questions about the family's past to herself. "They are fine, but hungry."

He stood, gripping the back of the chair as if he needed support, then nearly sat again as he looked at his wife's face.

Ruby stepped into the room and picked the baby up from the floor.

"Go," she said, her voice firm. "You need to eat. I'll sit with your wife and call you if she needs anything."

He took the baby from her arms as he nodded his acceptance. "Her name is Lovinia. I'll be back as soon as I can."

Ruby shook her head. "I'll stay until you see to your children and get them settled for the night."

"What about your supper?"

"I'll eat after I get home tonight."

"You don't live here?"

"My sister and I live at the top of the hill. It's only a short distance."

He sighed, sounding very much like his daughter. "If you think Lovinia will be all right . . ."

"For sure, she will."

His eyes met hers as he moved toward the door. "I . . . I don't know how to thank you and your family for everything you're doing."

She smiled. "You heard what my father said."

" 'I was a stranger and you took me in.' " A shadow of a smile appeared on his face.

"You aren't strangers anymore. Your daughters kept me busy talking all afternoon."

"Still, I don't know what we would have done without your family."

Ruby sat in the chair next to the bed. "Don't even think about it. Enjoy your supper."

He paused in the doorway. "Have you ever seen soldiers around here? Armies?"

"Not here, but sometimes they pass by on the road to Farmerstown. We can hear the drums as they march. Once a group camped at the crossroads."

34

"But they don't come to Weaver's Creek?"

"They never have."

He nodded his thanks and left. His footsteps sounded on the stairway as Ruby took her first look at Lovinia. The woman's breathing was labored, as if each breath was a struggle, but she seemed to be sleeping soundly. Ruby laid her hand on the flushed forehead and felt the heat of her fever. Mamm had made a poultice for Lovinia earlier in the afternoon, and Ruby prayed that it would help.

The children's mother was a very sick woman.

2

On Sunday morning, Gideon emptied cups of oats into the horses' feed boxes. He paused when he reached his own team. Samson and Delilah looked better for yesterday's rest, and they would be able to rest today too. Abraham had told him to grain his team. He said the oats would do them good.

But Gideon still hesitated. He was thankful for the Weavers' hospitality, but shame still crept up his spine as he considered the rich gift in his hand.

Samson whickered deep in his throat and extended his jug head toward the wooden scoop. The horse's nostrils opened wide as he breathed in the scent of the grain before Delilah shoved him aside and reached for the oats with bared teeth. Their hunger forced Gideon's decision to take advantage of Abraham's offer. His pride was no reason to withhold grain from the starving horses.

Later, sitting at the breakfast table with his family and Abraham, Gideon was reminded that the horses weren't the only ones who had been on short rations this year. His children ate everything Lydia had prepared before she went upstairs to sit with Lovinia. Ezra even ate bacon, something he had refused when they had last had it at home.

As he spooned oatmeal into Daniel's mouth, he looked at his own plate. His eggs were getting cold, and the gravy that had smelled so appetizing when he had ladled it over his biscuits no longer steamed. He had no appetite, but he needed to eat to keep up his strength. While Roseanna shared her eggs with her baby brother, Gideon forced himself to take a bite of his biscuit before he pushed the plate away. The little food he had eaten settled like a stone in his stomach. How could he enjoy his breakfast while his wife was so ill?

"You're coming to Sunday meeting with us?" Abraham asked as he scraped his plate clean.

Abraham's voice was pleasant, and the question was casual, but Gideon wasn't sure what to answer. "I don't want to leave Lovinia alone."

"Ruby will stay with your wife today."

Abraham went to the stove to refill his coffee cup. "A father needs to take his family to worship."

Gideon nodded. He had preached a sermon on that very subject, but it had been months since they had attended a worship service.

Lydia came down the stairs, a poultice in her hands.

"Your wife is awake and asking for you," she said. "She's feeling better today and breathing easier. The poultices are just what she needed."

Gideon rose. "I am beholden to you for all that you've done. I'll go and speak with Lovinia before we leave for the service." He paused, cupping his hand over Ezra's head. "I've been neglectful in so many things concerning my family, and if Lovinia is doing better, I will be glad to take my children to church."

Roseanna bounced in her chair. "Will you be preaching, Daed?"

Gideon glanced toward Abraham. "Not today, daughter."

"You're a minister?" Abraham asked.

The stone in his stomach turned. "That was a long time ago, and too much has happened since then." Gideon shook his head. "My preaching days are over."

Abraham leaned toward him, his elbows on the table. "If you were called to be a minister, that calling doesn't end."

"Unless the Good Lord himself makes it clear. I no longer have a church. There is no longer a flock for me to shepherd." He shook his head again. "Ne, I am no longer a minister."

Abraham didn't say any more, and Gideon went up the stairs, feeling the older man's gaze upon him. Abraham was right. When a minister was called, it was for life. But whose life? His? Or the congregation's?

Lovinia's eyes were bright and she smiled when he appeared in the doorway. She reached her hand toward him. "How are the children this morning?"

"Eating a good breakfast and happy that we aren't traveling today."

Gideon took his wife's hand as he sat in the chair. It was cool and dry. With his other hand he brushed her hair back from her forehead and let his palm rest on her brow. The fever seemed to be less today.

"Lydia said that her daughter Ruby would keep me company while you take the children to Meeting this morning."

"Do you mind being alone with her? I know how you dislike meeting strangers."

Lovinia gave him one of her beautiful

smiles. "She was here last evening, and I like her. She isn't fussy like some women can be." She squeezed his hand. "Besides, the children haven't been to a Sunday meeting for months. They need to go. But will you leave Daniel here?"

"Are you sure he won't be too much trouble?"

"I don't want to miss spending time with him . . . with any of them. And he will only fuss during the service." A shadow passed over her face as she spoke, and she averted her gaze.

Gideon took her hand in both of his and kissed it. "You're gaining strength quickly. Rest and good food are what you need, and the Weavers are generous with both. You'll soon be caring for the children again."

She met his eyes and smiled again. "Ja, for sure. You're right."

Hearing footsteps on the stairs, Gideon leaned over and kissed Lovinia's forehead. "I'll come back as soon as I can."

She tugged at his hand. "You will not. You will stay for the fellowship meal and learn to know the folks from this church. Then when you get home, I want to hear everything."

With a soft knock on the doorframe, Ruby Weaver came into the room. "You look

40

much better today, Lovinia."

She nodded at Gideon as she crossed the room and opened the window. The day promised to be warm and humid, with soft clouds scattered across the sky. Ruby's red hair was as wild as on the first day he had met her, with strands dancing above her kapp in the breeze from the open window.

"Are you sure it's a good idea to have the wind blowing into the room when Lovinia is so ill?"

Ruby flashed a grin in his direction as she tucked the blankets under Lovinia's mattress. "Mamm believes that fresh air is the best cure, as long as the sick person doesn't get chilly." She pulled a rocking chair from the corner of the room and took a seat. "As long as the breeze is as light as it is now, we shouldn't have a problem."

Gideon cleared his throat, chasing away the comment he longed to make about bossy women. Lovinia was smiling at Ruby as she rested on her pillows. Roseanna had been right. Ruby's presence was enough to make Lovinia feel better.

"Is it all right with you if Daniel stays with the two of you this morning?" Gideon tried to look everywhere but the young woman's face. "Lovinia asked if he could."

"For sure and for certain," Ruby said.

41

"Having the baby around will make the morning go quickly, won't it?"

Gideon was sure a wink passed between the two women, and Lovinia actually giggled. What did his family see in this forward girl that he didn't? No decorum, no sense of propriety. Not even the proper solemn mood fit for the Sabbath.

"Don't frown so, Gideon," Lovinia said. "It is so refreshing to feel a bit of joy after our long time of suffering."

A sudden fit of coughing caught them all by surprise. Gideon's heart pounded as he lifted Lovinia upright in the bed. He pounded her back with his fist, trying to loosen whatever was making her cough, but Ruby grabbed his hand.

"Don't hit her like that. You might break her ribs. Just support her."

Ruby grabbed a towel and Lovinia clutched it, holding it to her mouth. Her body was racked with the violence of the coughs, and every time she took air into her lungs, it triggered another bout. Gideon clung to her shoulders until Ruby loosened his grip and showed him how to allow Lovinia to lean on his arm.

Once the coughing fit was over, Ruby laid his wife back on the pillows. Her closed eyes were shadowed and thread-like blue veins

42

lined the paper-thin eyelids. Her body trembled with each breath.

"I should stay with her." Gideon's voice shook as he looked across the bed at Ruby. "If something should happen while I'm gone —"

"Nothing will happen." Ruby's lips were stretched in a thin line. "It's the poultice. It has loosened the congestion, and that is good. She needs to cough to clear her lungs." She smoothed Lovinia's hair from her cheeks. "If you were to panic like that while you were alone with her, I hate to think what might happen."

Gideon felt his face heat. "I didn't panic." He ground his teeth together to keep his voice even. "I was only concerned about my wife."

"You panicked. If I hadn't been here —"

Ruby stopped when Lovinia laid a hand on her arm.

"Don't argue about it." She opened her eyes, her color back to normal. "Gideon, you are going to take the children to Sunday Meeting. You will stay for the entire day, and when you get home, you will tell me all about the good people who live here in the Weaver's Creek community." She smiled at him. "I will be fine. Ruby and I will take care of Daniel, and I promise that I will rest

43

as much as I can."

Gideon hesitated, his gaze shifting from his wife's weak but confident smile to Ruby's composed expression. Roseanna's feet pounded on the stairs.

"Daed, we're ready to go," she said as she came into the room.

Lovinia held her arms out for Roseanna's hug, and then the girl tugged at Gideon's shirt.

"The Weavers said that it is time to go."

"Calm down," Gideon said. "I'm coming. You go on ahead and I'll catch up with you before you reach the road."

"I'll come downstairs with you," Ruby said, taking Roseanna's hand. "I need to get Daniel and bring him up."

Once they left, Gideon took Lovinia's hand again. "Are you sure you'll be all right?"

She smoothed his forehead with her other hand, then patted his cheek. "For sure, I will. Ruby will take good care of me."

Gideon kissed her forehead, then stepped out of the room. Before he descended the staircase, he glanced back at Lovinia. She had closed her eyes again, and her chest rose and fell with every quick, shallow breath. In spite of her assurances, Gideon felt a sudden fear that she would not recover from this illness. She was too weak, and she had been ill for too long. Even the Weavers' hospitality couldn't cure every illness.

By the time Ruby ascended the stairs with the baby in her arms, the families had crossed the stone bridge on their way to the Sunday meeting at the Beilers' home. Lovinia struggled to sit up when she saw Daniel.

"Let me help you," Ruby said, setting the baby on the floor.

Daniel crawled to the bed and grasped the quilt that hung over the edge, grinning at his mother while Ruby placed another pillow behind Lovinia's back. Then lifting Daniel, Ruby perched the baby on the edge of the bed where Lovinia could hold him close.

"This poor child," Lovinia said. "All he knows is a sick mother."

"He's almost nine months old, isn't he? Has your illness lasted that long?"

Ruby sat on the chair by the bed, ready to catch Daniel if he decided to try to crawl off the edge.

"I never felt like I recovered from his birth." Lovinia brushed Daniel's fine hair off his forehead. "I just couldn't get my strength back, even though the women from

45

our church brought nourishing meals and cared for the older children. Then when the soldiers started passing along our road, it was like a plague of locusts. They took every bit of food they could find, leaving us with only the little we managed to hide."

Ruby had no experience with soldiers, except when her brother, Jonas, had come home from the army for a visit during the winter. His uniform had caused no end of gossip in their little community, even though he worked in the army hospitals rather than carrying a gun.

"You mean the soldiers stole your food?"

Lovinia nodded. "Even if they had asked, I couldn't have refused them. The poor men were so hungry. I could see it in their eyes." She paused, her eyes focused on memories Ruby couldn't see. "One group butchered our milk cow, then the next took the sow and all the piglets. They tore down the fences to feed their campfires and harvested the oats before they were even ripe."

Daniel yawned, then laid his head down, snuggled in his mother's arms. Ruby looked out the window toward the neat, prosperous fields of her father's farm. Could the ravaging armies come as far north as Ohio?

"Where was your husband when all this was happening?"

Lovinia stroked the baby's back. "When the first group came, he tried to reason with them. But there were too many. After that, he would take us to hide in the woods to wait until the soldiers left." She rested her head on the pillow. "But then Gideon was gone."

"Gone?"

"He planned a trip to Oakland, fifteen miles away, to trade for some food for us. Most of our church had moved already, taking their families to Pennsylvania until the war is over, but the few that were left asked Gideon to make the trip for all of us."

Ruby leaned forward. "What happened?"

Lovinia shook her head. "I didn't know. He didn't come home from that trip. As the weeks went by, the other families gave up hope. They left, one by one, moving farther north, away from the armies. But I couldn't abandon our farm. Not without knowing what had happened to Gideon."

"You were all alone with the children." Now Roseanna's story made sense. "That's when you became ill."

"I was so afraid for them." Lovinia's voice was a whisper. "What would happen to them when I died? I prayed that I would survive long enough to make certain they would be brought up in a Christian home."

"But your husband did come home." Ruby smiled at her. "And you didn't die."

The corners of Lovinia's mouth trembled as she smiled. "Ja, Gideon came home. He had been forced to use his team and wagon to haul supplies for one of the armies. He finally came home when the company he was with was destroyed in a battle. He said the soldiers who weren't killed were captured, but the officers of the other side let him come back to us."

Daniel had fallen asleep, so Ruby laid him in the cot next to his mother's bed.

"Can I get anything for you?" Ruby asked. "Some tea? Or something to eat?"

Lovinia's face was pale against the linen pillow cover, and her lips had a pale blue tinge.

"Could you read to me from the Good Book? Gideon used to read to me in the evenings before he went away, but he hasn't since he got back."

Ruby ran downstairs to fetch Daed's old Bible from the shelf in the front room and a cup of water for Lovinia. By the time she returned upstairs, Lovinia had turned on her side and was watching Daniel sleep in his cot.

"I can't seem to look at him enough." She let Ruby help her sit up enough to drink some water. "My time with him has been so short, and I wonder if he'll remember me."

"Why wouldn't he remember you?" Ruby sat on the chair by the bed again. "You're so much better today than you were yesterday, and in another week, you'll be back to normal."

Lovinia shook her head as she settled back on her pillow. "I don't believe I'm going to recover from this illness." She grasped Ruby's hand. "Sometimes, I feel death in the room, as if it's waiting for me."

"Don't talk that way," Ruby said. "You're not going to die. Mamm knows all about nursing sick people back to health."

Lovinia smiled again. "I like you, Ruby. Every time you come into this room you bring sunshine with you."

Ruby grinned and squeezed her hand. "Most folks say I bring trouble with me."

"Why?"

"I know I'm too outspoken but can't seem to keep myself from saying whatever comes into my head."

"I consider that to be a good quality. You can always tell me what you think."

Lovinia pulled her hand from Ruby's and closed her eyes. Her face was still pale, and her breathing was shallow. For the first time, Ruby wondered if Lovinia's illness might be worse than it appeared.

"If you would rather sleep, I can read to you later."

"Ne, don't go. I don't want to be alone."

"Then I'll read while you rest." Ruby settled back in her chair.

Lovinia opened her eyes again. "I'm sorry I'm so selfish. You are missing the Sunday meeting and an opportunity to see your friends."

Ruby leafed through the pages of the heavy book. "Don't worry about that. I don't have many friends, so I won't be missed."

She turned the pages until she found the beginning of the book of Matthew in the New Testament. Glancing at Lovinia, she saw that the woman was staring at her. "What is wrong?"

"I can't believe you don't have friends. Kind people gather friends like daisies."

Ruby smoothed the stiff page of the old book. "I suppose Katie is my friend." She glanced at Lovinia. "Katie Stuckey, who lives just up the road. She is quite a bit younger than I am, but she is going to marry my brother Jonas as soon as the war is over and he comes home."

Lovinia smiled. "I knew you had a friend. Who else?"

"Elizabeth is my sister, and she's a friend too. But I live with her, so we spend a lot of time together. We get along well."

"What about the other women? The girls you grew up with?"

Ruby's thoughts went back to her school days. "They never liked me. When we were young, they used to tease me about —" Ruby pressed her lips together and stared at the page on her lap as the letters blurred together. The three other girls her age had always shunned her. "Now that we're all grown, they don't include me in their talk and gossiping." She shrugged. "They are all married and busy with little ones." Ruby let her gaze drift to Daniel, sleeping in his cot.

"So, you don't have anything in common with them?" Lovinia's face was still pale against her pillow, but the blue of her lips had turned to a healthier pink color.

Ruby shrugged again. "I don't care. I don't want to be friends with them, anyway."

"I don't think that's true. Every woman needs a friend. Someone you can giggle with and share secrets with. Can you do those things with Katie or Elizabeth?"

"Katie is preoccupied with her plans for the future, and Elizabeth . . ." Ruby didn't want to gossip about her sister. "Elizabeth has her own life to worry about."

51

"Then I'll be your friend, if you'll let me." Lovinia was smiling, her face brighter than Ruby had seen her before.

"You don't even know me."

"But I like you, and I'll grow to love you, just as you'll learn to love me." Lovinia reached out and Ruby took her hand. "Please, Ruby. I've been so lonely."

Something tickled in the back of Ruby's throat, and she swallowed. She knew what it was like to be lonely. "All right." She couldn't keep back a smile as Lovinia squeezed her hand. "I'll be your friend."

"And I'll be yours." Lovinia relaxed against the pillow, still smiling.

"But now you need to rest." Ruby turned to the book in her lap again. "I'll only read as long as you close your eyes and don't talk."

"I promise," Lovinia said, but she didn't close her eyes right away. A tear slid from the corner of her eye. "Thank you, Ruby. You don't know how much better I feel, knowing you're here."

Ruby pasted a frown on her face. "I mean it. No talking."

Lovinia smiled and closed her eyes. Ruby started reading aloud, concentrating on the list of names in the genealogy of Christ. When she reached the end of chapter one of Matthew, she glanced at her charge. Lovinia's face was relaxed, her breathing even, but a trace of a smile still rested on her lips.

A friend.

Ruby closed the Bible, rose from her chair, and started to go downstairs. She paused at the top of the stairs and glanced back into the room to make sure both mother and son were still sleeping. Lovinia coughed a little and turned on her side but didn't awaken.

Would the friendship Lovinia offered last once she was well again? Or would she recoil at Ruby's outspoken ways like everyone else did?

Gideon sat on the backless bench next to Abraham, his head bowed. Abraham would think he was praying, but no prayers would come.

Mein Herr . . .

Did he even belong here anymore? Since he had last been to a Sunday meeting, he had witnessed horrible things. He had never known that men could be so cruel to each other. The worst part was that he had done nothing to stop the madness. He had only stood as a silent witness, even when death fell at his own feet.

Mein Herr, forgive me.

How could he even ask for mercy?

Someone sitting toward the front of the room started singing the first hymn, and the rest of the congregation joined in. Gideon knew it well and forced himself to mouth the words. He raised his head and glanced across the aisle at Roseanna and Sophia, sitting with Lydia. Roseanna knew the hymn as well as he did, and Sophia watched her face, repeating each slow word that rose and fell with the chanting music.

When the hymn reached the end of the second stanza, "He who on earth does Thy will, know us as Thy children," Gideon's voice broke. He had never felt farther from God. The Lord was silent.

Gideon cleared his throat and continued singing the next verse. The words spoke of praising Christ and thanking him for his favors and his protection from sin. His heart beat so loudly that Abraham must be able to hear it, but the older man made no sign that anything was amiss. Gideon took a deep breath, then another. His knees shook and he wiped beads of sweat from his nose, but he could not make himself conspicuous by leaving the service.

Mein Herr, have mercy.

He took another deep breath and joined

54

in the fourth verse of the song. This verse was about how sorry the sinner is in his sins. Unrepentant sins. The plight of the man who nurtures his soul-destroying pride and who ignores God's warnings.

Mein Herr, I heed your warnings. Help me humble myself under your righteous hand.

His gaze found Roseanna again, and he felt strength returning to his limbs. The Lord knew he didn't participate in the war more than he had been forced to. Hauling supplies, helping the cooks, splitting wood . . . he did only what they forced him to do, but he did nothing against his conscience. Except that one, terrible moment.

How many times did he need to ask for forgiveness before he felt the peace of being part of God's family again?

When the service was over, Gideon left the house with the other men, leaving the youths to convert the benches into tables for the fellowship meal. Instead of following the men to the shaded area by the barn, though, Gideon walked to a fence that lined the crest of the hill behind the house. A panorama of peaceful farms lay at his feet. Farms that had never known the ravaging forces of an army.

"It's beautiful, isn't it?"

Gideon's overwrought nerves jumped at

the sudden intrusion. He hadn't been aware that anyone followed him, but the young man striding toward him wore a friendly expression. His round face was red from the exertion of climbing the hill, but his smile never faltered.

"Ja," Gideon said. "It is lovely. And so peaceful."

The younger man joined him and gazed at the scene, his hands resting on the top board of the fence. "From here you can see most of the farms in the community. The stream is Weaver's Creek, and you can see the Weavers' barn behind the trees down there in the valley." Then he turned to Gideon and held out his hand. "I'm Levi Beiler. I understand you and your family are staying with the Weavers."

Gideon shook his hand. "We are traveling, and Abraham was kind to offer to let us stay with him and his family for a time."

"Abraham said you might consider settling here."

Gideon kept his tone noncommittal. "We might. My wife is ill, so we'll stay at least until she is able to travel again."

Levi looked back toward the house where the men stood in groups near the barn and the children played a game of tag in the shady yard. "Do you know what illness she

56

suffers from?"

Gideon caught the shadow of a frown flash across the younger man's face, and he felt the stiff wall of resentment rising in his own heart. "Ne, but it is not catching. None of the children or myself have experienced any illness."

Levi flushed, his face turning a deeper shade of red than it had held before. "I'm sorry. I didn't mean to be rude. I heard some folks talking, and I only want to set their minds at ease."

Gideon relaxed. Levi was young, but he spoke with a reassurance in his voice that was sincere. It told Gideon that Levi had discerned the defensiveness he had tried to conceal but still pressed on to get the information he needed to protect the community from an unknown disease. It was an unusual quality for a man his age.

"Your last name is Beiler?" Gideon asked, changing the subject. "Are you related to Amos Beiler, who preached this morning?"

"Ja, for sure." Levi smiled. "I am his son."

"How many ministers are in the church?"

"Only one now, since Bishop Miller moved west to Indiana a few months ago." Levi dug into the grass with the toe of his shoe. "Abraham mentioned that you are a minister. My father has been saying that our community could use another."

Gideon shook his head. Not him. "I have a sick wife and a family to care for, and I don't know how long we'll be staying around Weaver's Creek. If there are nominations for a new minister, I won't let my name be put in."

Levi's shoulders relaxed. "Unless God ordains it . . ."

Gideon nodded, an automatic response to Levi's words. "For sure, unless God ordains it."

But God wouldn't. God didn't use men like him in his church.

"Well then," Levi said, taking a deep breath. "That's settled."

His words were quiet, not directed at Gideon.

"What is settled?"

Levi's eyes widened, as if he hadn't meant to say the words out loud. "I just meant that I'll know not to nominate you, that's all."

"Did you have someone else in mind?"

Levi didn't answer but kicked the grass again. "Since you're a minister, can I ask you something? And you won't tell anyone else?"

"I'm not a minister anymore, remember?" Gideon leaned against a fence post. "But I won't share anything you tell me if you don't want me to."

"Before you became a minister, did you already have a . . . a feeling that God was calling you to be one?"

Levi's face was serious as he waited. Gideon looked out over the valley, thinking back to that Sunday meeting more than five years ago when his name had been put forward in the nominations.

"Not until my name was called as one of the men who had been nominated." Gideon turned to Levi. "Then I knew, as if God had spoken the words out loud. I knew the lot would fall to me."

Levi nodded. "I know that feeling. It's as clear as opening a door and seeing beyond it to a different world on the other side." He wiped his forehead with the back of his hand. "I've never heard anyone else talk about it, though."

"I've never mentioned it, not even to my wife." Gideon frowned as he looked out over the scene below. "It is prideful to claim that God has spoken to you."

The younger man nodded. "He speaks in Scripture, in his Word. But this other . . . he doesn't use words, but somehow I know that I will be a minister someday."

"But you haven't told your father or your friends?"

"For sure and certain I would never do that." His face reddened again. "My friends would laugh at me, and Father would be angry. He scolds me for reading his books, saying that a boy like me can't possibly understand them. But I do, and I can't stop reading them."

"What kind of books?"

"The Good Book, of course. And the *Martyr's Mirror.* Father also has Augustine, Luther, and Zwingli. He recently bought a book by Menno Simons, and that is one I long to read."

"Then you are a scholar?"

Levi's face flushed again. "I can't stop reading and memorizing. I've memorized the hymns in the *Ausbund,* and now I'm working through the prayers in the *Christenflicht.* Sometimes I feel that it's wrong to fill my head with all these things, but I can't stop. I have a thirst that can't be quenched."

"Has your father told you that it is wrong?"

"Not in so many words, but he doesn't want me to speak of what I'm reading or discuss it with me. He wants me to spend my time working on the farm, as if he's the only one who should be concerned with books." He kicked the grass again. "Sometimes he acts like he's ashamed of me. I

60

know he would like me to be more like his other sons."

"I take it that your brothers don't spend their time reading." Gideon covered his mouth to keep from smiling. He remembered feeling the same way about his uncle when he was Levi's age. It seemed that every decision he made displeased Uncle Eli, but even as a young man, Gideon had known how he wanted to live his life.

"I don't know what they do. But they don't take after Father. They are tall and strong and work hard. They live in Illinois, and from the news they share in their letters, they have large, successful farms."

Taking in Levi's soft face and round body, Gideon could see that this young man would have a hard time keeping up with most farmers.

"I have a volume of Menno Simons's writings. You're welcome to borrow it."

"Could I?" Levi's eyes lit up. "You wouldn't mind?"

"Come by the Weavers' sometime. I'll have it waiting for you."

"This afternoon? Or this evening?"

Gideon grinned. Levi's eagerness was contagious. "I'll have to get it from the box in our wagon, but this evening would be all right."

Levi nodded, his hat nearly falling off. "I'll be there."

"Won't you miss the young people's Singing tonight?"

"It doesn't matter." Levi looked at the sun as if he was calculating how many hours he would have to wait until evening. "Books are more important."

Gideon found himself laughing. Suddenly, he felt far away from the struggles of the last several months.

3

By the time the last of the families had left the Beilers' farm on Sunday afternoon, the sun was finally heading toward the horizon. As far as Levi could tell, everything was ready for the Singing tonight. Millie and a couple of her friends were in the kitchen, giggling as they set out the snacks for the evening. Mother had gone to her room to lie down for a nap before the rest of the young people returned, and Father was in his study where he spent every Sunday afternoon.

He knocked on the closed door.

"Come," Father said.

When Levi opened the door, Father looked up from notes he was writing. He sat at his desk, just as he always did when he wasn't working in the farm fields. Levi had never seen him sit in the front room with Mother, or even linger at the table after meals. The study was Father's, and his alone. Levi stood in the doorway, not daring to set a foot in the quiet room while Father was there. He waited until Father finished writing a sentence, then looked at him.

"Well?"

"I wanted to let you know that I'm going to the Weavers' for an hour or two. I won't be too late."

Father frowned. "The Singing is here tonight. You should stay home."

"I'll be back before it ends."

Blowing on the page to dry the ink, Father perused what he had written before closing the notebook. "You won't find a wife that way."

Levi sighed. He had given up on finding a wife after Rosie Keck had married and moved to Wayne County, and Katie Stuckey had refused him last fall. He would never find another girl like Katie.

"I saw you talking with that new man this afternoon." Father's eyes pierced as he started the interrogation Levi knew would come. "What was his name again?"

"Gideon Fischer." Levi knew better than to try to hurry Father through his questions.

"Did he say why his wife wasn't here with him?"

"He said that she is ill."

Father smoothed his beard with one hand, a gesture Levi recognized as the prelude to a long interview. "You made certain that it is nothing catching? We never know what illnesses outsiders may bring into the community with them."

Levi let the comment pass. "I asked him, and Gideon assured me that only his wife is ill. He and the children are well. I don't think her condition is contagious."

"How did this . . . Gideon?" Father paused, looking for Levi's nod that he had remembered the name correctly. "How did this Gideon seem to you?"

"You mean, will he and his family fit in with the rest of the community."

Father's sharp look told Levi that he came close to overstepping his bounds. "Did he seem acceptable of our ways?"

"He didn't speak as if he felt anything was other than he expected."

"Abraham Weaver said this man was a minister in Maryland before he came here. Did you ask him about that?"

"He said he wasn't interested in taking on that role here. He isn't certain how long he will be staying."

Father nodded. "Good. Then we don't need to worry about him pushing in before we learn to know him."

"I liked him." Levi had never volunteered information in a discussion with Father before. He stood straighter. "He looked tired and worried, but he was also friendly and willing to talk. I think he needs a safe place to rest and help his wife recover from her illness. He isn't looking for anything more."

"So far." Father smoothed his beard again. "Will you see him when you visit the Weavers?"

Levi couldn't do anything but give Father a straight answer. "For sure, I will."

"Why is it so important that you go over there tonight?"

"Gideon has a book he said I could borrow."

Father threw his hands up in the air in a dramatic gesture. "A book! Now the next week will be wasted while you read a book instead of applying yourself to your work on the farm."

"I promise I won't let it interfere with my responsibilities."

"It already has. It's taking you away from home when you're needed here to help your sister and your mother." Father tapped his finger on the desk blotter. "You are too quick to forget your duties on the farm and stick your nose in a book. I don't know how

66

you expect to get married and start a family if you're reading all the time."

Levi didn't have an answer to that comment. He had heard it too many times. He waited.

Father turned back to his notebook, opening it to the page where he had been writing, and dipped his pen in the inkwell. "Go now and get the book. But don't dawdle and be back here as soon as you can."

"Yes, Father."

Levi closed the door behind him and went toward the kitchen. If Mother was still resting, he could slip through to the door without Millie and her friends taking too much of a notice of him.

Silence fell as soon as he appeared in the big kitchen. The girls were making sandwiches and slices of bread covered the table. All three girls had been buttering the slices while they talked. When Levi paused, the girls looked at each other and giggled.

"Am I interrupting anything?" He grinned at Millie.

"Nothing we want you to listen to," she said, then giggled again. "And the sooner you get out of here, the sooner we can get back to our visiting."

"Don't mind me." Levi stopped behind Millie on his way through the kitchen, leaning over her shoulder to snatch a slice of bread from the table. "I'm on my way to the Weavers'."

"Aren't you coming to the Singing?" Millie's round eyes showed her disappointment.

"I'll be back before too long. If I'm not here when it starts, I'll be here soon after."

Millie smiled at that. "There are cookies on the cupboard shelf. But don't take too many."

Levi wrapped two cookies in his handkerchief, then he was out the door and on his way to the Weavers'.

The bread was good, as Mother's baking always was, and Millie had spread a generous amount of fresh butter on it. But as satisfying as it was, it didn't match the anticipation of reading a new book, and with Father's permission. Perhaps this meant that Father was finally recognizing that Levi was more like him than he thought.

Levi finished the slice of bread in two bites, brushing crumbs off his fingers. Father would see that he had one son who wanted to follow in his footsteps.

Ruby's days quickly fell into a new routine. She and Elizabeth would have breakfast together, but then instead of working in the garden with her sister, Ruby would head down the road to the home farm to help Mamm with the Fischer children and spend time with Lovinia. Even though Lovinia's health didn't worsen, it didn't seem to be improving, either.

After two weeks, Lovinia still didn't feel strong enough to come downstairs. Rising to care for her personal needs exhausted her, and afterward she would sink back into the bed, pale and breathing as hard as if she had run to Millersburg and back.

On Friday morning when Ruby arrived, Mamm, Daed, and Gideon were still sitting around the breakfast table. Ruby had seen the three older children playing near the barn, but Daniel was in his high chair chewing on a crust of bread. He grinned when he saw her, but the adults' faces were grim. Mamm rose to fetch a cup of tea for her, and Ruby sat between Mamm and Gideon.

"Lovinia took a turn for the worse last night," Mamm said as she set the teacup in front of Ruby and sat down. "I don't know what more I can do."

"The poultices aren't helping?"

Mamm shook her head. "They seemed to ease the congestion, but she isn't getting stronger."

Ruby looked at Gideon. "Do you have any idea what is wrong with her?"

He gripped his cup, not looking at her. "I don't know. She hasn't had a fever since the day after we arrived, but she is so weak."

"Should we call a doctor?" Daed looked around the table. "He might be able to tell us what she has and help us treat her the correct way."

Gideon sighed. "I don't have money for a doctor."

"I do." All three of them looked at Ruby. "Remember when I went to help the Hostetler family when their baby was born? They insisted on paying me, but I've never spent any of it."

"I can't take your money," Gideon said, frowning. "I'll have to think of another way."

"Why can't you use my money for a doctor?"

"She's my wife. My responsibility."

"She's my friend, and we're a community. We help each other. I'm not using the money for anything else, and I'm not likely to. So I'll give it to you for the doctor." As Gideon's frown deepened, she stood up. "Don't argue with me. You know I'm right."

Gideon slumped in his chair. "All right. Where do I go to find the doctor?"

"There is one in Berlin," Daed said. He

stood too, ready to stop talking and act. "I'll hitch up the wagon and go with you."

Ruby got a cloth to clean up Daniel's messy hands and face. "Stop by Elizabeth's on your way. She knows where I keep the money."

Suddenly, she was anxious to see Lovinia. Surely, she couldn't be as ill as the others thought. Yesterday she had been fine.

Ruby picked Daniel up in her arms, giving him a noisy kiss on the cheek. She caught Gideon watching her, his frown gone. Mamm was at the sink, starting to wash the dishes, and Daed had already gone out the door toward the barn. The sound of the children's voices greeting him drifted in through the open window, but Gideon didn't move to follow him. He reached to take Daniel from her arms, but the baby buried his face in Ruby's shoulder, teasing him, and Gideon patted his back instead.

"He likes you."

Ruby kissed the top of the baby's head. "Only because I've spent so much time with him and Lovinia."

"All the children like you."

Gideon's face held a sad expression Ruby couldn't interpret. Perhaps it was resignation.

"And I like them." She smiled, wanting to

pull him out of his mood. "Things will get better, I'm sure of it. The doctor will prescribe a treatment and Lovinia will get well."

He gave her a small smile. "Lovinia says you're her sunshine, and I can see why. You're a good friend for her, and I thank you for that."

As Gideon followed Daed to the barn, Ruby climbed the stairs with Daniel. She peered in the bedroom door and found Lovinia lying in bed waiting for her.

"How are you this morning?" Ruby set Daniel on the floor where he could play with the toys she had put in a basket for him.

Lovinia's face was pale, but she looked peaceful. "I'm all right, but I know Gideon is worried. What were you all talking about downstairs?"

"Daed and Gideon are going to Berlin to fetch the doctor. They are afraid you aren't getting better."

"The coughing has come back, and I had a bad spell last night."

"Then I should take Daniel downstairs and let you sleep. You need your rest so you can get better."

"I'm only tired, but not sleepy. I'd like for you to read to me, but I have something to ask you first." Lovinia opened her eyes again. They shone bright blue in her pale face. "You might be right, that I will recover from this illness, but if I don't —" Her words broke off as she started coughing.

Ruby helped her turn over and gave her the towel to hold to her mouth. When the coughing fit finally ended, Lovinia lay back down on the pillow, exhausted and even more pale than before, and the flecks of blood on the towel were larger than they had been last week. She breathed slowly, then looked at Ruby again.

"If I don't survive, I want to make sure my children have a loving mother to raise them." The corners of her mouth trembled. "And Gideon . . . he's a good man. A man of God. Kind, hardworking, and loving. He needs a wife that can help him learn to laugh again."

A tear trickled from the corner of her eye to the pillow, and she wiped it away. Ruby's own eyes filled with tears as Lovinia reached for Daniel, resting one hand on his head as he played on the floor.

"I'm sure Gideon will be able to find another woman to marry if it comes to that." Ruby blinked to chase the tears away. "You don't need to worry about that now."

"Ja, I do. Gideon won't know what to do,

and he will think he's betraying me if he marries again. But he needs to, for his sake and for the children." Lovinia paused to catch her breath. "I want you to marry him, Ruby. You're the kind of woman Gideon needs for a wife and the kind of mother I want for my children."

If Lovinia's face hadn't been so pale, Ruby might have laughed. But the woman was serious.

"Not me." Ruby shook her head. "I'm not the right type of woman to take on a family. You need to look for someone like my mother."

A smile crept across Lovinia's face. "You don't realize how much like Lydia you are." She took another breath. "Please tell me you'll consider it. That's all I ask. I'll rest easier if I know that you're thinking about it."

"All right." Ruby took the Good Book from its place on the bedside table and opened it. "I'll consider the idea, but it won't be necessary. You'll be well again before you know it." She turned the pages to the book of Psalms. "Should I read the Shepherd's Psalm?"

"Ja, I like that one." Lovinia turned on her side, her face peaceful. "And after that, would you read the Gospel of John? Start at

74

the beginning and keep reading, even if you think I might be asleep. I'll be listening." She gave Ruby a smile. "I am so glad the Good Lord brought us here. You are like a sister to me."

"The Good Lord certainly brought us together." Ruby patted Lovinia's hand, then turned to the Twenty-Third Psalm and started reading. " 'The Lord is my shepherd, I shall not want.' "

She glanced at Lovinia. Her friend's expression was peaceful, but her lips and fingernails were tinged with blue. She bit her bottom lip. What if Lovinia was right? After all this suffering, would her illness only lead to death?

Ruby turned back to the book on her lap. Only the Good Lord knew the future, and she could trust it to his hands.

Gideon stood with his hands clasped behind his back as the doctor examined Lovinia. Curling tendrils of gray encircled the man's bald head, bent in concentration as he moved his listening instrument over Lovinia's chest. The little man leaned over the sick woman, his short body bent at nearly a right angle.

Glancing up at Gideon, the doctor beckoned him. "Help me turn her onto her side."

Gideon crouched beside the bed as he turned Lovinia to face him.

"Don't look so worried," she whispered.

"We need absolute quiet, please," the doctor said as he pressed the stethoscope to Lovinia's back.

Gideon answered his wife with a smile. But why shouldn't he be worried? Her skin was nearly gray, and her breathing was labored. But her eyes remained the clear blue he remembered from their courting days.

"Take a deep breath, please."

As Lovinia obeyed the doctor's request, her breath hitched, then she coughed. Gideon gave her the cloth Lydia kept draped over the headboard. When she finished coughing, he saw the specks of blood that had become normal to him, but the doctor took the cloth and examined it closely.

"Hmm." He glanced at Gideon again, his bushy eyebrows thrust upward. "You can help her lie on her back."

The older man perched on the chair at Lovinia's bedside, hooking his heels on the rungs the way Sophia or Roseanna would.

"Now, my dear," he said, taking Lovinia's hand. "How long have you been ill?"

"A long time." She didn't look at Gideon. "Since before the baby was born."

Gideon ran his hand over his beard. He had been busy with the farm, with the church, studying for his sermons . . . How had he missed that she was ill? Or did she hide it from him?

"You have more than one child?" At Lovinia's nod, the doctor went on. "Tell me about the times before and after their births. Did you feel ill then, also?"

This time Lovinia gave Gideon an apologetic glance as she nodded. "Each time was harder, but I didn't want to worry my husband."

"Shortness of breath? Tiring easily? Feeling dizzy?"

"Ja, ja, ja. All of those things." When the doctor frowned, she said, "But it always went away after a few months. I thought this would too."

Gideon leaned forward, taking Lovinia's hand. "Do you know what it is, Doctor? What can we do to help her get better?"

The doctor glanced at Gideon, then spoke to Lovinia. "Keep resting and eat well. Let others do the worrying and the work." He laid both hands on his knees, pushing himself to his feet. "I'll have a word with your husband and then I'll be on my way."

Lovinia closed her eyes, exhausted by the doctor's visit, while Gideon followed him down the stairs and out to his carriage.

"How long will it take for her to get well, Doctor?"

The little man put his black bag in the carriage, then faced Gideon with a sigh. "She won't get well, young man. Not without a miracle."

Gideon's knees turned to water. "That can't be. She's only weak from so many months of hunger and worry. Now that we're here, away from the war, she'll get better."

"It's her heart, the poor child. It is very weak and has been for many years." He removed his glasses and polished them with his handkerchief. "Her heart is defective. It doesn't pump the blood in the correct way, and it never has. It affects her lungs and her ability to breathe well. It also affects how oxygen moves to other parts of her body."

"But rest will help, won't it? You told her to rest."

The doctor gripped Gideon's arm. "I am so sorry, but the only thing rest will do is to give her more time. Frankly, I am surprised that she has survived this long, especially after giving birth to four children."

"How much more time do we have?"

"A week, perhaps a month or two. There is no telling."

78

Gideon stiffened his legs, his mind searching for a way to understand the doctor's words.

The man continued. "You need to know what to expect. Her heart may give out suddenly, or it may just slowly stop beating. She may pass away in her sleep, and that would be a blessing." He wiped his eyes with the handkerchief and put his glasses in his vest pocket. "You need to be prepared for the end, and you need to prepare your family."

Gideon's gaze found Roseanna and Sophia playing near the barn with Ezra. Abraham had built a playhouse for his grandchildren, and the three were in the middle of a game, jumping in and out of the little building. Ezra's carefree giggles reached him from across the barnyard.

"How?" He looked at the doctor. "How do I tell my children that their mother is . . . is going away?"

"I can't tell you how to do that. But you're a religious man, aren't you? The Good Lord will help you when you need him."

The doctor climbed into his carriage while Gideon untied the horse from the hitching rail. His fingers were numb, and he fumbled with the knot, but then with a wave, the doctor was on his way.

Gideon gripped the hitching rail, his head reeling. He couldn't lose Lovinia. She had to get better. The children needed her. He needed her. How could someone who enjoyed life so much lose it when she was so young?

Footsteps on the porch reminded him that he was not alone. Ruby stepped to his side, her eyes searching his face.

"What did the doctor say? Lovinia is going to recover, isn't she?"

Gideon shook his head, not trusting his voice. He swallowed. "He said her heart is weak."

Ruby pressed her fingers to her lips. "It can't be. He could be wrong."

"I would like to believe that, but I know she is suffering —" His voice broke. She had been ill for years, and he hadn't noticed. He had been too wrapped up in his own work, believing that her tiredness was a passing thing. "I don't know how to tell the children."

"You should go to her, first," Ruby said. "I'll care for the children, but you need to be with her."

Ruby wiped away a tear that trickled down her cheek, pulling her bottom lip in between her teeth. The corners of her mouth quivered, but she gave him a smile.

"Lovinia needs you now. She needs you to be strong. Let her know that you and the children will be all right after she's gone. She worries about you."

Gideon glanced toward the upstairs window. The dark pane reflected the afternoon light. Even now, Lovinia's heart could be taking its last beat. He couldn't waste a minute of the time they had left together.

He laid his hand on Ruby's. "Will you tell the children? About Lovinia? They love you and trust you. I don't think I can do it."

She paused, then drew her hand out from under his. "I could give them the news, but they need to hear it from you. You're their father."

Ruby was right. He needed to be with his children when they heard this. He squeezed his eyes closed. How could he tell them something so painful? How could he comfort them when he couldn't find comfort for himself?

"Will you be there with me then, when I tell them?" His throat tightened, and he looked at the woman beside him. "If they ask questions, I won't have the answers for them."

She nodded, her freckles dark against her pale skin. "We will do it together with the Good Lord giving us strength."

Gideon turned away and headed toward the house and Lovinia. *Mein Herr. Where are you? I feel like you have abandoned me in my hour of need once again.*

He took the stairs two at a time, then paused in the doorway of the bedroom. Lydia had come to sit with his wife while he had been outside, and now the older woman rose from the chair.

"I'll be downstairs if you need me." She drew him out of the room and onto the landing at the top of the stairs. "When she goes to sleep, will you come down and let Abraham and me know what the doctor said?"

"Ja, for sure."

He slipped into the room and took Lydia's place in the chair.

Lovinia opened her eyes and smiled when she saw him. "I'm glad you came back."

"Shh. Don't talk. Save your strength."

She ignored him. "I know what the doctor told you. I'm going to die, aren't I?"

Gideon's throat squeezed at her words. "You've always been stronger than I am. The thought of losing you scares me like nothing else I've ever faced."

"You'll be fine without me." She took his hand. "The Good Lord will give you the strength you need."

Mein Herr, I don't need your strength. I need my wife.

"I want you to promise me something."

Gideon tightened his grip on her hand. "Anything. I'll do anything you want."

"I want my children to have a stepmother who loves them, and I want you to have a wife who can work alongside you in ways that I've never been able to do."

"Don't talk about that. We need to spend our energy on making you well."

Lovinia lay back against her pillows, waiting until her breathing returned to normal. "I'm not going to get well, and I don't want to spend the time I have left arguing with you and worrying about the children." She rested again. "I want you to marry Ruby."

The memory of his first sight of Ruby Weaver flashed through his mind, with her manly stride and curly red hair escaping from the confines of her kapp.

"I can't marry Ruby." He shook his head. "I can't even consider marrying someone else. Lovinia, don't ask this of me."

"I didn't ask you if you wanted to marry her, I asked you to promise me that you would." Lovinia's chest rose and fell as she struggled to catch her breath. "I love her like a sister, and I know you will grow to love her too." She squeezed his hand in hers, but her grip was weak. "Promise me, Gideon. Promise. Please."

"Lovinia, I —"

"Promise me. Then I can rest assured that you and the children will be taken care of."

Gideon watched Lovinia's face, the dark circles around her eyes and the blue-tinged lips. Her life was so fragile . . .

"Ja, for sure." At his words, her set mouth relaxed. "I promise. Whatever you want, I'll do."

4

The days passed quickly with early summer sunshine. Daed spent his time in the fields with Samuel and his sons, working to get the crop planted and growing well, but Ruby barely noticed anything that happened outside of Lovinia's sickroom and the time she spent with the children.

A week had passed since the doctor's visit. A week since Gideon had asked her to help him tell the children about their mother's health, but they still hadn't had that conversation. In fact, she hadn't talked with him at all except for the grunt he gave her as a greeting each morning. He gave no sign of when he planned to speak to the children. Ruby sighed as she finished putting away the breakfast dishes in Mamm's kitchen. Poor Gideon. The only thing he was thinking about now was his wife and his family. He had even refused Daed's offer to let him help in the fields, saying he didn't want to leave Lovinia's side for more than a few minutes.

Lovinia had told her that Gideon had promised to marry her, if Ruby agreed. She didn't know what his thoughts were regarding Lovinia's request, but as the possibility flitted through her mind, Ruby shuddered a bit. She didn't blame him for not speaking with her about that. She didn't want to look past this minute into the future without Lovinia, either.

Hearing the children's footsteps on the stairs, Ruby wiped off the table in preparation for the rest of the day. Each morning after breakfast, Gideon took the children to visit Lovinia, then Ruby kept them busy until dinnertime. Gideon would eat dinner with the children while Ruby sat with Lovinia, then she would take over the child care again while Gideon spent the afternoon at his wife's bedside.

Ezra and Sophia ran over to her.

"What are we going to do today?" Sophia asked.

"The garden needs weeding, so we'll start there. Mamm is already out there, working without us."

Ruby smiled at Sophia, then looked beyond the children to Gideon and Roseanna. Gideon held Daniel in one arm and Roseanna clung to his other hand, her face sober. Ruby's heart sank at the sight. The young girl knew, even without anyone telling her, that her mother was dying. Ruby blinked back tears that threatened to fall and took Daniel from his father's arms. Now was the time when Gideon needed to tell his children. They needed to be prepared for the storm that would shake their young lives.

She glanced at Gideon, his face carefully still and flat. No sign of emotion showed beyond the pinched lines around his eyes and mouth.

"Gideon?" Ruby waited until those sad eyes turned toward her. "It's time."

She had spoken softly, but Sophia had heard her. "Time for what?"

Gideon held her gaze for a slow second, then turned toward Sophia. "I have some news for you. Let's go into the other room and talk."

The children gathered around their father as he sat in Daed's big chair. Ruby sat on a footstool nearby with Daniel on her lap. Oblivious to the growing tension in the room, Daniel stood on her knees, holding her hands while he bounced. Ruby set the baby on the floor where he teetered, the edge of her apron knotted in his hands as he balanced on his feet.

Roseanna said, "I know what you're going to tell us." She lifted her chin, standing with her feet slightly apart as if she was expecting a blow.

"What is it?" Sophia asked.

"Mamm is —" Roseanna broke off and her shoulders sagged.

"Mamm is very sick," Gideon finished for her.

"Is she going to die? Will we have a funeral? Can I wear my Sunday dress?" Sophia looked from her father to her sister as she asked the questions.

"Hush up." Roseanna turned toward her sister, her face twisted in a frown. "It isn't a party. Don't be so stupid."

Gideon lifted panicked eyes toward Ruby, and she tried to give him a reassuring smile. He was asking for her help.

"Roseanna, you must be patient with Sophia," she said.

The eight-year-old turned her fury on Ruby. "You don't know anything about it." Her red face crumpled as tears streamed down her cheeks. "Your mamm never died. Your mamm never got sick." She pushed past Ruby and ran out the door.

Gideon buried his face in his hands while Sophia and Ezra stared after their sister. Sophia had also started crying and Ruby reached for her.

"This wasn't the best way to tell you about your mamm," she said, drawing the little girl close.

"I know she is sick," Sophia said, taking a breath. "Is she going to die today?"

Ruby glanced at Gideon for help, but he stared at the floor, one arm around Ezra, who leaned against his knee with his thumb in his mouth.

"We don't know when she will pass on," Ruby said. "That is in the Good Lord's hands, and only he knows how soon it will be."

"Why is Roseanna angry with me?"

Ruby kissed the top of her head. "She isn't angry with you. She's angry and sad and doesn't know what to do."

Sophia nodded as if Ruby's explanation was enough. "Can we go play?"

Ruby glanced at Gideon again. He hadn't moved.

"You and Ezra can go help my mother in the garden. She would like your company."

Sophia took her brother's hand and led him outside. Part of Ruby wanted to follow them, to find Roseanna and comfort the girl, but Gideon still sat in the chair, a picture of desolation. Should she leave him alone?

"Are you all right?"

He lifted his head and stared at her. "I don't know what to do with them. I don't know what Lovinia would say to comfort them." He gave a short, barking laugh. "Part of me wants to do exactly what Roseanna did. I want to yell and hurt people and run away." He ran one hand over his face. "I don't want this to happen. I don't want to go through this, and I don't want to live without Lovinia."

Ruby stroked Daniel's hair. He had stuck the knotted fabric of her apron in his mouth and was chewing on it. She had no words of comfort for Gideon, but she felt the same frustration.

"It doesn't seem fair that she should suffer this way." Ruby looked back at him, struck by the open anguish in his face.

"Lovinia told me she asked you to —" His voice broke. "To take her place in our family."

Ruby felt her face grow hot. Discussing that possibility with Lovinia had been difficult, but she hadn't realized how embarrassing it would be to hear her husband mention it.

He swallowed. "I want you to know, I'm not going to hold you to any promises you might have made to her."

She cupped Daniel's head in her palm. "I wouldn't expect you to, except I promised I would take care of the children, and I would consider . . ." She wiped away a tear that tickled her cheek. "I will take care of the children, just as I have been. I won't break that promise."

Gideon looked away with a long sigh. "*Denki.* I'm grateful." He gripped his knees. "I won't expect anything more from you. Lovinia can't expect me to keep such a promise."

Ruby narrowed her eyes. "You should. Lovinia was clear that she thought you would need my help too, as well as the children."

"Did she say that?"

"She said she wanted me to help you learn to laugh again." Ruby leaned toward him, this stranger that Lovinia loved so much. "She is my friend, and I love her dearly. She loves you and worries about you, and I won't let her down."

"Did she . . . did she say anything about . . . marrying me?"

Ruby nodded. "I didn't promise I would, though. She seemed content that I would think about it."

"My wife is a stubborn woman sometimes." He lifted his head again and

91

searched her face. "She made me promise. She wouldn't rest until I did."

Ruby's stomach flipped.

"I can't go back on my promise, as much as I want to." His eyes opened wide as he realized what he had said. "Not that I don't think you would be someone I might marry someday. I didn't mean to imply that you aren't good enough."

Ruby smiled. Even with her grief at losing her friend at any time consuming her, the situation still struck her as funny. Ironic. "I understand. You would rather not be in the position to fulfill that promise."

He nodded, relief flooding his face. "Maybe Lovinia is right, that I need you to help me laugh again. I tend to take myself much too seriously."

"And I don't take myself seriously enough."

Gideon smiled at her. "We do have one thing in common."

Ruby nodded. "We both love Lovinia and want what is best for her."

"If she knows we have discussed this and are considering fulfilling her wishes, do you think that will be enough to let her rest easy and not worry about the future?"

"I hope so." Ruby felt Daniel sagging against her knee, so she picked him up and held him close. "I don't want to mislead her, though."

"We won't." Gideon stood. "I'm going to go find Roseanna and talk to her. Do you mind sitting with Lovinia until I get back?"

"Not at all. Daniel is ready for a nap, and she'll be happy to spend some time with him until he falls asleep."

Ruby stood just as Gideon took a step toward the door. Their near-collision brought them closer together than was proper, and Ruby took a step back. But not before she felt the solid presence of the man. He put out a hand to steady her, then went on his way. Watching him, all she could think of were Lovinia's words, how he was strong, kindhearted, and loving. A man of God. No matter what happened, she could see herself loving him for Lovinia's sake. Loving him like a brother and a partner in raising his children.

Gideon knew where Roseanna had gone when she fled the house. Even though the Weavers' farm was large, Roseanna had found a favorite spot in the big haymow. He found her there now, snuggled in the soft hay and looking out the big open window toward the east.

Mein Herr, help me.

"Roseanna?"

Her shoulder twitched, but she didn't turn toward him.

"Daughter. We must talk. I don't want you to be so sad."

She turned toward him then, her eyes red and puffy from her tears. "I don't want her to die. I want to go home and have things be the way they were . . . before."

When Roseanna reached her arms toward him, he crossed the nearly empty loft in two strides and sat next to her, taking her in his lap. He hadn't realized how much she had grown in the past months until he saw that her long legs no longer fit on his knees the way they used to. He held her against his chest as she cried, tears flowing down his own cheeks.

After a few minutes, he gave her a quick squeeze. "It is all right to cry. Even Jesus cried when his friend died."

Roseanna hiccupped. "Which friend?"

"Lazarus. When Jesus came to see him, he had been dead for four days. The Good Book tells us that he wept at Lazarus's tomb."

"Mamm says she's a friend of Jesus. Will he cry when she dies?"

Gideon swallowed. "I don't know. I do know that he will be with us in our sorrow."

"But what about Mamm? Doesn't he care about her?"

"For sure, he does." He shifted so he could look into his daughter's face. "Do you know what happens to us when we die?"

She nodded. "When one of the soldiers died, the others buried him in the ground."

Gideon didn't want to think about the war. "Do you remember when Viola Hostetter passed away?"

"She looked like she was asleep. But she wasn't."

"That was her body, and it was dead. But her soul wasn't. She was a righteous woman who loved the Lord, just like your mother is."

"Where was she?"

"In heaven. The Blessed Land. After our bodies die, our souls go to heaven if we love and trust our Lord Jesus Christ."

"That is where God is."

"And we can be assured that Viola, and all who die in the Lord, are there also."

Roseanna laid her head on his shoulder and looked out the window again. "Is it a happy place?"

"The Good Book tells us that there is no sorrow there. No tears. No sickness. No death. I think it is the happiest place of all. It is a blessed place."

"How will Mamm be happy if we aren't there with her?"

Gideon kissed Roseanna's kapp. "She will be happy knowing that someday, when the Good Lord determines, we will be there with her."

"Forever?"

"Forever."

"Is Jesus's friend there?"

Gideon nodded. "For sure he is. And a lot of other people too."

"I still don't want Mamm to die."

"I don't either. But if it is the Lord's will, then we must learn to accept it."

Roseanna settled against him, still looking out the window. Gideon gazed out over the distant trees to the hazy blue horizon. Somewhere out there was the home they had left behind and the battles of the war. In spite of what he had told Roseanna, he had his doubts about whether God knew what was happening to one family, and he had no idea how he would learn to accept what was happening. There were so many dying on the battlefields, so many breathing their last breaths. Why would God see him?

He shut his eyes at the memory of the soldier who had fallen at his feet at the battle in the mountains of Virginia. The man, just a boy, had rolled down into the ravine where Gideon held the horses and landed in a sprawled heap. Had that boy entered heaven in the moment that he died? Or had the Good Lord forgotten him too?

Mein Herr . . .

Gideon shook his head, pulling his thoughts back to the present. The sound of children's voices rose in the clear air.

"Do you hear Ezra and Sophia?" he asked.

Roseanna nodded.

"When I'm sitting with your mother in her room, she can hear the three of you laughing and talking outside. Every time, she stops whatever she's doing and listens. Then a smile comes. She gets so much joy out of listening to your laughter."

"Even though she is . . . is dying?"

"For sure. She loves you very much, and when her children are happy, then she is happy."

"Do I have to be happy? I don't know if I'll ever be happy again." Threatening tears strangled Roseanna's words.

"You won't think you will be, but someday you'll find that you can laugh again." Gideon combed his beard with his fingers. "I was six years old when my daed passed on, so I know a little about what you're feeling."

"Were you sad?"

Gideon nodded. "But as time went by, I found that I wasn't as sad anymore. I still missed Daed, and I always will, but it didn't hurt as much."

"How long did it take?"

"My daed died in the summer, and all winter I was sad. But when spring came again, I was happy sometimes. That's when I knew I was beginning to feel better. It might not take as long for you, or it might take longer."

"Will I forget her?"

Gideon gave her another squeeze. "Never. You'll never forget your mamm."

"But . . ." Roseanna let the word hang in the air between them.

"But what?"

"Who is going to be our mother?"

"Ruby said that she will take care of you. You don't need to worry. There will always be someone to take care of you and Sophia and your brothers."

Roseanna stood up and brushed the hay off her skirt. "I'm going to go help in the garden."

"Lydia will like that."

When Roseanna had gone, Gideon stood also. Lovinia was waiting for him, and he didn't want to miss spending time with her, but Roseanna's question echoed in his mind. Ruby's promise to take care of the children was a good thing, but it wasn't the same as the children having a mother. Was Lovinia right? Should he marry again? Could he marry again?

He shook his head at the thought. No one could take Lovinia's place in his heart and his life. But how could he hope to care for his children and support his family without the help of a wife? The Weavers had been kind to let them live with them during Lovinia's illness, but once she was . . . He took a deep breath at the thought. Once she was gone, there would be no excuse for not finding a place in the area and starting to farm again. And it would have to be soon if he was going to get crops in the field before winter.

Abraham would know where a farm might be available to buy, if he could borrow money to do it, but that could wait. He pushed away from the open window. It was time for him to be with Lovinia now. He could plan for the future after.

The kitchen was empty as he entered the house. He heard the rise and fall of Ruby's and Lovinia's voices from the room upstairs, and then soft laughter. Lovinia was laughing.

Gideon took the steps two at a time, pausing on the top step where he could look into Lovinia's room. Ruby sat in the chair, her back to the door, supporting Daniel on the edge of the bed while Lovinia held his hand. For sure, she was laughing, and Ruby's shoulders were shaking. At that moment, Lovinia's gaze met his. He had never seen her look so peaceful.

"Gideon, I'm glad you're here." Lovinia's voice was weak, but she smiled at him.

Ruby stood and turned toward him, the laughter lingering on her face. "I'll leave the two of you alone. Do you want me to take Daniel or leave him with you?" She looked at Lovinia as she asked the question.

"He is ready for a nap," Lovinia said with a little cough, "and I feel like sleeping too." She grasped Ruby's hand when she reached for the baby. "Denki, Ruby. I don't know what I would do without you."

"It is what friends do, isn't it?"

With that, Ruby left and Gideon took her place on the chair next to Lovinia's bed.

"What did Ruby do?" He took Lovinia's hand in his, then covered it with his other one. Her fingers were cold.

Lovinia smiled at him. "She reminded me of my future."

What future? Gideon almost asked the question but kept his mouth closed. He didn't want to spoil Lovinia's peaceful mood.

She went on. "She reminded me of what the Good Book tells us about heaven. That there will be no more pain, no more tears." She looked toward the open window and her voice grew soft. "I feel like I'm resting on the bank of a wide river. Some days the water is turbulent, barring the passage across. But other days, like today . . ." She paused to take a few breaths. "Today the water is placid. I can see the other side and the beautiful trees growing there. The grass is so soft and clean. I want to cross the gentle river and rest in the shade of the trees."

Gideon swallowed, a bitter taste filling his mouth. "Don't, Lovinia. Don't leave me."

She smiled at him again. "I don't want to leave you. I don't want to leave the children. But it seems to be the Lord's will, and I am content."

Tears filled Gideon's eyes, but Lovinia didn't see them. She had gone to sleep, her chest rising and falling with each shallow breath. He buried his face in his hands and let the tears fall.

Levi followed Mother and Father on the dusty road, trailing behind Millie. They were

walking home from Meeting at Karl Stuckey's farm, and on this Sunday afternoon the
overcast sky and heavy air added to his
impatient mood.

Katie Stuckey had received a letter from
Jonas and had shared it with him. Since
Jonas now worked at a hospital in Washington City, they no longer feared for his safety
the way they had last year, but Jonas's
description of his work was depressing.
Jonas had skimmed over the details, but his
stories were disturbing. Tales of the constant
groaning and cries of the wounded men,
the stench of the festering wounds, and the
appalling number of men who died from
their wounds or from disease. Levi was
certain Jonas had meant his letter to be
uplifting as he wrote about the lives that
were saved in the hospital, but underneath
Levi had seen his friend's despair over the
many who would never return to their families.

As much as he disapproved of Jonas's
term in the military, in some ways Levi
envied him. He was doing something with
his life, and when he returned home he
would marry Katie and start a family.
Meanwhile, Levi felt like he was stuck. Each
year followed the ones that had gone before
with no change in his life. For sure, he could

read and study, but where was that leading him? He had no guarantee that he would ever be a minister. Perhaps the Lord wasn't calling him in that direction after all.

Millie dropped behind their parents and nudged his shoulder. "I have a favor to ask you."

His sister walked slower, letting Mother and Father go ahead until they were far enough away that they wouldn't hear their conversation.

"I'm not going to talk to any boys for you." Levi grinned.

Millie blushed as she threaded her hand through his elbow. "That isn't what I wanted to ask you." She stopped in the road, turning him to face her. "Would you mind staying home from the Singing tonight?"

"Father wouldn't want me to. He says I need to go to the Singings to meet the right girl."

"But you never do. You never take anyone home."

"That doesn't matter."

Millie nodded. She knew as well as he did that no one argued with Father when he had made up his mind. They started walking again, passing Elizabeth Kaufman's house as they crested the hill leading out of the Weaver's Creek valley. Home was only a mile farther.

"Why do you want me to stay home?"

"There's a boy that I want to get to know better, but he won't talk to me if you're around."

Levi wiped the perspiration off his nose. The day was warm and humid. "I'm not that scary, am I?"

"He thinks you might be like Father. I've told him you aren't, but he is still intimidated by you."

"If I stay home, how will you get to the Singing?"

"Becky will come by on her way, with Henry. He'll walk with both of us."

Becky's brother Henry was one of Levi's best friends.

"Who is this boy, anyway? I thought Caleb Lehman was interested in you."

"Caleb only has his mind on horses. Whenever he walks me home from a Singing, all he talks about is the new horse he's training. If he thinks that is enough to court me, he's wrong."

Levi chuckled, thinking he had better give Caleb a word of advice the next time they saw each other. "This fellow must be new."

"He is Becky's cousin, Wilmer. He's staying with their family for a few weeks. You must have seen him with Henry at the meeting today."

Levi had spent most of his time talking with Gideon and Abraham, but he had seen the stranger with Henry. "He's from up at Oak Grove, isn't he? From the family Rosie was visiting when she met that Schrock boy she ended up marrying?"

"That's exactly why Wilmer doesn't want to talk to me when you're around. He knows you had been thinking of marrying Rosie and is afraid you're angry with the whole family."

"I don't hold any grudges about that. I've realized that Rosie was never the girl for me." Levi looked sideways at his sister. Her chin was set in that stubborn way he knew so well. "But I would stay away from those Oak Grove fellows. That congregation is change-minded. They don't think it's important to stick to the old ways."

"Wilmer is right. You do sound like Father." She met his gaze. "But I'm not like you and Father. I think the old ways are over and done. We don't have to live like this anymore, do we? Why can't we wear nicer clothes and —" She closed her mouth.

"And what?"

Millie sighed. "I want to have pretty things and have fun. I hate obeying all these rules."

"I remember you saying the opposite last

year, when you admired everything Father said and did. I think this Wilmer has turned your head in more ways than one."

She shook her head. "I haven't talked with Wilmer about this at all. I've only started thinking for myself. Is there anything wrong with that?"

"Not in itself." Levi thought back to the book he had borrowed from Gideon. "But wanting fancy clothes and such shows a love for the world that can pull you away from the things of God."

"Maybe I don't think God is all that important. I can always worry about him when I'm older."

Levi stared at her. He had had no thought that she held such ideas.

"What about tonight?" she asked, reminding him of her first question. "Will you stay home? We can pretend you've gone with me so that Father doesn't ask you about it."

"I'm not going to lie to Father."

"It wouldn't be a lie. We're just keeping Father happy."

Levi increased his pace as they neared their house. "I'm not going to lie, but I'll stay home and let Father think what he will. I have a book I want to read and that will keep me busy."

Like most Sunday afternoons, Mother

went into her bedroom to lie down for a rest and Father closed himself in his study, so when Millie left for the Singing with Becky and Henry, neither of his parents saw Levi slip up to his own room. He sat in his chair with the big book open on his desk and found the spot where he had left off reading last night.

He heard Mother in the kitchen but didn't pay attention to the familiar sounds. Then her footsteps clicked on the wooden floor as she walked from the kitchen to the door of Father's study at the bottom of the stairs.

"Amos, now that the children have gone to the Singing, I need to talk to you about something." Levi heard Mother open the study door. "It's that Ruby Weaver. Did you see her today?"

"What about her?"

Father sounded a little irritated, just like he did when Levi interrupted him. Levi could see him in his imagination, turning in his chair and looking toward the door.

"Did you see the way she was caring for those new children as if they were her own?"

"I had heard that she was helping with the children while the mother was ill."

Mother's voice rose. "But did you see her with that Gideon Fischer? It was scandalous."

Levi suddenly realized he was eavesdropping. If he rose to close the door, though, they would realize he was here, and then he would be on Father's bad side again. He decided to try to concentrate on his reading.

"I saw them talking together," Father said. "I understand that Lydia stayed home with the sick woman today. She was probably only asking him a question about the children."

"It just isn't proper. The poor woman isn't even dead yet and Ruby Weaver has already claimed her husband."

Father's chair squeaked as he shifted in it. "Do you think it is something we should be concerned about? Surely Abraham is aware of what is going on under his own roof and can stop things before they go too far."

Mother sniffed. "You and I both know how quickly things can go too far."

Levi put his finger on the page. What did she mean by that?

"Salome, that wasn't my fault."

"Do you think it was mine? I was an innocent young girl."

"You weren't so innocent, if I remember right. Besides, I was a widower with three young boys. Our situation was different."

Levi couldn't stop listening. They were

talking about the time before he was born, when the family still lived in Pennsylvania.

"Not that different. Gideon Fischer will be a widower soon. And even though Ruby doesn't live with him now, what will he do when he leaves the Weavers' home? He won't be able to care for those children by himself. He'll ask her to continue to help him, and you know what that means."

"So, they will marry. No one will blame them."

"What if —" Mother's words broke off and Levi strained to hear what she was going to say next. "If they don't marry, then you will need to confront them. You know that. It is your duty as a minister."

"That is the deacon's job, not mine."

"But the minister will be involved."

Silence. Father's toe tapped against the floor the way it always did when he was thinking through a problem. "You might be wrong, Salome. We don't know if anything has happened, or if it will happen. We will have to wait and see."

"Gideon Fischer is a man, just like you. And Ruby Weaver is past the marrying age. If I was her, I would be desperate to find a man and hold on to him."

"You were her. Have you forgotten why we had to leave Pennsylvania? No one believed that Levi was born three months early."

Now Mother's toe tapped the floor. She was irritated. "I'm not the one who decided to sneak around the house at night."

"I'm not the one who left the bedroom door open and a light burning."

They were silent. Levi could imagine the glare they were giving each other.

When Mother spoke again, her voice was hesitant. "If things had happened differently, would you have still married me?"

"You mean if Levi hadn't come along?" Father's chair scraped on the floor. "We'll never know the answer to that question, so there is no use asking it. You have your son and the daughter you wanted, and the scandal didn't follow us to Ohio. We don't need to bring it up again."

The conversation faded, but Levi didn't want to hear more. His stomach churned, and his skin was clammy. He leaned over with his head between his knees, waiting for the dizzy feeling to disappear. Mother . . . and . . . and Father. . . . He swallowed. No wonder Father had never been proud of him like he was of his other sons. Levi was the source of shame and disgrace for the family, and the reason they had left their home in Pennsylvania. Nothing he could do would make that right or change Father's opinion of him.

Late Sunday evening, Lovinia's health took a turn downward. Gideon was shocked by the gray pallor of her skin and the way her eyes seemed sunken, her cheekbones standing out in high relief.

Monday passed quickly. Tuesday came, and then it was gone too. Each hour emptied itself relentlessly as Gideon sat by Lovinia's bed. She slept nearly all the time now, as if life itself exhausted her body. Gideon read sometimes, trying to find answers in God's Word or in the writings of Ulrich Zwingli, the early Anabaptist theologian. Sometimes he stood at the window of the little bedroom, watching the children play or the crops growing in the summer sunshine.

The promise he had made to Lovinia was ever foremost in his mind. The promise he couldn't think of keeping. Lovinia was his wife and he couldn't consider marrying another. That would betray his love for her, his vows to her. He couldn't imagine being one with another woman the way he was with Lovinia. She knew his thoughts before they entered his mind. She knew his moods before he could express them. She knew his deepest fears and his struggle with sin . . .

How could he ever be as close to someone else? A stranger? When Lovinia passed on, part of him would die too. He couldn't — wouldn't — share his life with another again.

Gideon didn't dare nap while Lovinia slept. He waited for the moments when Lovinia's eyes would flutter open. Then she would smile at him. He would spoon some water between her dry lips or feed her some of the nourishing broth Lydia kept hot on the stove, even though the kitchen was sweltering with the extra heat. But she would stay awake for only a few minutes before her eyes closed again.

By Wednesday, when there was still no change, Lydia came upstairs at midmorning.

"Gideon, you need to get out of this room for a while. I will stay with your wife, but you need to take a walk. Get some fresh air. Talk with your children. It won't do Lovinia or your family a speck of good if you don't take care of yourself."

Gideon closed his eyes. "I can't leave. What if . . . what if the end comes, and I'm not here?"

Lydia laid a hand on his shoulder. "She will pass on knowing that you love her. I will not leave her alone, but you must have

112

some rest before you come back to your vigil."

The older woman's touch stopped his protests.

Resigned, he said, "You're right. I should spend a few minutes with the children. I've been neglecting them."

"Ruby took them up to Elizabeth's for the day. She said it was time she helped with the chores at her own home, but I think she is trying to distract them." Lydia patted his shoulder before she stepped to the window to raise the sash. "They know what is happening here, and they feel your absence."

Gideon stood. Lovinia hadn't stirred since early morning when he and Lydia had changed the linens on the bed and he had fed her some sweet porridge for breakfast.

"Perhaps you're right. I won't be gone long, though. No more than a quarter hour." He stroked the paper-like skin on Lovinia's cheek. She seemed to be sleeping peacefully.

"I won't let you back into this house until an entire hour has passed." Lydia frowned at him, then sighed. "I will send word to you if there is any change, but I'm sure she will sleep until dinnertime, at least."

Gideon left the house, the fresh fragrance of lilacs awakening his senses to the early summer world outside Lovinia's room. He had grown used to the odor of perspiration, decay, and . . . death. He shook his head and took a deep breath. Lydia was right. He needed a break but then caught himself. A break? When did Lovinia get a break? How could he think of escaping from her sickroom when she couldn't? He nearly turned to go back into the house, but the thought of Lydia's reaction stopped him. She would only turn him around and make him go out again.

He looked up the hill. Ruby lived somewhere in that direction with her sister, and that was where he could find the children. As he started walking, his stiff muscles loosened, and he rolled his shoulders to stretch them more. The days of inactivity were taking their toll. Again, the thought of Lovinia confined to her bed swept over him and he longed to go back to her, but he turned his mind toward his children. Crossing the stone bridge, he turned onto the dirt road and walked up the hill.

As he approached the top, where the gentle slope climbed out of the shallow valley, he heard voices. On the right, set back from the road, sat an old log cabin, its door propped open to the morning air and sunshine. Beyond it was a large garden where his children and Ruby were working, digging in the dirt. Another woman sat in the shade of an apple tree with Daniel on her lap. Laughter filled the air.

"Daed!" Roseanna spied him before the others. "Come see what we're doing. Ruby says the one who finds the most grubs gets to choose what kind of cake to make."

Ruby straightened, shading her eyes with one hand. Her hair was even messier than usual, escaping from the scarf she had tied around her head. Like the children, her feet were bare, and the breeze blew her dark green skirt and black apron around her legs.

"Is everything all right?" she asked as he came closer, Roseanna tugging at his hand. Ruby's gaze held her concern.

"For sure. Lovinia is sleeping peacefully this morning, so I thought I would spend some time with the children while Lydia sits with her."

He met her eyes and tried to give her a reassuring smile. Roseanna let go of his hand to join Sophia as she dug in the soft dirt.

Ruby stepped closer to him, keeping her voice low so the children wouldn't hear. "I was worried when I saw you walking up the hill alone. You've been spending all your time at her side, and I didn't think you would leave unless . . ." She glanced at the children again.

"Your mother shoved me out of the house. I think she's worried about me."

"We all are." Ruby's brow rose as Sophia shrieked at the sight of another grub. "I brought the children up here to meet Elizabeth and give them something different to do, and they're having a wonderful time."

"Come see," Ezra said, running over to Gideon and pulling on his trouser leg. "My grubs. Come see."

Gideon followed his son to the edge of the garden plot where Ruby's sister sat with Daniel. Three flat stones at her feet held a collection of white grubs, curled tightly against their exposed location.

"I have ten," Ezra said, holding up two fingers.

Roseanna grabbed her brother's hand and forced one more finger to join the others. "You have three, Ezra. Three. One, two, three."

"I have two." Sophia said, squatting next to her stone. "I hate them." She poked at one with a stick.

"I found five," Roseanna said. She picked one up. "You can have one of mine, Sophia. Then you and Ezra will have the same."

Gideon nodded to the woman who was

holding Daniel. "I'm Gideon Fischer."

"Elizabeth Kaufman." Her voice was soft. "I'm sorry I haven't come down to the folks' house to meet you. The garden has been keeping me busy."

"I don't think I met you at Sunday Meeting, did I?"

She blushed, turning her gaze away from him and focusing on Daniel. "I don't go to Meeting. My husband wouldn't like it."

Before Gideon could ask her about her husband, another shriek rose from Sophia.

"Ne, ne, Ezra. Don't pick it up."

Ezra didn't react to his sister's yells as he snatched a grub from his pile and squeezed it, fascinated as the sticky ooze covered his fingers.

"Eww!" Roseanna turned toward Gideon, her eyes wide with panic.

He turned her away from Ezra, holding her, while Ruby grasped Ezra's hand before he could reach for another grub.

"Sophia, stop crying," Ruby said over the din, wiping Ezra's hand with her apron.

"But it's so . . . awful," Sophia said between sobs.

Now all three children were crying, and on Elizabeth's lap, Daniel's mouth turned down, ready to add his voice to the noise. Gideon looked from child to child, helpless in the bedlam.

"Come with me." Ruby took Ezra and Sophia by the hands and led them away from the grubs. "Roseanna, you come too."

She sat down on the grass by Elizabeth, pulling Sophia onto her lap. Ezra screamed with frustration, reaching for the grubs, while Roseanna sat next to Ruby, as far from her little brother as she could get.

"Gideon, would you take the grubs to the chickens? I think it would be best if they were out of sight." Her calm voice pierced through the children's crying.

As he gathered up the grubs, Ezra's angry howls subsided. At Ruby's suggestion, the little boy followed Gideon to the chicken coop and helped drop the grubs on the ground for the hungry birds. By the time they returned, the girls had stopped crying, but Roseanna still glared at Ezra.

Gideon watched Ruby as she settled Ezra next to her again.

"Boys will be boys, won't they?" she asked Roseanna, smoothing the girl's hair.

"Boys are awful."

"God made Ezra different than you are. He is curious, and he isn't afraid to get his hands dirty."

Roseanna made a face.

"Why, Ruby?" Sophia asked. "Why can't

118

Ezra be like us?"

"You didn't like the grubs, did you, Sophia?"

His daughter shook her head.

"What if, when Ezra was a man, he didn't like to take care of a sick animal or dig in the dirt? He wouldn't be a very good farmer, would he?"

Roseanna looked thoughtful. "So, God made Ezra like yucky things on purpose?"

Ruby smiled. "God doesn't make accidents. Ezra is just the way he should be, just like you are the way you should be."

Sophia settled against Ruby, while Roseanna picked a dandelion. Gideon sat on the grass nearby and Daniel crawled over to his lap. As a robin flew up to a branch above his head, Gideon thought about what had just happened. Ruby had dealt with his upset children with patience and grace while his first response had been anger. He would have punished Ezra for starting the whole thing, but Ruby was right. He was only a curious little boy.

More than that, Ruby responded the way Lovinia would have. The way a mother would have.

He glanced at the headstrong, red-haired woman as she showed his daughters how to make a chain with the dandelions they found.

Lovinia was right. His children needed a mother. Not just someone to feed them and wash their clothes, but a mother who understood them and loved them. A mother who would nurture them and help them grow into men and women. They needed Ruby.

Gideon sighed, resigned. He would keep his promise to Lovinia. He would marry again. He would even marry Ruby, if the woman would have him. At least he liked her, even if he couldn't imagine her as his wife.

Perhaps in a year or two, he would keep that promise.

5

The next day, when Ruby visited Lovinia, the change in her appearance drove home how quickly her friend would be leaving them. The sick woman seemed to have sunk into the bedding, she had lost so much flesh so quickly. Ruby slipped into the chair Gideon vacated as he went to the kitchen to have breakfast with the children and took Lovinia's thin, pale hand in her own.

Her friend's eyes fluttered open. "Ruby? What day is it?"

"It's Thursday."

"How are the . . ." Lovinia stopped talking to pull in a breath.

"The children?" Ruby finished her question. "They are fine, but they miss you. I've been trying to keep them busy."

"I want to see them." Lovinia struggled to sit up and Ruby tucked another pillow behind her back. "I need to . . ." She took another breath. ". . . say goodbye."

"I'll bring them upstairs after they have finished their breakfast."

Ruby tucked in the edges of the blanket, making sure Lovinia wouldn't get chilled, then opened the window to the fresh June air. The day promised to be hot. She returned to her seat and offered Lovinia a drink of water, spooning the liquid into her mouth. When she had finished drinking, Lovinia closed her eyes.

"You will remember your promise?" she asked, her eyes still closed.

"Ja, for sure I will remember."

"When I'm gone, Gideon will try to talk you out of it."

Ruby smiled and squeezed Lovinia's hand. "Don't worry about that now. We will make sure the children are taken care of."

Lovinia was quiet then, and Ruby thought she had gone to sleep. She refused to think about marrying Gideon right now. The most important thing was that Lovinia's time was short. Like Gideon, she only wanted Lovinia's last days and hours to be peaceful.

"He will think he's betraying me by marrying you."

"That's just what he said."

Gideon's footsteps sounded in the doorway. Ruby hadn't heard him climbing the stairs, but his presence brought strength into the room.

"What did I say?"

Lovinia opened her eyes and smiled at Ruby, sharing the joke between them.

Ruby smiled back and kissed her friend's forehead. "I'll bring the children up to see you as soon as they're done eating."

She left Gideon and Lovinia talking together and went downstairs. Daniel still sat in his chair, eating a crust of bread, while Ezra finished a piece of toast. Mamm and the girls were washing the dishes.

"What are we going to do today?" Roseanna asked when she saw Ruby. "Are we going to work in your garden again?"

"First, we're going to visit your mother."

Roseanna frowned, but Sophia grinned.

"Can she play a game with us?" Sophia ran to take Ruby's hand. "Is she better now?"

Ruby swallowed, thinking of the pale woman in the bed upstairs, her flesh wasting away as death drew near. "She isn't better. She is still very sick, but she misses you and wants to see you."

Mamm took her hands from the dishwater and wiped them on a towel. "You had better go right away, then, before she falls asleep again."

Mamm wiped Ezra's hands while Ruby cleaned up Daniel with a wet rag. Mamm drew close to Ruby. "Don't let them stay too long. Lovinia gets tired very easily."

Ruby nodded as she lifted Daniel into her arms. She took Ezra's hand and led the way to Lovinia's room upstairs.

When they reached the doorway, Ezra pulled away from Ruby and ran to the bed, climbing on it before Gideon could stop him. Lovinia, smiling, waved his help away as she put one arm around her son, holding him close. Roseanna and Sophia stood next to the bed and Lovinia let her free hand touch each one's face in turn.

"I've missed you —" Lovinia's words were cut short as she began coughing.

Gideon thrust Ezra toward Ruby, then helped Lovinia turn on her side and gave her a clean cloth to hold. Gideon's actions pushed Roseanna and Sophia to the side, and they came to the door where Ruby still stood. Silently, they all waited for Lovinia's coughing spell to end. When Ruby spied blood on the cloth and the coughing continued, she pulled the children away, urging them down the stairs again.

Mamm looked up. "You weren't up there very long."

"Lovinia is coughing, and Gideon needs

your help."

Mamm didn't answer but ran up the steps, wiping her hands on her apron.

Ruby looked at the children who stood around her, quiet and subdued. A tear traced a path down Sophia's cheek.

"I want Mamm," she said, looking back up the stairs.

Lovinia's coughing spell had ended, but Ruby couldn't tell if that was a good sign or not.

Roseanna's frown was stony. "She doesn't want to talk to us. She's too sick." She pulled away from Ruby. "Let's go outside. I don't want to be here anymore."

Ruby grabbed Roseanna's hand. "You can go out and play, but remember that your mamm loves you. She would rather be with you than be sick."

The girl shook her head. "If Mamm loved us, she would get well. She would come downstairs. She doesn't love us anymore. Nobody does."

Roseanna turned and ran out the door while Sophia and Ezra stared after her.

Ruby sat down on a kitchen chair with Daniel on her lap. She pulled the other two children close.

"Roseanna is wrong. Your mother loves you very much, but she can't make herself get well." She looked into Sophia's face. "Do you believe me?"

Sophia nodded. "But I want Mamm."

"I know you do, and she wants to see you too. I'll talk to your father and we'll decide if we can try again."

Ezra leaned against Ruby's lap as Daniel pounded on his head with his fist. Ruby smiled. At least two of the children seemed to be happy.

"Why don't you and Ezra go outside to play. See if you can find Roseanna and ask her to play too."

Sophia nodded and took Ezra's hand, pulling him toward the door. Ruby stood at the kitchen window, watching them until they coaxed Roseanna out of the playhouse and started another game of family time, a game the girls had made up and played endlessly. Roseanna placed some leaves on the big stump they used for a table, and Sophia pretended to ladle something into the "dishes." They would be content playing that game until dinnertime.

Then she glanced up the stairway. All was quiet, but Mamm hadn't come back down. Ruby climbed the steps slowly, not certain what she would find.

Mamm looked up as she came to the doorway. "It's all right. Lovinia is resting, but all the children coming at once might have been too taxing."

Ruby stepped closer to the bed, next to Gideon's chair. Lovinia seemed to be sleeping, but she held Gideon's hand in a tight grip.

Gideon glanced at Ruby. "She wanted to spend time with the children, but she just isn't strong enough."

"We don't dare to try again," Mamm said. She smoothed Lovinia's hair back from her face. "It must have upset the children to see her like this."

"Roseanna is affected the most," Ruby said, taking a seat on the end of the bed with Daniel on her lap. "The others only want to see their mother."

"Let them come." Lovinia's voice was raspy and weak, but she opened her eyes to look at all three of them. "Don't keep them from me."

"We can't risk it." Mamm leaned forward. "Lovinia, think how terrible it would be if you passed on while they were here."

A tear trickled down Lovinia's cheek. The sight of that one lone tear made Ruby long to do something. Anything to fulfill Lovinia's longing to see her children.

"What if they visited one at a time?" She looked at Mamm. "We could start with

Roseanna and limit the time so that Lovinia doesn't get too tired."

Mamm nodded. "What do you think, Gideon?"

He stared at Lovinia, their eyes meeting in silent communication. Ruby looked away from the intimate moment.

"I think we should try it. We'll give Lovinia a chance to rest, then bring Roseanna up to see her the next time she's awake."

Ruby stood, balancing Daniel on her hip. "I'll tell the children, so they know what to expect."

She found Sophia and Ezra still involved in their game by the playhouse, but Roseanna was hanging over the pasture fence, watching the horses graze. With Gideon's team available, Daed used one team in the forenoon and the other in the afternoon, keeping both teams in good condition by dividing the work between them. Gideon's team grazed in the lush pasture this morning, paying no attention to the girl who was calling them.

"They don't come when you call?" Ruby asked as she joined Roseanna.

Roseanna didn't look at Ruby. "They don't like me. Our other team was better. Brownie and Socks were their names, and Daed let us ride on their backs sometimes."

"What happened to them?"

"The soldiers took them and left these two in their place. Daed says that they are afraid of children, so we stay away from them."

"I know how to help them learn to like you."

Ruby went into the barn and took a few carrots from the bucket Daed kept near the stalls. Wiping the dirt off one, she let Daniel chew on it as she took the others to Roseanna.

"Try this." Ruby held a carrot up. They paid no attention.

"You have to call them," Roseanna said, impatient.

"What are their names?"

"Samson and Delilah."

Ruby glanced at the girl, but she wasn't teasing. "Like in the Bible?"

Roseanna nodded.

Ruby held the carrot up again. "Samson! Delilah!"

Samson kept grazing, but Delilah lifted her head.

Encouraged, Roseanna joined in. "Delilah! I have a carrot for you!"

The big horse took a step closer, her nose raised. Then she started walking toward the fence.

Roseanna gasped. "She's coming. What

do I do?"

Ruby snapped off the end of a carrot and gave it to the girl. "Hold this out for her, on your palm, with your fingers flat."

When Delilah reached them, she lipped the carrot out of Roseanna's hand and crunched it, watching the girl with one eye.

"She likes it," Roseanna said. "Can I give her another one?"

Ruby gave her the rest of the carrot and Delilah finished it. Then the big horse put her nose over the fence and nudged Roseanna's hair, taking a deep breath.

Roseanna fed her the rest of the carrots, then Delilah went back to grazing. But she stayed close to the fence rather than wandering away.

"I think she likes you." Ruby shifted Daniel to her other hip.

"Can I feed her more carrots?"

"Another time. She needs to eat more grass than carrots."

Roseanna wrinkled her nose. "I wouldn't want to eat grass."

"Horses like it." Ruby grinned at the expression on Roseanna's face. "Your daed wanted me to tell you that you'll be able to see your mother later today, after she sleeps for a little while."

Staring at the horse, Roseanna rested her

chin on the fence rail. "She doesn't want to see me."

The memory of Lovinia's single tear gave strength to Ruby's words. "She wants to spend as much time with you as she can. She misses you very much."

"Then why doesn't she get better? Why did we have to come here? Why doesn't Daed make things better?"

Delilah cropped the grass, took a step forward, then grabbed another bite of the green blades. Mamm would know how to answer Roseanna's questions.

"We don't always get what we want." She glanced at Roseanna, who still watched the horses, her back straight and stiff. "Your mamm and daed left your home because they thought it was the best thing for your family. Your mother doesn't want to be sick, and she doesn't want to leave you."

Roseanna was silent.

"But you can help give her the one thing she wants desperately, and that's to spend a few minutes with you. Just the two of you together. Can you give her that?"

When the girl nodded, Ruby glanced up at the bedroom window. Gideon stood at the open window, watching them. When she waved, he lifted his hand, signaling that all was well.

As he disappeared back into the room, Ruby found that she was smiling. Because of Gideon? He was a good man, and she could tell why Lovinia loved him so dearly. But as the thought of her promise to her friend rose to the surface again, she pushed it down. She wouldn't think about that now. There would be plenty of time to face that afterward.

On Saturday morning, Lovinia didn't wake up.

Gideon had spent the night dozing in the chair next to her bed, ready to help her whenever she stirred. Then sometime, in the darkest hours of the night, she had whispered his name.

"Gideon?"

He took her hand, the light from the low lantern giving her face a golden glow.

"I'm right here. What do you need?"

"Could you lie next to me? You haven't held me in such a long time."

Gideon considered the narrow bed. "Are you sure I won't crowd you?"

"I need to feel you close to me."

He maneuvered onto the bed and settled in close, his arm under her and her head pillowed on his shoulder. She was so thin. So frail.

Lovinia sighed and relaxed. "I love you, Gideon." And then she was asleep.

He had held her, feeling her body grow warm against his, feeling her breath against his cheek, and then fallen into a deeper sleep than he had enjoyed for a week.

Gideon woke the next morning to sunlight streaming in the window. He tightened his arm around his wife, but the chill of her body and her stillness told him she was gone. She had fled in the night.

"Ach, Lovinia . . ."

He stayed still, reluctant to let her go. Finally, he rose, arranging her body in a natural pose, and sat on his chair again. Burying his face in his hands, he waited for the tears to come.

Mein Herr . . .

She looked peaceful. Happy. Content. No longer struggling for breath. No longer in pain. No longer so weak that she could barely raise her hand to cup his cheek.

He couldn't be sad for her . . . but . . .

Mein Herr. I can't do this . . .

A great weight settled on his shoulders, filling his chest, pushing him down. He folded his arms on the edge of the bed and laid his head on them, just as he had slept for so many nights during the past week.

His wife was gone.

The early morning sounds of the family rising drifted up the stairs. Soon Lydia would come to wake the children. Soon she would have breakfast prepared. Soon . . . too soon . . . Ruby would knock lightly on the door . . . ready to stay with Lovinia while he ate his breakfast . . .

Why would he ever eat again?

Lovinia was gone.

How could he tell their children?

Mein Herr, strengthen me . . .

A light knock on the door roused him. Had he slept?

Ruby opened the door. "It's time for your breakfast. Mamm has it all ready —"

He didn't have to turn. He didn't have to say anything. As soon as she saw the still form on the bed, she knew.

She knelt next to him, one hand resting on Lovinia's arm.

"I'm so sorry, Gideon. So sorry." Tears trickled down her cheeks and she wiped them away. "We will miss her so much."

He could only nod in agreement. He couldn't seem to speak.

"Do you want to tell the children?"

"I can't." The words blurted out. "I can't face them now." He ran his fingers through his hair, his hands shaking. "I can't face anyone right now."

134

Ruby put an arm around his shoulders and he found himself in her arms, finally crying. The depths of his sadness clawed at him, chewing him up inside. He had never felt so alone. Sob followed sob, wrenching him away from Ruby's comfort, the shame at showing his vulnerability at war with the longing to surrender to the peace of another person's presence.

Finally, Ruby handed him one of Lovinia's soft towels, and he sat up, wiping his face and beard. He looked at her, her tear-filled eyes meeting his.

"I'm sorry." He blew his nose. "I shouldn't have wept like that in front of you."

"There is no need to be sorry." She blinked as another tear slid down her cheek. "It's a sad day for all of us, but especially for you."

Gideon took her hand. "Lovinia said I would need you. You have been a great comfort for me already today."

Her face was red and splotchy. She had been crying too.

"We both love her, so we have something in common, like we've said before." Ruby's smile trembled. "You can come to me any time. And if I think you've cried enough tears, I'll let you know."

Gideon smiled back, clasping her hand in

135

his. He took in a shuddering breath, looking in Lovinia's face for what he felt was the last time. "She told me that she felt like she was standing at the edge of a river."

"And on the other side was a meadow of soft grass and shade trees. A cool and pleasant place." Ruby squeezed his hand. "She told me about it too. It makes me glad to think of her there in that meadow."

"In the presence of our Lord. Light and warmth all around." Gideon sighed again. *Mein Herr, what do I do now?*

"It is time to tell the others. I'll tell the children, but would you tell your folks?"

"Ja, for sure." She rose to her feet. "I'll tell the family and anyone else who needs to know."

As Ruby opened the door, Gideon glanced at Lovinia's body once more. She was no longer there. She had left him to grieve alone.

Lovinia's passing left a wound in Ruby's heart that nothing else seemed to fill. The funeral had been held on Tuesday, the third day after her death, and somehow, they had gotten through it. Ruby hadn't seen Gideon weep since the morning his wife died. At the funeral service he had looked resigned, standing in a quiet group with the children.

136

Even Ezra leaned against his father, his thumb in his mouth, not understanding this great change in their lives.

During that first week, Ruby had spent her days with the children, either at Mamm's house or at Elizabeth's, while Gideon worked with Daed in the fields. The children seemed to adapt to their new routine, but whenever Gideon came in for dinner or at the end of the day, he didn't meet Ruby's gaze. He kept his red-rimmed eyes down, and she only saw his sunburned cheeks above his beard.

On Saturday, a week to the day after they lost Lovinia, she and Elizabeth took the children berry picking in the clearing where the old salt lick attracted deer and all kinds of wildlife. The girls skipped down the dusty road ahead of Ruby and her sister with Ezra running behind them, empty pails swinging in their hands. Ruby and Elizabeth carried the rest of the pails. They had left Daniel in Mamm's eager care.

"It's going to be a hot day, ain't?" Elizabeth asked, borrowing the Englisch phrase from Mrs. Lawrence, the postmistress in Farmerstown.

"It's a scorcher," Ruby answered, using Mr. Lawrence's answer to his wife. They had heard the couple exchange the same phrases on every summer visit to the store and post office as long as they could remember.

"At least it's cool this morning." Elizabeth switched back to Deitsch. "And perfect for picking berries."

"We should take the children to play in the creek this afternoon," Ruby said. "That will be fun in the afternoon heat."

"You can do that while I help Mamm lay the berries out to dry."

They crossed the creek on the bridge their brother Jonas had made last year, walked past the foundation of the house he had been building for Katie before he joined the army, and took the trail leading to the clearing. Ruby walked behind the children and her sister. She hated this spot in the woods, even though it was a place of beauty all through the year. It reminded her too much of Ned Hamlin and the stolen moments she had spent here with him so many summers ago.

"I haven't come here to pick berries for years," Elizabeth said. She hurried along the path, following the children.

"Remember when Miriam and Rachel used to bring us? We were probably the same ages as Roseanna and Sophia."

"I remember how frustrated they got with

us when we kept eating berries instead of dropping them in our pails." Elizabeth stopped and faced Ruby, her voice low. "Do you remember the time we saw the bear? You don't think we'll see one today, do you?"

"Daed says there haven't been bears in these woods for years. There are too many farmers around." She looked around the clearing as her sister turned and kept walking. "It would be nice to see a deer, but I'm afraid we're too noisy. We'll chase all the animals away."

When they emerged from the cover of the trees into the sunny clearing, Elizabeth and the children turned to the right, toward the largest stand of black raspberry bushes. It had grown and spread over the past few years until it covered nearly a third of the acre-sized clearing. Ruby turned to the left, toward a much smaller clump of brambles, as far away from old memories as she could get.

"Ruby!" Elizabeth called to her from the prickly bushes. "Come over here with us. Ezra needs help picking, and so does Sophia."

Dropping a handful of berries into her pail, Ruby walked toward the others. She held her hand out toward the little boy.

"Ezra, come and pick with me, over here."

"I want to stay by Sophia." Ezra's voice was muffled, his mouth full of berries.

"Bring her with you."

Sophia plucked a thorny raspberry cane from her skirt. "I want to stay by Roseanna."

Elizabeth shaded her eyes as she looked at Ruby. "Why don't you just join us? There are a lot of berries here."

Ruby took a step closer to the giant bramble patch. She eyed the raspberry canes. Too well she knew of the bare center in the berry patch, a fine hiding place. She shuddered, pushing the memories back.

Elizabeth needed her to help with the children. She closed her eyes. The memories were old, from years ago. Ned was gone and wasn't going to return. He had died last year while in Mississippi with the Confederate army, with Elizabeth's husband Reuben at his side.

Reuben. If it wasn't for her, Elizabeth would never have made the mistake of marrying him.

"Ruby? Can you hold my pail?"

Little Sophia was standing by her, one hand balancing her pail and the other full of crushed black raspberries. The thoughts of the past flew out of her mind as she bent to hold Sophia's pail and help her scrape the raspberry mess off her palm.

"I don't like the juice," Sophia said, her voice trembling a little. "I don't want my hands to be purple."

"Don't worry. The stain will wear off in a few days." She went around the brambles to a fresh bunch of canes, Sophia following. "I'll hold your pail and mine, and we'll both pick the berries."

Roseanna moved closer to them, picking almost as quickly as Elizabeth.

"Do you like picking berries, Roseanna?" Ruby asked.

The girl looked at her, then held up her arm. "The prickers scratch, but I like to eat the berries."

Elizabeth looked up from the lower canes where she was helping Ezra find berries for his pail. "Just like everything else, we learn to take a bit of bad with the good."

"I don't like the prickers," Sophia said, gingerly grasping a berry and dropping it in her pail. "Why do berries have them?"

Ruby had never considered the question. "Maybe it's to protect the berries from the animals who would eat all of them."

"We're going to eat all of them," Roseanna said. "The prickers won't stop us."

"We'll only pick until our pails are full. There will still be a lot of berries left."

Sophia dropped another berry in her pail. "Does God like it when we eat the berries?"

"Remember what Mamm said?" Roseanna stopped picking. "She said that God made them specially for us to enjoy. She said he made the whole world for us." She turned to Ruby, a frown on her face. "Is that right? Was Mamm right?"

"Your mamm was right." Ruby smiled. She could almost hear her friend's voice imparting those words of wisdom to her daughters. "Did you pick berries with her when you lived in Maryland?"

The frown on Roseanna's face deepened as she nodded. "We'll never do it again, though. We'll never get to do anything with Mamm again."

"You have your memories with her."

Roseanna didn't look at her but went back to her picking. "I'd rather have her. I wish she hadn't died."

Putting an arm around the girl's narrow shoulders, Ruby tried to give her a reassuring hug, but Roseanna pulled away. Ruby let her go, wondering what Mamm would have done.

Elizabeth had been watching their conversation and came closer to Ruby. "Don't worry. She'll get over her mother's passing in time. You're doing your best." She kept her voice low so the children wouldn't hear her.

Ruby shook her head. "I don't think I'll ever be able to take their mother's place. Lovinia chose the wrong person."

"Why? I think you're just the person those children need right now."

"They need someone who can help them grieve. Someone who can be a good influence as they grow. I'm not that person."

"You might not think so, but I do, and so does Mamm. But most important, Lovinia and Gideon thought you were the right person. Rely on the Lord and he will help you."

"But I've made so many mistakes in my life." Ruby bit her lip. She had never talked to Elizabeth about how she had misled her when they were both younger. Why would anyone think she wouldn't do the same for these children?

Elizabeth looked at her, her gaze steady. "Past mistakes are something we live with, but that doesn't mean we have to continue to make the same decisions over again. We learn from our mistakes and move on." She was silent for a moment, watching the children. "If I could live my life over, I wouldn't marry Reuben. Marrying against Mamm and Daed's wishes was bad enough, but marrying a non-Amish man has been harder as the years have gone by. I would like to be baptized and join the church, but Reuben won't hear of it." She laid a hand on Ruby's arm. "If I had the opportunity to do it again, I wouldn't make the same decision. But I made my decision and I have to live with it."

Ruby's thoughts went to Reuben. Elizabeth hadn't heard from him in almost a year, ever since he left to join the Confederate army. "What if he never comes home?"

"I've thought of that. Worse than that, sometimes I wish it was true, and then I have to ask for the Good Lord's forgiveness for even thinking such a thing."

"Would you marry again?"

Elizabeth's eyes narrowed and her voice was steady. "If I ever marry again, I will marry an Amish man. I wouldn't consider anyone who wasn't Amish."

At a call from Sophia, Ruby went back to helping her pick the berries, but her thoughts were still with Elizabeth. Even though Ruby was older by two years, it seemed that Elizabeth was much wiser than she was. Even after knowing she had made a mistake when she married Reuben, Elizabeth still believed that God was with her. Still believed that God would accept her as a member of the church.

Ruby turned a berry over in her fingers. One little round part was hard and dark, a single flaw in an otherwise perfect fruit. The berry blurred, and Ruby dropped it into the pail, blinking her eyes against the threatening tears as she reached for the next one. Her sin was hidden. No one but Elizabeth knew about Ned, and she only knew part of what had happened. Even when Ruby had joined the church, she had never confessed her sin.

She dropped more berries into the pail, covering the flawed one.

But nothing would cover the memory of the mistake . . . the lie she lived with.

6

Gideon wiped the sweat off his forehead and grasped the scythe handles again. Abraham's fields were large, filling the rolling land along the creek for a half mile or more beyond the house and barn, and on this hot Monday in late June, it was time to cut the lush grass of the hay meadows.

He leaned into the rhythm of the scythe, letting the monotonous action free his mind for other thoughts.

Gideon had once hoped his land in Maryland would be this fruitful someday. Ten years ago, when he and Lovinia were first married and joined the settlers seeking to establish a new Amish community south of Somerset County, Pennsylvania, he had been full of plans. Young, strong, and never a thought his life would be other than good.

Good?

Gideon shifted his grip on the handles once more.

Could he call his life good now that Lovinia was no longer with him?

He swung the scythe, watching the swath of tall grass fall like water over a dam.

Ja. Good. The children were all healthy, he had work to keep him busy, and they were away from the war.

As he stopped to sharpen the scythe's blade, the war crowded in on his thoughts. The cries of the dying haunted him, drowning out the song of the meadowlarks at the hayfield's edge.

He pushed against the memories, applying the scythe to the lush grass once again.

Echoes of the past assailed him, and he sorted through them until he found ones he could dwell on. Lovinia. Their early days, and the joy of Roseanna's birth. He couldn't stop a chuckle as he thought of the troubles she had caused them as a toddler, inexperienced parents that they were. Lovinia's face, lit by joy as she placed his dinner on the table in the cabin that smelled of roast pork and freshly sawn lumber. The weariness of falling into bed at night after a day of hard, satisfying labor.

The scythe caught in a tangle of thick grass, throwing off Gideon's rhythm. At the same time, Abraham hailed him from the other end of the field.

"It's nearly noon," the older man called. "Time to head to the house for dinner."

Gideon glanced at the position of the sun. The morning had passed quickly, but they were more than halfway through the field. Abraham's son Samuel and grandsons Bram and Henry had been working across the creek through the morning, and they met at the end of the fields where a single-board bridge spanned the creek. Then the five of them walked along the narrow lane toward the house, their scythes over their shoulders.

"It's a good day for haying," Samuel said, taking Henry's scythe and carrying it along with his own. "What do you think, Henry?"

"I think it is hard work."

Gideon grinned. "Is this your first time in the hayfield?"

The boy shook his head. "I started when I was eight years old."

"This is his first year with the scythe, though." Samuel gripped the boy's shoulder.

Abraham chuckled. "I noticed you had a few wild swings before you figured out how to handle it. Reminded me of Bram's first time."

"I can work all day now, though." Bram was a tall, quiet young man. "As long as there is a dinner break."

Laughing, Samuel and his boys turned toward their house across the road. Abraham's barnyard was quiet. The children were with Ruby at Elizabeth's cabin for the day.

"Bram and Henry are good workers," Gideon said as he and Abraham continued toward the house.

"They are. Samuel has taught them well. They remind me of my boys when they were young."

"You have two sons?" Gideon hadn't tried to keep Abraham and Lydia's extended family straight in his mind while Lovinia was ill. "I haven't met your other son, have I?"

Abraham led the way to the barn where they cleaned the scythe blades before hanging them on the wall. Abraham gave a last swipe to the wooden handle that was damp with sweat.

"Jonas is in the army." The older man's words were clipped. He sighed. "I'm thankful that he works in the hospital rather than fighting on the field."

Gideon couldn't speak. An Amish man in the army?

"I don't understand. Was he forced to join?"

"Samuel was on the conscription list and

149

Jonas took his place." Abraham's eyes were troubled. Gideon waited for him to continue. "Jonas hasn't joined the church yet, but Samuel has, of course. When Samuel chose to object to the conscription by not cooperating with the authorities, Jonas took his place to keep him from being arrested or suffering other consequences of his decision."

"So he volunteered, and yet he avoided the fighting?"

"Not at first. He doesn't speak of the fighting he saw, only the medical training he received. His transfer to the hospital corps was a relief to all of us."

"He will be safer there."

Abraham's eyes met his. "I pray for his safety, but before he was transferred, I worried more about the possibility that he would take a life. Where he is now, he shouldn't be called upon to do any fighting, but rather extend mercy to the wounded and dying."

Mercy. Where was mercy in war? Gideon pushed his thoughts to the side and brought himself back to the conversation. "Will he come home when the war is over?"

"That is our hope." Abraham started toward the house. "He plans on getting married when he returns and will need to join the church."

"Joining the church may be a problem for a soldier." Gideon's gut twisted. Even though he hadn't been a soldier, the guilt of the weeks he spent with the army still weighed on him. "I hope I'm here to meet him when he comes back."

"I wanted to talk to you about that."

They had reached the washing porch where a basin and towel were waiting for them. Gideon hung his hat on a nearby nail and splashed the cool water over his head. Abraham did the same, then reached for the towel.

"I hope you will remain here in Weaver's Creek with us. Have you made any plans?"

Plans? "I hadn't thought much beyond Lovinia's illness. But now that she's —" He couldn't say the words. "I'm not sure what I'll do."

"You should consider marrying again. A man with a young family shouldn't be without a wife."

Gideon had buried his face in the towel and now lowered it to look at Abraham.

"That is what Lovinia said, but I can't —" He shook his head and hung the towel on its hook. "I can't imagine marrying again so soon."

"I understand," Abraham said. "But a

man can't farm and raise a family on his own. It is a labor that requires two people working together."

Gideon nodded. But knowing the situation and doing something about it were two different things.

Abraham peered in the kitchen door, then indicated a couple chairs on the porch. "It looks like we're early for dinner. We have time to sit and rest before we eat."

It felt good to sit down. Gideon stretched his legs out in front of him, crossing them at the ankles.

"My father settled on this land almost fifty years ago," Abraham said, folding his hands over his chest as he stretched his own legs out. "He eventually built the farm up to eight quarter sections, including the land on either side of the creek." He waved his hand toward the trees beyond the barn. "We kept that quarter as forest, but we are clearing the rest of the land as we need it. Jonas chose the timberland for his home. He'll be taking over this place when Lydia and I are too old to care for it anymore. I sold the quarter section north of the timber section to Gustav Stuckey when he brought his family from Germany twenty years ago." He rubbed his beard. "Hmm. More than twenty, now. Poor Gustav is gone, but his sons do well since they have taken over farming the land."

"Does Samuel have a quarter?"

"For sure." Abraham waved toward the stone bridge. "Across the road, there. You can just see the peak of his barn roof. We farm his acres and mine together, along with Jonas when he's home."

"And then you have this quarter section, where the farm buildings and pastures are, and the parcel that you've cultivated on either side of the creek to the west." Gideon counted on his fingers. "That makes five. Where are the other three?"

"Two of them lie farther to the west and are still wooded. Someday we'll clear those. Samuel's boys will each get a parcel, Bram and Henry. Their younger brother, William, will continue on Samuel's place when he's old enough." Abraham turned toward Gideon. "The last one is the original homestead. Lydia and I lived there in the early years, until our family grew larger. When my parents passed away, we moved into this house. The old house is still there." He pointed beyond the corner of the white farmhouse toward the north. "The quarter section, one hundred sixty acres, is on the south-facing slope there, across the road to the west of Samuel's. It's good land with

153

trees surrounding the house and outbuildings. I had the thought that you and Ruby might marry, live in the house, and that you will share in the family's work the way Samuel does."

Gideon cleared his throat. "Marry Ruby?"

Abraham covered his smile with one hand. "I seem to have spoken too many thoughts out loud. Lydia had mentioned that Lovinia wanted you to marry our Ruby. Didn't Lovinia talk to you about it?"

"Ja, she did." Gideon shifted in his chair. "She was convinced it was the right thing to do."

"But you aren't?"

"I haven't . . . I mean, I told her I would . . . think about it." He wiped the beaded sweat off his upper lip and glanced at Abraham's calm face. "She made me promise . . . but it's too soon. I can't consider it."

"You should. She asked you to promise to marry again for a reason." The older man paused, silent for a long moment.

Abraham was right. Gideon wiped his upper lip again. Lovinia wouldn't have asked him to marry Ruby unless she thought he needed to. Perhaps it was more that the children needed a mother rather than him needing a wife. And the children certainly needed someone like Ruby.

"Your family needs a home."

Gideon nodded. They needed security, comfort, permanence. All things he hadn't been able to provide for the last year or two, ever since the war had started.

"I . . . I don't have money to buy such a large piece of land."

"It's a gift, son. For you and your family."

Eyes filling, Gideon shook his head. "I can't take it . . . I don't deserve something like this."

Abraham drew in his feet and leaned forward, his elbows on his knees. "It isn't a question of deserving something or paying for it."

"But if you knew . . ." Gideon stopped, his throat filling. If Abraham knew the depths of his sin, he wouldn't even welcome him onto his porch. "You don't know what I've done." He closed his eyes. "I'm responsible for Lovinia's death, and for our church breaking apart." He stopped, not able to continue.

"How are you responsible? You didn't cause Lovinia's heart to give out. You didn't drive the people away from your community, did you?"

"I was their shepherd. I was Lovinia's

husband. God gave them to my care and I failed."

"Those things were out of your control."

Gideon drew his hand over his beard as he straightened up. "But they shouldn't have been."

Abraham was silent for a few minutes. The sound of Lydia setting the plates on the wooden table drifted out the door.

"Be careful of pride, Gideon. *Hochmut,* soul-destroying pride, can be your downfall."

Gideon shook his head. "I'm not proud. I know how sinful I am."

"But you just told me that your life should be in your control. You told me that you're responsible for everyone's well-being."

"I am." When Abraham didn't answer, Gideon looked at him. "Aren't I?"

"You aren't that powerful. Only the Good Lord himself has the kind of control you're talking about. When you wrest that control from his grasp, that's an act of pride that can destroy your soul." He rubbed the palm of his right hand with his left thumb, massaging the tired muscles. "Remember to practice *Gelassenheit.* Letting go of your own control and surrendering to the Good Lord's will is the only way for a man to live."

Gideon stared at the wooden porch floor.

Lydia's voice drifted through the screen door, calling them to dinner.

Abraham stood, clapping him on the shoulder. "Consider my offer and consider marrying our Ruby. Nothing could make me happier than to have you and your children as part of our family." He opened the door, then glanced at Gideon again. "And I'll be able to rest well, knowing Ruby has a fine man for a husband."

Standing to follow Abraham, Gideon glanced up the road toward the section of land. Lovinia's suggestion . . . ne, her request that he marry Ruby weighed heavily. Was Lovinia telling him what God's will was for their family? He only wanted to do what was right, but did that mean he should marry a woman he barely knew?

He shook his head as he followed Abraham into the house. It was too soon to think about it.

Wednesday was the full moon, ten days past midsummer. The men had been working long hours in the fields, trying to get the hay cut, dried, and in the barn before the next rainstorm. Ruby, Elizabeth, and Mamm, along with Samuel's wife, Anna, had been hard at work too, storing the first garden vegetables and fruits for the families.

After a cold supper of cottage cheese, fresh bread, and greens with vinegar dressing, the families rested in the cooler air outside the house before the men went back to the fields. There they would work until nearly dawn, taking advantage of the bright moon during the cool of the night.

Ruby sat on a quilt with Daniel. Gideon stretched out on the other side of the baby, his hat over his face.

"Katie came by the house this afternoon," Elizabeth said. "She had a letter from Jonas."

"What did he say?" Mamm sat on a chair brought from the house, her ever-present knitting in her hands.

"I wish I could read it to you, but Katie kept a close hold on it." She laughed along with Anna. Ruby only smiled, sure that Gideon was sleeping and not wanting to wake him.

"Is he all right? Is he coming home soon for a visit?" Daed asked.

"Jonas said he is doing well. The work is keeping him busy, but he didn't say much more about it. He only said how hard it was to see so many wounded and dying men. Most of what Katie shared with me was about how the Federals are worried that the Confederates might try to attack Washington

City, where he is working."

There was silence at this news, then Daed said, "We must always pray for his safety and for a quick ending to this terrible war."

Daniel rattled the string of wooden beads he was playing with and Gideon lifted his hat, reaching over to pat his son on the back. Daniel crawled to him and laid his head on his father's chest.

"Did Jonas say anything else in his letter?" Anna asked, her watchful gaze on the children's game at the playhouse.

Elizabeth smiled. "Only private things for Katie. She didn't let me read that part of the letter."

Mamm laughed at that. "He had better come home soon, or Katie will find another beau."

"I don't think there's much danger in that," Ruby said. "I've seen the way her eyes light up whenever someone mentions his name."

Daniel pounded on his father's chest, and Gideon rolled over on his side, his head propped on one hand. He pulled the baby close for a kiss on his soft cheek. Ruby smiled at the sight. She had rarely witnessed such affection between a father and his children, but Gideon often hugged and kissed his little ones.

"How much of the hay is done, Abraham?" Mamm asked.

"We should finish raking it tonight, and then tomorrow afternoon we'll start storing it in the barn, as long as it doesn't rain."

Daed glanced toward the northwest and Ruby followed his gaze, but the sky was almost clear. The setting sun had turned the haze on the horizon to a soft orange and twilight had descended.

Anna stood, dusting off the back of her skirt. "I must get home. It is the children's bedtime." She nudged Samuel's foot with her toe. "Are Bram and Henry both going to work with you tonight?"

Samuel lifted his head and looked at the boys. Bram was sitting up, eager to get to work, but Henry had fallen asleep on the grass.

"It looks like Henry will be going home with you."

He stood up and lifted the boy in his arms while Anna walked over to where her younger children were playing yet another game of family time. Roseanna and Sophia had convinced William and his little sister Dorcas to join in their endless imaginary world. Roseanna and William were pretending to be the parents while Sophia and the others were the children, although with the

160

raised voices coming from the playhouse, it sounded like all of them were very tired children.

Ruby stood up and reached for Daniel. "It's bedtime for these four too."

Gideon stood at the same time and handed Daniel to her. "I'll help with the older three if you take care of him. I've spent so much time in the fields this week that I've hardly seen them."

He headed toward the playhouse while Ruby carried Daniel up to the children's bedroom. By the time Daniel's diaper was changed and Ruby had settled in the little rocking chair with the baby and a cup of milk, Gideon brought the other children up the stairs.

"Will you stay with us, Daed?" Sophia asked as Gideon helped her change into her nightdress.

"I have to work tonight, but I'll stay for a few minutes."

He turned down the covers on the bed and the children climbed in. By the time Ezra was settled between the two girls, Sophia was nearly asleep. He kissed all three foreheads, then Roseanna wrapped her arms around his neck in a fierce hug.

Ruby put the sleeping baby in his cot, then crept out of the quiet room. The children seemed to be happy during the day while she cared for them, but Roseanna's hug told Ruby that they craved their father's attention in their mother's absence. A substitute might see to their basic needs, but a parent's love was what they really needed.

In the kitchen, Ruby put away the few dishes that Mamm had left on the sideboard to dry, then checked the sponge for tomorrow's bread baking. From the kitchen window, she saw that Mamm, Daed, and Elizabeth still sat under the tree, slapping mosquitoes as they talked. Just when she decided she should see if Elizabeth was ready to walk home, Gideon came down the stairs.

She blew out the lamp in the center of the table as he stopped at the bottom step, his hat in his hand. The room was dark enough that she couldn't read the expression on his face.

"I haven't thanked you for taking care of the children so well."

Ruby's face grew even warmer than the hot kitchen had made it. "I'm not sure I'm doing as well as I should. Roseanna doesn't seem to like to be around me."

Gideon glanced up the stairs and then led her out the kitchen door to the washing porch.

"I don't know what we can do for her other than wait." He ran his fingers through his thick brown hair, so like Roseanna's. "Losing a mother is hard for a child, but she will get through this time of grief." He took his hat from the hook by the door and put it on. "Meanwhile, I'm glad she has you."

He turned to go down the steps, but Ruby grasped his sleeve, stopping him. "I've been thinking about the promise we made to Lovinia."

"I have too." He moved closer and kept his voice low so they wouldn't be overheard. "I won't hold you to that promise. I know how difficult —" He cleared his throat. "I think Lovinia would understand if you . . . if we didn't go through with it."

Ruby nodded, ignoring the sinking disappointment at his words. "I think she would too. But I want to continue to care for the children and keep at least that part of my promise to her. I was wondering if you have thought about the future. Are you going to stay here, living with Mamm and Daed? Or will you look for your own place in the area?"

"Your daed reminded me that it's time that I made plans. After Lovinia —"

His voice broke and he looked away from

163

her, into the growing darkness. The full moon was rising, round and glowing silvery-white.

He cleared his throat and continued. "I haven't been able to think about the future since we left Maryland."

Ruby laid her hand on his forearm, trying to give him some comfort. The fragrance of work, dirt, and drying hay clung to him. The smells of summer.

"I miss Lovinia too, and I think I always will. I wish we had been able to spend more time together."

Gideon didn't move and didn't speak as a long, quiet moment stretched between them. "Your daed assumes that I will marry you, and soon. Your mother told him about Lovinia's request."

"I haven't discussed it with anyone else, but other people will begin to wonder what your plans are. It's common for a widower to marry sooner than later."

"I know, and I've counseled other men to take that step when they're in this situation. It only makes sense with children to care for and the demands of farming." He sighed and put his calloused hand on top of hers. "I certainly won't be so quick to mention it in the future, though. I can't imagine . . ." He shook his head. "I just can't imagine be-

164

ing married to anyone but Lovinia."

Ruby's throat was dry as she tried to swallow. This was what Lovinia had been worried about when she had asked her to take care of Gideon, but she couldn't force the man to act against his conscience, could she? "I think I understand."

"Abraham offered me a quarter section of land, the one next to Samuel's."

Ruby met his gaze. "He did? Years ago, he told me that farm would be mine."

Gideon smiled. "I think it was a kind of wedding present, because he talked of giving it to both of us."

"So in order to get the land, you would need to marry me." Ruby pressed her lips together, glad that Daed wasn't close enough for her to tell him what she thought of that proposal.

"That quarter would be welcome, and close to Elizabeth's house and your parents." He rubbed her hand with an absent motion. "I don't have any money to buy it, but I suppose he might let me work it off."

Ruby shook her head. "That wouldn't be right for you to be indebted like that." His hand was rough, telling of his long days of work in the fields. "I have an idea, though. If Daed has been waiting for me to marry so he could give that land to me and my

165

future husband, perhaps he'll give it to me now. We can fix up the house that's there, and you can live there with the children. I'll be able to care for the children easily, since you'll be living so close to Elizabeth's."

Gideon looked toward the rising moon again, thinking. "What happens when Elizabeth's husband comes home?"

"Then I'll build a little cabin for myself. There are one hundred sixty acres and we should be able to share it without a problem."

"You're a good friend, Ruby. I may take you up on that offer." He smiled, the moonlight striking the side of his face with a white glow. "I like the thought of being close to you. I know you love the children, and I'm happy you'll be caring for them."

As Gideon went on down the steps, Ruby leaned against the doorframe. For sure, the arrangement sounded simple. There would be no danger of her marrying and forcing Gideon to move off her land, since no man would have her. But if he found someone else to marry someday . . .

Ruby slapped at a mosquito. She would worry about that when the time came, but not before.

Samuel came back from his house across the road, his shadow long in the moonlight.

Gideon and Daed picked up the rakes they had left leaning against a tree when they came in for supper and headed out to the hayfield with him and Bram. Gideon was tall and strong, but gentle and caring. He had a way of letting an easy silence fall in a conversation so that it invited her to share anything with him.

Anything except what was really on her heart. Because even if he didn't want to marry her, she couldn't keep herself from wondering what it would be like to keep her promise to Lovinia. Ruby felt the place where Gideon's hand had lain on hers, still warm from his touch. Lovinia had said that she wouldn't find a better husband anywhere.

Ruby shrugged off that thought. A husband would want to change her to fit his idea of what a good Amish wife should be. No man was going to force her into that mold. She would rather remain independent and single.

Stepping off the porch into the soft grass, she went to help Mamm and Elizabeth fold the quilts, damp and cool from the evening air.

The first Sunday in July was a church Sunday. Gideon woke early, the growing discomfort at the thought of attending the meeting keeping him from the restful slumber he needed.

Mein Herr . . .

Why was the Good Lord silent? He had confessed to God. His sin was against God, and only God, wasn't it? But the boy still haunted his dreams, tumbled in the fallen leaves and mud at Gideon's feet, his face still twisted in agony, his eyes continuing to plead with him.

Mein Herr . . . forgive me.

Lovinia's face, as peaceful as if she was only sleeping, but frozen in the moment of her death, took the boy's place in his mind.

Gideon sat up and pushed the heels of his palms into his eyes. His life had become a series of memories he couldn't erase, with no relief. Layers of regrets as relentless as the tall grass falling before his scythe.

A woven wool rug covered the floor next to Lovinia's bed, but some nights that slight padding was not enough. He couldn't sleep in the bed, even though he knew others wouldn't understand his reluctance. But that was where Lovinia's soul had fled. That was where he had held her for the final time. He couldn't bring himself to take his ease on the soft mattress.

Rain spattered the windowpane in an early

morning shower. They had gotten the hay into the barn in time, working far into the night through the end of the week. Abraham had said a change in the weather was coming, and he had been right. But as Gideon prepared for the day ahead, the rain ended and sunshine broke through the clouds. It looked like they might be able to walk to church between showers.

Before he finished shaving his upper lip, he heard Ruby's footsteps on the landing, then her voice as she woke the children.

"It's a lovely Sunday morning and time to get up."

Daniel's cry was the first answer he heard.

"Are you hungry?"

Gideon smiled as he imagined Daniel burying his face in Ruby's shoulder.

"Let's change your diaper first." After a short pause, Ruby said, "Ezra, do you need to go to the outhouse?"

"I used the pot."

"He didn't," Roseanna said. "He wet the bed again."

Even this news didn't upset Ruby.

"We'll change the sheets after you get dressed. But we must hurry now. Mamm has breakfast ready and she's waiting for the four sleepyheads."

"Five, you mean." Roseanna's voice was

muffled. She must have been pulling her dress over her head. "Daed is still asleep."

"If your daed misses his breakfast, then that is his concern."

Gideon slipped his shoes on, chuckling. He wouldn't miss breakfast, not with a stomach as hollow as his felt this morning.

"Is today a church day?" Sophia asked.

"For sure it is. We're going to Samuel's for Meeting today. It is only across the road, so we don't have to leave so early."

"Will Dorcas be there?"

"She will. It's her house."

"She's my friend." Sophia's voice held a confident note Gideon had never heard before. "Can I play with Dorcas?"

"After church and after we eat dinner. I'm sure Dorcas is looking forward to playing with you too."

"And William?"

"William won't want to play with us," Roseanna said. "There will be other boys, so he'll only want to play with them."

Gideon opened the bedroom door and looked into the room across the landing. Ruby had managed to get all four children dressed and was braiding the girls' hair. None of them noticed him as he stood watching Ruby's deft fingers.

"Remember, though," she said as she

170

finished Roseanna's second braid and turned to Sophia's fine blonde hair, "church comes first. We must worship the Lord our God with our whole hearts."

Roseanna nodded. "And our whole minds, and everything." She pulled one braid to the front and examined it. "Where did you learn how to braid hair?"

Ruby started on Sophia's second braid. "I have sisters, remember? Elizabeth and I used to braid each other's hair. When Sophia is a little bit older, you can do that."

"Can I braid Sophia's hair tomorrow?"

"I think that is a wonderful idea." Ruby finished Sophia's braid and turned to Ezra, straightening his suspender straps.

Gideon suddenly realized that he was smiling. He had forgotten the memories of the past as he had witnessed Ruby perform the simple task of helping the children ready themselves for the day. With Ruby around, perhaps someday he could break free of his regrets and look toward the future.

Ruby rose and lifted Daniel in her arms. "Are we ready for breakfast?"

"I have to use the pot," Ezra said, pulling it out from under the bed.

Gideon stepped onto the landing. "I'll take you to the outhouse, Ezra."

He held out his hand to his son, glancing

at Ruby. Her face turned pink as his glance lingered. She was an extraordinary woman, and he could understand why Lovinia had considered her a good friend.

Then Ezra grabbed his hand and pulled him toward the stairs. "Hurry, Daed. Hurry."

Gideon wasn't alone with his thoughts again until silence fell before the service started. Samuel and Anna's living room and kitchen, one large room after the portable walls had been moved away, were filled with more than one hundred men, women, and children of all ages. The room quieted as the people sat, yielding, waiting. He fought against the pressing memories that roared into the quiet. Why would they not leave him alone?

He looked across the aisle to the bench where the children were crowded next to Ruby and Lydia. Roseanna wiggled in her seat, her fingers tangled in her apron. Ruby laid her hand on top of Roseanna's to still the fidgeting, then helped her smooth the white fabric again. Ruby was teaching his daughter Gelassenheit, just as Lovinia would have. Teaching her, and Sophia and Ezra, to yield to the silence, to let go of their busyness, to trust . . .

A sudden prickling brought Gideon's

hand to his eyes, pressing the corners to keep the tears from spilling out. Abraham had been right. He had been trying to control his life rather than yielding to the Lord.

Mein Herr, I have forgotten.

How long had it been since he trusted God and his ways? How long had it been since he had felt that peace of the soul? Gelassenheit didn't come naturally, it had to be taught. It had to be remembered. It had to be practiced.

He had been fighting against God's will for months, ever since he had been forced to haul the army's supplies from camp to camp, witnessing battle after battle. His time with the army couldn't have been God's will. He was in the wrong place. He was outside of God's will . . .

But could a man, unless he was rebellious against God, ever be out of the Lord's will? Could he fall out of his Lord's sight, through no fault of his own?

With a sigh, he centered his thoughts, trying to empty himself of the memories, the worries, the grief. He waited, working to release the tight ball of blackness lodged in his breast.

But even after the first song was announced and the congregation began singing the long, drawn-out syllables of the hymn of prayerful contemplation, the peace he sought still eluded him. The church service dragged on.

After the first seating of the fellowship meal, when Gideon ate with the rest of the men, he wandered to the edge of Samuel's yard while he waited for the children to finish their meal. Across the road was the section of land Abraham had offered to give him. The price, whether Abraham had intended it to be or not, was clear. Take Ruby as his wife, and the land would be his. Through the trees he could see the house. It had been empty since Ruby's grandparents had passed away and Abraham and Lydia had moved their family to the bigger house across the creek.

The little house, a log cabin built into the slope on a stone foundation, had been located a dozen yards or so from the road, directly opposite from Samuel's yard. He looked at the cabin, picturing it in his mind. If he sided the logs with boards, painted it white, and also painted the barn and outbuildings, the place would look new and fresh.

His mind continued on into the future. As time went by, Ezra and Daniel would join him in his work, while Roseanna and Sophia helped their mother in the house . . .

His thoughts faltered. For a sweet moment, he had forgotten that this future he was imagining was a future without Lovinia. She would never be part of their lives again.

He could create a home for his family here in Ohio, but he couldn't imagine doing it without Lovinia, without his wife. Even with Ruby helping him, her daily presence would only be a shadow of what he and Lovinia had shared.

"Daed, can I play with Dorcas and the others?" Sophia tugged on his trouser leg, pulling his thoughts back to Sunday afternoon.

Ruby followed Sophia, carrying Daniel across the yard, with Ezra and Roseanna following behind.

"For sure, you can play." He glanced toward the house where the young children were gathering with some older girls to care for them. "We don't have far to go home, so you'll be able to play all afternoon." He smiled into her sky-blue eyes and tugged on the string of her kapp. "Obey Roseanna and help take care of Ezra."

Ruby stood beside him as he watched the children run toward their friends. Daniel reached for him and he took the baby from her arms.

"They are feeling very much at home here," Ruby said. "Even though they miss their mother, they seem to be happy."

"Children get over their hurts quickly."

Her eyebrows raised as she turned toward him. "You mustn't assume that. Roseanna, especially, feels her loss very deeply. It doesn't always show, but it's there."

"I only meant that they are able to go on. They aren't held to the past." Gideon felt the prickle in his eyes again, but he bounced Daniel in his arms, making the baby laugh.

Ruby watched his face and stepped closer. "I miss Lovinia too, but she wouldn't want you to grieve too long." She crossed her arms. "Lovinia loved you and didn't want you to live in the past. She was afraid you would forget to think of your children and their needs."

"Is that what the two of you talked about during your long hours together?"

"We talked about a lot of things, but mostly about the future."

"Her future?"

Ruby nodded. "She looked forward to heaven, and to the ceasing of her cares and weakness. But she also talked about her dreams for the children's future, and yours. She told me that she prayed for you every day."

176

"I miss those prayers."

Gideon didn't realize he had spoken out loud until Ruby squeezed his arm. He wasn't surprised that Lovinia had been thinking of him in her last days, but she had shared more of what was on her heart and mind with Ruby than she had with him. And Ruby . . . As much as he missed Lovinia, he was surprised that a simple, brief touch from Ruby had shown him that he wasn't alone. Lovinia had given him a gift of a companion in his grief.

He shifted Daniel to his other arm and nodded toward the section across the road. "I was just considering your idea, to live in that old house. It needs to be cleaned and fixed up. And I think I'd build a new barn closer to the creek, in that flat space between the trees."

Ruby stood on her toes, frowning. "I don't see the place you're talking about."

He put his hand on her shoulder, turning her slightly. "There." He put his head level with hers to make sure she could see the spot. "On this side of those pine trees."

"Now I see it. That's a good level place, perfect for a new barn. The old log one is beginning to fall apart."

She turned her face toward him at the same time he looked at her. Their noses were inches apart. She blushed and stepped back.

"I'll talk to Daed and see what he says about giving the land and the house to me, even if we don't marry. I hate the thought of it being a bride-price."

"A bride-price?"

She laughed a bit and blushed harder. "I read about it somewhere. Some fathers provide money, or land, or livestock to a future husband to make their daughters a more attractive bride. Like a dowry."

"Your father has no need to provide such a thing."

Her smile disappeared. "I don't know. No man has ever considered me as a bride. Perhaps Daed should offer a bride-price."

Gideon's stomach clenched at the thought. The promise he had made to Lovinia rang in his memory, but then Ruby's red hair stirred in the breeze, floating beyond the confines of her kapp. The sunlight glinted on it, turning it to burnished gold.

"Someone like you shouldn't require a dowry. You are valuable enough on your own."

"It doesn't seem like anyone else shares your opinion."

She dropped her gaze and kicked at a

dandelion in the grass. Gideon suddenly saw beyond her confidence and brashness to the lonely girl she kept hidden.

"Maybe the right person just hasn't met you yet."

Ruby glanced up at him, her vulnerability fading. "Maybe you're right." She reached for Daniel. "It's time for his nap."

As he watched Ruby carry the baby toward the house, his gaze slid beyond her and met the stare of Salome, Preacher Amos's wife. She raised her eyebrows, then turned away.

Gideon went to help move the tables out onto the grass on the shady side of the house, converting them back into benches so folks could sit in the shade while they visited. He glanced at Salome again, but she was engrossed in a conversation with another woman. Why had she been staring at him?

7

As Abraham stepped off the porch, he looked toward the eastern sky. The first Monday of July, and the early morning air already held the promise of a hot, humid day ahead.

The barn was still dark in the gray hour before dawn, so Abraham lit the lantern. The soft, golden glow reflected off the wood beams and rose into the shadowy heights of the loft.

Taking a deep breath, Abraham smiled. The fragrance of fresh hay mingled with the scent of the animals. A barn filled with blessings from the Lord and the promise of another year of provision. Harvest was still ahead, but the haymow, filled to the rafters, was the early note of the hymn of praise to come.

As he went about his chores, feeding, milking, checking the stock, his mind flitted from one thing to another, bringing each one to the feet of God.

He poured measures of grain into the horses' feed boxes as he considered the picture in his mind. He had no trouble imagining himself looking no higher than God's feet, but was it prideful to even think that his prayers reached that far? Not prideful, he decided. Not when God himself had asked his people to bring their prayers to him.

Moving on to the cows, he sat to milk each one in turn. There were only two, and soon they would be down to one. Millie was aging quickly, and he would not be getting another calf from her. This year's heifer had nearly been the end of her, and he wouldn't risk breeding her again. But with their family grown and mostly gone, he and Lydia had no need for more than one cow. He could even give the cow away and get enough milk for the two of them from Samuel.

Abraham leaned his head against Millie's flank. Who needed another cow, though? Bett was only five years old, with plenty more years of milking ahead of her. Samuel already had four cows, and the Stuckey boys each had one or two for their families.

As the milk drummed into the pail, Gideon's name came to mind. For sure, Gid-

181

eon needed a cow for his growing family. Abraham chuckled. And when he married Ruby, there would be even more grandchildren to provide for. He closed his eyes, imagining the red-haired sons and daughters Ruby could be blessed with. His daughter's reluctance worried him a bit. Ruby might not think she was going to marry Gideon, but it was only a matter of time if it was God's will. If it wasn't?

Abraham aimed a squirt of milk into a waiting cat's mouth. If it wasn't God's will for the two of them to marry, then they wouldn't. The whole question wasn't something for him to worry about. He chuckled again as he patted Bett's flank and picked up the bucket full of warm, frothy milk. That wouldn't stop him from praying for the marriage to happen, though. He couldn't think of a better solution to both Gideon's and Ruby's problems.

By the time he left the barn with the pail of milk, the sun was up, and the morning's coolness was wearing away. Ruby greeted him from the bridge and hurried to meet him even before he reached the porch.

"I have something to ask you," she said. Her bright eyes and flushed cheeks were certain signs that this might be an idea he wouldn't like.

"What is it?"

Ruby stood between him and his breakfast, her arms crossed. "It's about the quarter section of land."

Abraham set the milk pail on the ground. "The quarter section I offered to Gideon?"

She nodded.

"Does this mean the two of you are planning to marry soon?"

Ruby blushed. He had never seen her face so pink.

"We're not planning on getting married, but Gideon needs a house for his family."

"I agree, but what does this have to do with that land?"

"Gideon said you offered it to him, as a gift."

"For sure, I did. A wedding gift for the two of you."

She twisted her fingers together. "But since I'm not marrying Gideon, what will happen to the land and the house?"

Abraham's eyes narrowed. Now they were getting to the point. "I suppose I would wait until you did marry, either Gideon or someone else."

She kicked at a stray dandelion plant with her toe.

"What is wrong with Gideon? I thought the two of you were getting along very well."

"Nothing is wrong with him. It's just that —" She bit her bottom lip. "Neither one of us is interested in marriage."

"What about the children? Who will care for them?"

"I will." She met his gaze. "Here's my idea. If you give me the land now, I can let Gideon live in the house. I'll still live at Elizabeth's but take care of the children and Gideon's house during the day."

Abraham combed his fingers through his beard. The fragrance of bacon frying drifted through the open kitchen window, reminding him that Lydia would have breakfast ready soon, but this problem needed to be resolved first, and in a way that would be pleasing to him and to God. This scheme of Ruby's might be the path toward her marriage.

Of course, he could just let Gideon live in the house and not involve Ruby at all. He owned the land and could do anything he wanted with it until he actually gave it to her. That gift would be an unnecessary extra step.

But if he gave the land to her, he wouldn't need to be involved in the arrangements between the young folks. And the two of them would have to work together in that arrangement, and that could lead to their eventual marriage.

"Daed, what are you thinking about?"

He smiled. "I was thinking of Caleb's daughter in the Bible. She asked her father for land also, and he gave it to her. Could I do any less?"

Ruby blushed again, then kissed him on the cheek. "Thank you, Daed." She squeezed his arm, her eyes shining again. "I must go in to get the children ready for the day."

"And tell Gideon the news?"

She grinned, nodding. "For sure. I think he'll be happy about it, don't you?"

She didn't wait for an answer but ran into the house. Abraham picked up the milk pail, a smile still on his face as he carried it inside.

As he set the pail on the sideboard, Lydia glanced at him.

"What has Ruby so excited this morning? She came in and ran upstairs without even a good morning for me." She looked at him again. "And what has you grinning like that?"

"We may be having a wedding soon."

She had been turning the bacon strips in the skillet, but now her hand paused in midair, a slice of bacon hanging from her tongs. "Ruby?"

He nodded, coming close to her as she continued turning the bacon.

"I was going to give Gideon and Ruby the homestead for a wedding present, but both of them said they weren't getting married."

"That's what I thought. So why do you think they will change their minds?"

Abraham picked a piece of bacon from the plate of cooked slices keeping warm on the back of the stove. "I gave the land to Ruby, and she'll let Gideon live in the house. She said she'll keep house for him and care for the children."

"How will that change things?"

"Remember the days after our wedding? We worked together to get that old house ready for us to live in it, and you told me that there is nothing like her own kitchen to make a woman feel like a wife."

Lydia put the spatula down and turned to him. "You think that Ruby will change her mind as she spends her days cooking for Gideon and caring for the children in that old house?"

"For sure, I do."

She smiled and tugged on his beard. "You are a crafty man, you know that, don't you?"

Abraham brought her closer, wrapping his arms around her waist.

"Do you think it will work?" He nuzzled her ear.

"If it doesn't, I don't know what else will."

The next Tuesday morning, after more than a week of working on the old house, Ruby was exhausted but pleased with the progress. Gideon had the idea of covering the old dry and warped logs with board siding rather than trying to rechink the walls, and the result was a house that looked new. At least on the outside.

Samuel and his boys had cleaned out the inside of the house, ridding it of old mouse nests and some newer ones that were occupied. Ruby's job was to scrub the walls, ceilings, and floors with Mamm's help, and she was glad they didn't need to worry about being surprised by vermin.

"I can't get over how much dirt has accumulated in only ten years," Mamm said. "I left it clean when we moved out, but the years do take their toll."

"If I remember right," Ruby said, "you didn't think anyone else would live in this old house again."

"For sure. It was old, and we were certain that you children would want to build your own houses and start fresh."

"That's what Samuel did, and what Jonas

is planning. But Gideon doesn't have time to wait for a new house. He says this one will be as good as new when we get done with it."

Mamm sprinkled sand on the wet wooden kitchen shelf, then started scrubbing it with a brush, leaning into each stroke.

"I'm glad your daed thought of using the boards Jonas had cut for his house to use for the siding," she said. "He has been worried about the lumber deteriorating while Jonas is away."

"Gideon wasn't sure he should use it, but Daed said he could replace the boards."

"I think the children are going to like it here." Mamm rested from her scrubbing. "Just listen to them playing in the attic upstairs."

Ruby listened as she wrung her rag out in the bucket of water at her feet. Roseanna's and Sophia's voices shouted as they ran from one end of the big empty room to the other. But there were only two sets of feet. She walked around the main floor of the house, looking into the rooms.

"What are you looking for?" Mamm asked.

"Ezra." Ruby stood in the center of the kitchen, her hands on her hips. "Daniel is here, and the girls are upstairs. I thought

Ezra was with them, but I don't hear him."

"He's probably just watching his sisters. Do you want me to go check?"

Ruby shook her head. "I'll do it. I need to take a break after scrubbing the bedroom floor."

She climbed the steep, narrow steps until her head rose above the level of the attic floor. She only saw the girls. "Is Ezra here with you?"

Roseanna stopped her progress across the attic floor, crawling this time instead of running. "He said he was going outside to help Daed work."

"How long ago?"

"Not long. He went downstairs while we were playing house."

Ruby backed down the steps. The little boy must have gone out the front door without being seen. She stepped out onto the wooden porch and walked around the house to where Gideon was on a ladder, applying whitewash to the new siding.

"Did Ezra come find you?"

"Ne, I haven't seen him." He stopped painting and looked at her. "Isn't he in the house with you?"

Ruby's lungs were tight, as if they wouldn't allow her to get a breath. "He told Roseanna and Sophia he was coming out here to help you, but I didn't see him leave the house."

Gideon climbed down the ladder. "He couldn't have gotten far. You look around the house, and I'll check the barn and the other buildings." He stopped, looking into her face. "Don't worry. Little boys wander off all the time. We'll find him."

As Gideon headed for the barn, Ruby walked around the house, trying to peer into the woods around it, but the underbrush was too thick. By the time she reached Gideon's ladder again, she was sweating, but she shivered. She had lost Ezra. She was responsible for him and she had lost him. Where could he be?

Suddenly she remembered the well. What if the wooden cover had rotted . . . She ran to the spot, just a few yards from the back door. The strong cover Daed had made years ago was weathered but still solid. When she tried to lift it, she knew Ezra could never have lifted it on his own. She sat down on the cover, her hands over her face. Where could he be?

The woods behind the house were silent except for the drone of insects. No sound of a boy playing or scared or calling. Her knees quivered. Who had given her this responsibility? Didn't they know she wasn't the person to take charge of four children? Lovinia should have known better. Mamm should have stopped her.

Ruby swallowed and wiped a tear from her cheek. She wasn't the person Lovinia thought she was. She wasn't the person anyone thought she was. She wasn't strong enough or smart enough to take care of others . . . she could barely take care of herself. Look what had happened with Ned. She hugged her knees and rocked as she sat on the well cover. It all started with Ned. And now Ezra was the one to pay. She knew she shouldn't have offered to care for the children, and now Ezra was lost. She dashed away another tear.

Suddenly, Gideon appeared around the corner of the house, Ezra in his arms.

"Look who I found," he said.

Ruby turned away. Her face must be blotchy, and she hadn't been able to stop the tears.

Gideon opened the back door and sent Ezra inside to play with his sisters, then came and sat next to her on the well cover. "What is wrong? Ezra hadn't gotten far, he was down by the old chicken coop."

Ruby shook her head. "I'm glad you found him." She turned so her back was to him. "This isn't going to work, Gideon. Eliza-

191

beth will have to help you with the children. I can't do it."

"I told you, little boys wander off all the time. It isn't anything to cry about."

She shrugged his hand off her shoulder. "I'm not crying. I'm just not the person for this task. It's too much responsibility."

"What do you mean?"

"I mean that I can't do anything to help. Everything I try turns out wrong. Roseanna barely tolerates my presence, and Sophia has started sucking her thumb again. Ezra . . ." She waved a hand toward the outbuildings. "Who knows what Ezra is doing? He used to talk, but now he never says anything."

"That isn't true, and you know it. He talks all the time."

"Not as much as he used to. Not as much as before . . . before he lost his mother." Gideon was silent, and she turned toward him again. "Even Daniel cries all the time."

"He's getting new teeth. It doesn't have anything to do with you." Gideon took her hand. "The children miss Lovinia, but they're young. This is the first time they have lost someone important to them, and they don't know how they're supposed to act."

"I thought . . . I hoped they would learn

to love me. Lovinia said they would, but —"

"They do love you. They just haven't been able to show it yet."

Ruby pressed her lips together. Gideon was wrong. The children didn't love her because she was unlovable. She was hard and brash, too quick to act and too slow to think. And she wasn't worthy of any man's . . . anyone's love.

Gideon tugged at the hand he was holding. "Lovinia was a wise woman. She could see into people's hearts and tell what they were like on the inside. That's why she loved you so much. She saw the Ruby that you don't show anyone else."

Looking into his eyes, Ruby saw that Gideon believed what he said.

"Don't give up on us," he said. "We need you. The children need you." He looked down at her hand, then released it. "Not many people around here knew Lovinia, but you were her friend. You, more than anyone else, understand what I —" He cleared his throat. "What the children lost when Lovinia passed away. You loved their mother, and you love them because of her. No one can take care of them better than you can."

Gideon leaned his forearms on his knees, lacing his fingers together.

"What if I lose Ezra again? What if Sophia never stops sucking her thumb?" Ruby took a deep breath. "What if I'm not the right person?" She didn't ask him what she was truly afraid of, that they would never learn to love her.

"I've been confused about many things over the past several months, but there's one thing I'm sure of." He looked at her. "You are the woman the Good Lord has provided to care for my children. Never doubt that."

He went back to his ladder on the other side of the house, but his words rang hollow in Ruby's heart. Gideon was wrong. God would never have chosen her for this task.

By the end of Wednesday afternoon, Ruby and Lydia had finished readying the house and had taken the children back to the farm while Gideon put the last coat of whitewash on the new siding. As he stood back to see if there were any spots he had missed, Ruby came walking along the lane from the road. He could hardly see her in the shadowed dusk under the trees.

"Did you finish painting?"

Gideon turned his head sideways, trying to see any imperfections. "It's hard to tell with the light fading so quickly."

She laughed. "It's nearly dark and I've already put the children to bed. I came to see if you were ready for your supper."

"Is it that late already?" Gideon sloshed the brush around in the bucket of water he set aside for cleanup.

"That late and past. It's after nine o'clock."

Suddenly Gideon's stomach rumbled. He left the brush in the water to soak until morning and placed a board on top of the pail of leftover whitewash to protect it until he needed it again. "Then I guess I'm ready for supper."

He started toward the road and Ruby fell into step beside him.

"Is the house done? Are you ready to move in?"

As they reached the end of the lane, they came out into the twilight of late evening. The sun had set, and the first stars were shining in the eastern sky. This was where Ruby would turn up the hill to Elizabeth's house and he would go down to Abraham and Lydia's home.

Gideon stopped, thinking of her question. "Not until I make some furniture. We need beds and a table, at least."

"I think Daed has some things stored in their attic. We'll have to look through them and see what you can use."

Gideon rubbed his right arm. The muscles were sore after painting all day. "We'll need some supplies too. Food, some kitchen-wares. Things like that."

He said the words before he thought. He had so little money. Not enough for a doctor, and certainly not enough to furnish a house.

"It sounds like you need to take a trip into Millersburg. Daed was saying at supper that he hoped someone was going soon. He needs a tool repaired before harvesttime."

"Never mind," he said, turning away. "It will have to wait."

"Wait for what?" She circled him until he had to look at her again. "If you're going to live here, you need to have food and other supplies for your family."

"We'll have to make do until I can afford store-bought things." He tried to smile. "I have only a few coins."

"But you still need to buy some food. Bacon, oats, flour, beans . . ." She listed the items off on her fingers, then glanced up at him. "How much money do you have?"

She was just as brash and nosy as ever.

"I have enough to buy a sack of beans, and maybe some flour."

"Then I'll buy the bacon and oats. I have

196

some money left. And I know where there is a bee tree. We can use honey for sweetener."

"I can't let you do that." Gideon felt his face heat.

"Why not? Honey is the best sweetener there is. I like it better than sugar."

"I meant that I can't let you buy food for my family. It isn't right."

She crossed her arms. "I won't let the children starve. Not when I have the means to buy food for them. You can pay me back later, if you think you need to."

"All right." Gideon gave up the argument. He had a feeling he would lose many arguments if he spent much time with Ruby. "Is Millersburg far away? Can I make the trip in one day?"

"It's about twelve miles, so it's a long day, but that's how we usually do it."

Gideon took a deep breath and let it out slowly. The last time he had gone to town, he hadn't come home for weeks. But this was Ohio. Perhaps the war hadn't reached its greedy fingers this far. "You'll have to tell me how to get there."

"I'll do better than that. I'll go along to show you the way. We can take the children and make it a fun trip for all of us."

"We'll have to leave early in the morning." Gideon watched her upturned face in the starlight. Her smile told how much she looked forward to the day away from her usual routine.

"I'll go to Mamm's house early, before Daed goes out to do the chores, and make sure the children are ready to go. And I'll pack a dinner for us to eat in town tomorrow. There is a nice grassy spot by the courthouse."

Gideon shrugged, amazed again at Ruby's energy. "We'll leave at first light, then."

She waved and ran up the hill. Her white kapp was all he could see, but he waited until she had turned off the road toward Elizabeth's cabin. Only Ruby would be so pleased at the thought of a trip to town. For him it was only an unwanted chore.

The next morning, Gideon woke in time to help Abraham with the barn work. Every night before he went to bed, he told the older man to wake him in the morning, but Abraham never did. Today though, he woke as soon as he heard Abraham stirring downstairs. Or perhaps he never really slept.

As Gideon milked the cows, he thought through the few coins he had brought with him from Maryland. There was enough to buy basic food, like salt and flour, but nothing extra. Meanwhile, he was grateful that Ruby had offered to buy some things. The children had endured enough privations over the past year.

They ate a quick breakfast, not wanting to wait for Lydia to fix a big meal. Ruby had gotten to the house while he had been out doing chores, so the children were awake and dressed. Sleepy, but excited about the day's plans.

"Leave Daniel here with me," Lydia said. "I'll enjoy having him around, and he won't enjoy the trip as much as the older children will."

She gave Gideon a list of her own, and Abraham handed him a scythe blade.

"Ruby knows where the smithy is. We need a new one just like this, and a new handle for this one."

Gideon wrapped the scythe blade in an old grain sack and laid it in the back of the wagon. He climbed onto the seat and held the horses still while Ruby got ready to get into the seat next to him, but Roseanna pushed past her.

"I want to sit by my daed," she said, not looking at Ruby. "You can sit in the back."

Gideon waited until Roseanna sat down. "What did you just do?"

The ever-present frown was on her face. "I wanted to sit by you."

"Did you ask if you could?"

She shook her head, looking at her feet.

"You pushed ahead of Ruby. Was that the right thing to do?"

She shook her head again.

"You need to take your place in the back. Ruby will sit up here."

Roseanna looked at him. "She doesn't belong here. She isn't our mamm."

Gideon glanced at Ruby, who was sitting in the back of the wagon, quiet and still for once, but listening to every word.

"She belongs here because she's our friend. She should sit in front because she is older than you are and must be respected."

Roseanna's frown deepened, and Gideon pushed down the anger rising at his daughter's disobedience. He didn't want to leave Roseanna at home to make Lydia's day miserable, but he couldn't let this defiance slide, could he?

"Gideon," Ruby said. "Is there room for three on the seat?"

When he nodded, Ruby climbed onto the bench with Roseanna sitting between them.

"Is this all right?" she asked Roseanna. "Can we share the wagon seat?"

Roseanna nodded and scooted closer to Gideon. Ruby made sure Ezra and Sophia were comfortable in the back of the wagon,

200

and Gideon jiggled the reins on the horses' backs. He looked sideways at his daughter who was looking straight ahead and as close to him as she could get on the crowded seat, and then at Ruby, who crowded the edge of the seat on the other side. After they came out of the valley, they reached a crossroad where Ruby indicated that he should turn left.

He looked into the back of the wagon. Sophia and Ezra had both gone back to sleep, their heads pillowed on some feed sacks in the bottom of the wagon bed. Roseanna yawned, then snuggled against him. Above them, the sky turned from dove gray to a pale blue, then streaks of yellow light covered the sky as the sun rose.

Ruby turned in her seat to look at it, shading her eyes. "I love to watch the sunrise. Do you?"

He chuckled. "I've rarely seen it. I'm usually in the barn doing chores when it comes up. But I do enjoy the early mornings."

They rode quietly for a few minutes, listening to the bird calls around them. The light grew stronger and mist rose from the open fields.

"I think the children have all gone back to sleep," Ruby said, her voice quiet.

"I'm not asleep," Roseanna said. She sat

up and stretched. "How long will it be until we get there?"

"It will take us a few hours." Ruby patted her lap. "Do you want to lay your head on my lap so you can sleep for a while? I woke you up very early, and a nap will help the time go by faster."

Roseanna snuggled closer to Gideon, then yawned. "I suppose so."

She laid her head on Ruby's lap but sat up again.

"Isn't it comfortable?" Ruby asked.

"I guess it is." Roseanna yawned again. "But it's crowded."

Gideon tried not to smile. "You could lie down in the back with Sophia and Ezra."

She looked at her brother and sister, now sound asleep, and nodded.

Ruby helped her climb down to the wagon bed, and soon Roseanna was asleep, her arm around Sophia.

"I'm sorry she acted the way she did," Gideon said as he and Ruby both moved away from the edges of the wagon seat toward the center. "I don't know what got into her this morning."

"I do." Ruby straightened her twisted skirts. "She misses her mother, but she doesn't want anyone else to take her place. I'm here, caring for her and the others, and she doesn't like it."

"She doesn't have a choice." Gideon stared at the horses' ears. None of them had a choice.

"She'll learn that I'm not trying to take her mother's place, and then she'll be better. I hope we'll be able to be friends, eventually."

"You're much more patient than I am. I was ready to leave her at home this morning."

Ruby took a deep breath, watching a pair of pigeons fly up from the dirt road as they approached. "This is better, I think. She learned that you're willing to compromise and to understand what she's feeling."

"I thought I just gave in to her."

She shook her head. "You let her give in a little, and she found out that she hasn't lost you. She can still be with you."

"And that's important?"

"A girl's father is always important."

Gideon let her words sink in. He had always felt the girls belonged to Lovinia and the boys belonged to him, but Ruby was right. Children needed both a mother and a father, and if they lost one, then they had double the need for the other. He had asked a lot from Roseanna during her mother's illness. No more than other children in the same situation, but that didn't mean she was an adult yet. She still had a child's need for love and reassurance.

"Yesterday you said you didn't think you were the right person to care for the children." He waited until she looked at him. "But you understand them and what they need better than anyone else, including me."

He glanced at the children to make sure they were still sleeping, then leaned closer to the woman next to him.

"This is what Lovinia saw in you, and why she made us promise what we promised."

Ruby's eyes grew wide, then she blushed and turned away from him.

Gideon didn't say anything more. He had already said too much.

8

Millersburg was busier than Ruby remembered it from her last trip. Gideon drove to the blacksmith shop first and ordered the new scythe while Ruby and the children waited in the wagon. Ruby held Ezra on her lap while the girls knelt in the wagon bed watching the people go by.

"Are there any children here?" Sophia asked, tugging on Ruby's skirt. "I only see grownups."

"The children might be in school today." Ruby wasn't sure of the Millersburg's school schedule, but she knew there was at least one in town.

"We never went to school," Roseanna said. "We didn't have one at home."

"We have one in Weaver's Creek, but it doesn't meet during the summer."

"Will we go there?" Roseanna's face was hopeful.

"I don't know why you wouldn't, but your

father will decide." Ruby watched a shiny black carriage drive by. "Henry and William go there, and the Stuckey children."

Gideon climbed into the wagon. "The scythes will be ready by midafternoon. You said there was a place we can park the wagon?"

"For sure." Ruby pointed ahead. "Another block farther, then turn left just before we reach the courthouse. The public square has a hitching rail in the shade and a water trough."

As they continued down the street, Gideon said, "Do you have Lydia's list?"

Ruby held it up. "Did you make one?"

He shook his head as he turned the team onto Monroe Street at the public square. "I'm not sure what we need. I hoped you would have an idea of how to stock a kitchen."

"We'll start at the store across the street. That's where Mamm usually buys her things."

The store was crowded, and Ruby saw they would need to wait for the clerk's attention. She read through Mamm's list.

"Roseanna, don't let go of Sophia's hand." She looked for Gideon. He had found a place to stand near the door, Ezra in his arms.

"What do we need to buy?" Roseanna slipped her right hand into Ruby's, keeping a tight grip on Sophia with her left.

Ruby read through the list. "Mamm needs some fabric and thread. Also, some coffee, salt, and cinnamon." She moved ahead in the line, following the woman in front of them. "And then we need things for your new house."

"Why are there so many people here?" Roseanna's face was blotchy, and her lips were dry. Elizabeth was the same way when she had to face strangers.

"It will be all right." Ruby smiled at the girl. "Many people live in Millersburg and even more come from their farms, the way we did today."

Roseanna tugged at her sleeve and Ruby bent down. "But I don't know any of them." Her eyes brimmed with tears. "What if they're bad?"

Ruby put one arm around Roseanna and drew Sophia closer with her other arm. "Most people aren't bad, and your daed and I are here to protect you if there is a bad person."

She glanced at the woman behind them, who smiled at the girls.

"It is certainly busy in the store today," she said. She spoke Englisch and the girls stared at her. "You look like you're the same ages as my granddaughters. What are your names?"

Ruby translated the woman's questions, and Roseanna blanched. "Do I have to tell her my name?"

"It's the friendly thing to do."

Roseanna swallowed, then said, "I'm Roseanna, and this is Sophia."

"Well, I didn't catch everything you said" — the woman laughed and winked at Ruby — "but I think you're Roseanna and the little one is Sophia." She turned to Ruby. "Is it all right if I give them some candy? I always carry some for my granddaughters."

"For sure." Ruby switched to Deitsch as she spoke to the girls. "You may have some candy. It's all right."

The woman took a small tin from her reticule and opened it. Inside were little candy balls covered in sugar. Roseanna and Sophia each took one.

"Denki," Roseanna said. She smiled at the woman. "Ruby was right. Most people aren't bad."

"Be sure to eat them before the sugar melts." The woman smiled again and turned to Ruby. "Such sweet girls. You must be so proud of them."

Ruby smiled, knowing that the woman

wouldn't understand the sin of pride. Very few Englischers did. "Thank you for giving them the candy. They were quite worried in this crowd of strangers, but your kindness has relieved their fears."

Then it was Ruby's turn at the counter and she gave her order to the clerk. After the goods were packaged and paid for, Gideon carried them to the wagon.

They ate dinner sitting under a tree near the courthouse, and afterward the children played in the soft, shady grass.

"Do we need to go anywhere else while we're in town?" Gideon asked.

"I was able to find everything we needed at the store, so all we have to do is wait until the scythes are ready."

Roseanna came over to them and sat next to Ruby. "That woman in the store was nice."

"She liked you and Sophia. She said you reminded her of her granddaughters."

"I wasn't nice to you this morning." Roseanna picked a blade of grass and twirled it between her fingers. "Am I a bad person?"

Ruby glanced at Gideon, but he was stretched out in the grass with his hat over his face and hadn't heard what Roseanna said. "You aren't a bad person. Sometimes even good people are tired and cross. But I understand how you were feeling this morning."

"I'm sorry. I don't know why I was so mean." Roseanna looked into her face. "I really do like you. I've liked you ever since the first day I saw you."

"I've liked you ever since then too." Ruby smiled. "I think we can be good friends, don't you?"

Roseanna stared at the grass in her hand. "I don't want to forget my mamm."

Ruby leaned down on her elbow, close to Roseanna, and picked her own blade of grass. "You won't forget your mamm. I know you miss her. I miss her too. She was my best friend."

The girl's eyebrows went up in surprise. "You miss her? I thought —" She stopped, her face turning bright red. "One of the girls at church said you were happy Mamm died because then you could marry Daed."

"That girl was wrong." Ruby grasped Roseanna's hand in hers. "I loved your mamm, and I will always miss her. I am very sad that she passed away."

"Are you and Daed going to get married?"

Ruby glanced at Gideon. His chest rose and fell in deep, even breaths.

"I don't know if your daed and I will get

210

married someday. But I do know that he loves you, and so do I. We will both continue to take care of you and Sophia and your brothers."

"I think you would be a nice mother." The corners of Roseanna's mouth lifted a little. "You're a lot of fun to be with."

Ruby drew her hand away. Being a mother was too much of a responsibility, and no matter what Gideon said, anyone else would be a better choice.

"Denki, Roseanna. But for now, we'll stick with being friends."

Shouting from the street nearby woke Gideon up from his nap on the lawn of the public square. A group of men had gathered in front of the courthouse.

"What is going on?" Ruby asked.

"I'm not sure." Gideon rose to his feet and put his hat on. "I'll go see. Stay here with the children."

He walked closer to the crowd, stopping when he reached the edge. A man was standing on the courthouse steps reading from a piece of paper in his hand.

"More folks are joining us, so I'll read the telegram again," the man said, his voice quieting the crowd. "It's a message that has come up the line from Cincinnati." He

211

cleared his throat. "Morgan's Raiders in Ohio."

Gideon's knees started shaking. He had heard of Morgan's Raiders, a band of freewheeling cavalry soldiers working on the outskirts of the Confederate army. Their presence in Ohio could only mean one thing: the war was coming this way.

The man continued reading. "Last seen in Jackson, seventy miles south of Columbus on Wednesday evening. Heading north and east. Troops sent to intercept. All citizens should be on alert."

"They're headin' our way!" A man a few feet away from Gideon shook his hand in the air as he shouted. "We have to stop them!"

"They tried that in Corydon, Indiana, last week," the man on the courthouse steps said. "Citizens were killed. We don't want that kind of bloodbath here."

Gideon stepped back as the crowd surged forward, each man shouting his opinion of what should be done. He made his way back to his family, dropping to the ground a little away from where the children were gathered around Ruby. His head pounded as he buried his face in his hands.

He had to run, take the children and go somewhere . . . anywhere away from the approaching raiders.

From the depths of his mind came the echo of cannon fire, gunshots, and the cries of the wounded. Screams of agony coming from the boy lying at Gideon's feet, his face mutilated by gunfire, one arm missing, and his eyes staring at Gideon, pleading with him. Then Gideon's eyes lowered to the place where his legs should have been . . .

Someone shook his arm.

"No, I can't. I can't." He twisted away from —

"Gideon? What happened?"

Then Roseanna's voice. "Daed? Are you all right?"

He opened his eyes and saw Ruby and the children staring at him. He wasn't in a forest in the mountains of Virginia. There was no gunfire. He willed his breathing to slow, his trembling limbs to still.

"Ja." He tried to smile. "Ja, I'm all right." He stood. His hat had fallen to the ground, and he picked it up, dusting it off before covering his head again. "We need to go home."

"Are the scythes ready?"

He forced himself to smile at Ruby but felt his chin quiver. "Ja, it's time to pick them up from the blacksmith and be on our way."

The children got into the wagon, but Ruby watched him carefully as he checked the horses' harnesses and led them to the watering trough.

"You aren't all right. What has happened?"

Gideon glanced at the crowd still gathered in front of the courthouse. "I'll tell you about it later. I don't want to risk the children overhearing."

"Are we in danger?"

He swallowed and shook his head. "Not right now, but we need to get home."

The children slept as they traveled along the quiet road toward Weaver's Creek, but Gideon couldn't relax. Phantom riders followed the wagon, their scabbards rattling against the horses' saddles, their faces grim and dark, the rolling beat of drums following them. But whenever Gideon turned to look, the road was empty. Peaceful.

Or maybe that was a deception. The riders could be just over the ridge ahead . . . His hands shook.

"Gideon." Ruby leaned closer. "What is wrong?"

He shook his head like a dog to clear the haunting memories. "There are Confederate soldiers heading this way. We need to get out of Ohio. We need to leave."

"How do you know?"

She laid one hand on his arm and that simple, gentle touch rippled through his consciousness like a pebble in a quiet pool. The phantom riders disappeared.

He turned toward her. The freckles on her nose stood out against her pale face. "I didn't mean to frighten you," he said. "I'm sorry. I don't know what came over me."

"You said soldiers were coming?"

"That was the news in town." He pushed at the panic that threatened to rise again. "Morgan's Raiders are in Ohio, and someone said they were coming this way."

She shrugged, letting her hand slide off his arm, and he wished for its calm pressure again. He gathered the reins in one hand and grasped her hand that rested on the seat between them.

"I don't understand," she said. "I thought the war was in the East, and the South, not here in Ohio. So why would you need to leave?"

Gideon glanced at the sleeping children in the wagon bed, surrounded by boxes and packages of supplies for their new home. If the raiders came to Weaver's Creek, how could he protect them? What if . . . what if he was taken again?

"I can't fight, and I won't stay to put my children in danger. If something happened

215

to them —"

"What would happen? We're safe in Weaver's Creek, aren't we? The soldiers wouldn't attack us."

"They might not attack, but they would steal supplies, horses, livestock." He glanced at her. He hadn't been able to protect his family in Maryland, and he wouldn't be able to in Weaver's Creek, either. If he lost the children . . . or Ruby . . . He swallowed, then went on. "They have no respect for people or communities. They are like a hungry leviathan, devouring everything in its path."

She looked across the fields, her hair gleaming in the sunlight where the strands had escaped her bonnet. "If they are hungry, then we should feed them."

"You don't understand. They take and take until they have devoured or destroyed everything. We would starve."

"Then we would starve." She turned toward him. "Remember what the Good Book says. 'I was a stranger . . .' "

Gideon shook his head. "This is different. These men are not needy strangers. They are soldiers. They are the enemy."

"You know the Good Book says something about enemies too."

He stared at her. She wasn't laughing.

"These aren't the enemies the Bible is talking about."

"What other kinds of enemies are there?"

He had no answer. She hadn't seen the power of an army, the disregard for life, the utter godlessness of a soldier who could kill a man as easily as look at him. A soldier who could send the final bullet into the heart of a dying boy . . .

Mein Herr . . .

She grasped his hand in both of hers, a solid anchor that pushed back the darkness. "Every soldier is a man. Or a boy. Someone's son, or brother, or husband."

"Every soldier is a killer."

"My brother isn't." She waited until he looked at her. "If soldiers came to Weaver's Creek, we would treat them the same as we would anyone else."

Her face was sincere, her eyes wide and innocent. She didn't know how cruel and heartless the world could be.

Gideon tore his gaze from her face and watched the horses plodding along the dusty road. In his imagination, he could see the cavalry thundering down the slope to the little community, riders peeling off to Elizabeth's house, his house, Samuel's farm. Then the main body galloping across the stone bridge into the yard of the home farm.

Abraham stepping out onto the porch to meet them . . . then crumpling, a blossom of red at his chest.

"You don't know what they are capable of." His jaw clenched.

"But I do know what God requires of us." Gideon knew also. Humility, kindness, service, love. Most of all, love. How many times did Jesus tell his followers to love their neighbors? Pray for their enemies? His shoulders slumped. He had built many sermons around those same themes. But when it came to living out what was required, it took a stronger man than he was.

9

When Sunday morning worship was over, Ruby helped the other women of the church set out the cold foods for the fellowship meal. Cold meat, cottage cheese, tomatoes, and loaves of sliced bread were all available for folks to eat. Feeding so many people would have been a lot of work, except that many women and girls pitched in, including Roseanna.

Ruby watched her carry a bowl of cottage cheese to one of the tables. Roseanna often reminded her of herself at that age. Different from the other girls and not knowing why. At the same time, Ruby had never formed any close friendships. She chewed her lower lip. She didn't want that same future for Lovinia's daughter.

"I appreciate your help," Ruby said, pulling the girl aside for a moment, "but the other girls your age are playing. Are you sure you don't want to join them?"

Roseanna moved closer to her, whispering into her ear. "I can play with them later. Mamm used to help with the meal after church, and I can too, can't I?"

"For sure you can." Ruby gave her a quick hug. "If your mamm was here, she would be pleased."

Roseanna grinned and went back to the kitchen for another dish. Ruby followed her, then stood back as Margaretta Stuckey came out the door with a plate of sliced tomatoes in one hand and a plate of cold meat in the other. Katie, Margaretta's daughter and Jonas's intended bride, was right behind her.

She stopped when she saw Ruby. Her eyes were rimmed with red. "Ruby, can I talk to you after the meal?"

"What's wrong?"

Katie stepped closer to her. "I received a letter from Jonas yesterday, and I'm so worried about him. You know I can't talk to Mama about it, and I don't want to worry Lydia."

"For sure." Ruby patted her arm. "We can go for a walk together."

Katie nodded her thanks as she went on.

An hour later, the meal was done, the dishes clean, and Ruby looked around for the children. Roseanna and Sophia were playing with the other girls, and Ezra was with Gideon, his head on his father's shoulder. Daniel was asleep in Mamm's lap, so she went to find Katie.

"We can walk along the road, if you'd like," Ruby said.

"I don't care where we go, as long as we're alone." Katie reached into the waistband of her apron, pulled out a folded letter, and handed it to Ruby. "I want you to read this and tell me if I should be as worried about Jonas as I am."

"Are you sure you want me to read this? After all, Jonas might be my brother, but he's your beau." Ruby smiled, trying to lighten the mood, but it didn't help.

"We can sit on that log there," Katie said, walking toward a log at the end of the Lehmans' farm lane.

Ruby opened the letter.

July 7, 1863, Gettysburg, Pennsylvania

My dearest Katie,

As you can see by the line above, I am not in Washington City at the moment. There was a large battle here in Pennsylvania during the first three days of July. On July fourth, the Confederate army left Gettysburg, and by all reports is heading south to cross the Potomac. But the battle was horrible. Many men died, perhaps thousands, and even more are wounded. I have come from Washington with many other doctors and even some women to tend to the wounded. We have set up a field hospital that many are calling Camp Letterman after the medical officer in charge.

The first thing I want to assure you of is that I am safe and well, but my heart is breaking. Death is everywhere. My first impression when I stepped off the train was the horrible, awful odor of decaying flesh. The dead, both human and horses, lie everywhere on the battlefield that stretches over a large area — thousands of acres in my estimation. The July sun has bloated the corpses, and the blood lies in pools on the soaked ground. The flies are terrible, and we have to wear a handkerchief over our faces to keep from breathing them in.

The wounded are to be pitied above all. The medical officers think that all have been brought in from the battlefields, but I can tell from the way they speak about it in hushed tones that they are not sure. No one can bear to think of a man left out there to die, helpless and alone. The wounded that have been found are housed everywhere that a space can be made for them. On my first evening here after getting off the train, I was sent to a church where the wounded were lying on boards laid across the tops of the high-backed pews. I aided the ones I could, but I quickly ran out of supplies, so all we could do — the two female nurses and myself — was to offer a drink of water to the men. When we ran out of water, I went to find some more, but every stream, every spring, stinks of blood and decay. Every mud puddle is reddish brown with filth. But it is the only water we have, and I must offer it to the men to relieve their suffering.

I spent that night writing letters. Every soldier who was conscious was aware he would most likely die soon, so I wrote countless letters to wives, families, and sweethearts. I prayed with many of the men and tried to give them what comfort I could.

The next day I went to Camp Letterman, where I've been ever since. The doctors require my assistance at the many amputations they perform, and I am loath to say I have nearly become immune to the pain of the patients. I tell them, and myself, that this trial will be over soon, and then they will be able to get well and go home. But those men and I both know that it is more likely they will die and never see their earthly home again.

But oh, Katie, when will this suffering be over? How much more loss of life and destruction of souls can we bear?

It seems like it has been months since I have seen the blue sky or breathed clean air.

I am sorry that I cannot be more encouraging in this letter. I hope I will be able to send you a happier one in the future. We don't know what will happen in the next few weeks. Will Lee, the Confederate general, try again to reach Washington City? I pray that he will surrender. The Union forces had a decisive victory here at Gettysburg, the officers say, and it should be the end of the war.

I don't think it will be, though. Some days I feel as if this war will never end.

Always keep me in your prayers as I keep you in mine,

Jonas

Ruby slowly folded the letter and gave it

back to Katie. She thought of Jonas the last time he had come home, last winter while he was on a short leave from the army. He had been smiling, and seemed healthy, but his eyes were shadowed, as if he had seen things he didn't want to remember. Gideon's eyes . . . Ruby's heart wrenched. Gideon's eyes were the same, especially after he heard about the raiders who were in Ohio. What had he experienced during the time he had been forced to haul supplies for the army?

"What do you think?" Katie held the letter close to her. "He sounds so sad. Do you think he will be all right?"

Ruby forced herself to smile. "For sure he will be. Remember, he isn't near the fighting anymore. He has his work to do, and then he will return home."

Katie shook her head. "I don't mean that. I know he will probably be safe." She drew a deep breath that shuddered at the end. "I mean in his mind. He has seen and experienced so many terrible things." She locked eyes with Ruby. "I can't imagine being so used to a person's screams of pain that he feels he is immune to them. What kind of horror has he seen that an amputation seems like a good thing?"

Ruby couldn't answer, but she took Ka-

225

tie's hand in her own and squeezed it. She had no other comfort to give.

As he often did on a Sunday afternoon, Gideon found himself talking with Levi. The younger man was serious and determined to learn as much as he could about the history, theology, and doctrine of the church. His thirst for knowledge far outweighed many ministers Gideon had known.

"So, when Menno Simons wrote that true evangelical faith is of such a nature it cannot lie dormant, what did he mean?" Levi leaned against the fence along the pasture next to the Lehmans' barn, the home where the Sunday meeting was held this week.

"I think he meant that our faith must be active. It isn't something we hold inside ourselves, to satisfy ourselves and no one else. Remember the last part of that sentence? He wrote that faith 'spreads itself out in all kinds of righteousness and fruits of love.' "

"Therefore," Levi went on, his face flushed as it always was when he spoke of what he had been reading, "we should do what he lists next. Die to flesh and blood, destroy all lusts and forbidden desires —"

"Wait a minute." Gideon interrupted him with a restraining hand on his arm. "What did Simons say? Do we do those things?"

Levi pondered the question, his pale eyebrows meeting in a pucker between his eyes. "You're right. We don't do those things. Our faith does."

"Menno Simons didn't give us a list to follow, things we must do, but he wrote examples of what a living, nondormant faith does. It clothes the naked, feeds the hungry, comforts the sorrowful, and all the other things he wrote. There is quite a number of them, if I remember right."

Levi nodded. "Seventeen."

"You counted them?"

The younger man grinned. "For sure, I did. Didn't you?" His brow puckered again. "But how do we know if it is faith doing those things or if it is our own selves? It seems like it should be the same, either way."

"Who gives us our faith?"

"The Lord God does."

"So, it isn't something we do ourselves, is it? If our faith came from ourselves, it would be weak and fallible just as we are." Gideon thought for a moment, the threat of the coming raiders on his mind. "If you were faced with an enemy determined to harm you, but your faith was grounded in yourself, how long would you be able to endure?"

"You mean like the martyrs? The ones who were burned at the stake?"

Gideon nodded. "How long would you last before you denied your Lord to save your body?"

"They wouldn't even light the fire before I gave up." Levi shook his head. "But I see what you're saying. When we have faith" — he glanced at Gideon — "faith given by God, then he is the one who is working in us to keep our faith strong."

Gideon looked out over the pasture at the mares grazing in the lush grass while their foals sprawled near them. Where was his faith when he was in Virginia? Where was his faith when the captain ordered him to fire? He didn't . . . he couldn't fire the gun in his hands, but was that the Lord who restrained him? Or was it only fear that froze his muscles?

"Gideon?"

He looked at the young man. "I'm sorry. My mind drifted somewhere else. What were you saying?"

"I said, is it all right if I ask you a question?"

When Gideon nodded, Levi looked across the pasture.

"If a man and a woman . . . well . . . um . . ." He rubbed his nose and started again. "If a couple who isn't married act like they are . . . I mean . . . when they are alone . . . Well, is it a sin?"

Gideon looked closer at him. "Are we talking about you or someone else?"

The poor boy turned so red he was nearly purple. "Someone else. You can't think that I . . ." Even his ears were pink. "I don't even know a girl. I mean, not one I want to marry. I was wondering, that's all."

"Isn't this something you should ask your father?"

"I . . . I can't. He . . . he wouldn't understand."

"All right. Yes. If a couple is intimate before they marry, then it is a sin."

"Intimate?"

Gideon nodded toward the stallion in the next pasture that had stretched his head over the fence toward the mares, and Levi's eyebrows rose in understanding.

"For sure, ja. A sin." The young man sighed and wiped his sweating face with a cloth. "But if they get married later, does that make it all right?"

"They should still confess their sin before the church."

Gideon glanced at his friend again, remembering the expression on Levi's mother's face two weeks ago when he had been talking with Ruby. She couldn't think that he and Ruby were acting in a sinful manner, could she?

Levi wiped his face again. "What if, well, the couple was expecting . . ." He gestured toward the foals in the pasture. "Would that child be sinful too?"

Shaking his head, Gideon relaxed. Levi wasn't talking about him. "The sin belongs to the parents, not the child. But our gracious and merciful God offers forgiveness to all who come to him in repentance." He turned around, leaning back against the fence and watching the crowd of children playing in the shade of an elm tree. "Is this someone you know, Levi? If it is someone in the church, you should go to them and remind them of their need to confess."

"I can't do that." Levi kicked at the fence post.

"What are you going to do?"

"I don't know." Levi balled his fists on the top fence rail and rested his chin on them while he watched the horses. "When I read the Bible or Menno Simons's writings or the *Confession,* it seems so simple. But when I think about facing the person, it's like I've turned to ice. I can't do it."

"Bringing up someone's sin is hard."

"But if I'm ever called to be a minister, I'll have to do that, won't I?" He looked at Gideon. "Did you ever have to confront someone like that?"

Gideon pushed at the memories that flooded into his mind. The regret of remaining silent when he should have spoken. Remaining frozen like ice when he should have acted.

He shook his head. "No one in the church. But my daed did, long ago. I remember that it was very difficult, and he spent many sleepless nights praying." Gideon saw himself, a little boy, creeping to the edge of the loft. The image of the man kneeling beside his chair night after night was the only clear memory he had of his father. "But the labor was worthwhile, because the man confessed his sin and was welcomed back into the church."

Levi was silent for a few minutes. Gideon watched Ezra running through the yard, being chased by another little boy. It was good to see his children happy. They felt secure and loved in this place. They didn't feel the shadow of the war that haunted him.

"I heard something," Levi said, interrupting Gideon's thoughts. "I think you should know. Someone thinks you and Ruby might be acting inappropriately."

"I don't know where someone would get that idea. My wife —" Gideon broke off. Sometimes the grief stayed in the background, but other times it came upon him like the rush of a stream over a waterfall. "My wife has only recently passed away." He cleared his throat. "I wouldn't . . . couldn't think of doing anything like that with Ruby."

But then the memory of how Ruby's freckles had stood out against her pale skin struck him. He wouldn't remember that if he felt no attraction toward the woman.

Then he remembered Salome, Levi's mother, again. She kept looking his way today, just as she had during the last church Sunday. Is that where this rumor had started?

"I didn't think so," Levi continued. "But you never know what people will believe." He paused, drumming his fingers on the top board of the fence. "Father announced that there will be an election for a new minister in two weeks."

"I was in the meeting this morning, remember?" Gideon smiled, but his stomach was churning. He wasn't ready to think about an election.

"I know you don't want me to, but I'm

going to nominate you."

"You're supposed to pray about it first." Gideon's mouth was dry. "Make sure your choice is God's choice."

"I've been praying about it, and there are only two names I can consider." Levi clapped him on the shoulder. "Your name is the one I'm going to nominate, no matter what you say. I thought you'd want to know."

Before Gideon could protest, Levi went back to the house where the women had set out plates of cookies. Gideon stayed where he was, watching the folks in the yard.

The children were getting tired, so they should start toward home soon. Roseanna ran to where Ruby sat with another young woman Gideon didn't know. Ruby bent her head toward Roseanna, listening to her. Paying close attention. Any other adult would brush the child aside. Roseanna must have asked about him, because Ruby turned toward him and waved along with his daughter. He waved back, then Ruby and Roseanna went back to their conversation and Gideon turned to watch the horses again.

He missed Lovinia. He missed talking with her, spending quiet evenings by her side, planning for the future with her. He missed sharing his life with her. She would know what to do about his calling to be a minister, and she had always helped him when he had a tough decision to make. She would know what to say to Levi about the coming nomination.

God was right when he created men and women to join their lives together. Was this loneliness what Lovinia foresaw when she told him to marry Ruby? He sighed, pulling one hand over his face. Someday the loneliness might be enough to make him want to take that step.

Ruby was at Gideon's cabin early the next morning. The sky was gray with hanging clouds promising a cool, damp day. In the distance, she heard thunder rumble softly. Perhaps they would get some rain.

Gideon had already gone to the barn by the time she got there, so she crept up the stairs to the loft where she had slept with her sisters when she was a young girl. The room didn't seem as large as it had when she was a child, but then everything seemed smaller than it had then. Gideon had built a large bed and placed it on one side of the room, and on Saturday Ruby had stuffed a ticking full of fresh straw. All three of the older children were sound asleep on the soft mattress, Ezra lying sideways above his sisters' heads. Daniel's cot was next to the bed and he was awake, lying on his back, the toes of one foot grasped in his hands.

When he saw her, he grinned and sat up.

"How are you this morning, little one?" Ruby asked in a soft voice.

He pulled himself to his feet, reaching for her. She left the other children sleeping while she took him downstairs to change him into dry clothes, then poured some milk into his cup.

By the time Daniel had finished his milk, Gideon came in from his chores. He gave her a quick nod, then went straight to the sink to wash up.

"We need to set up a washing bench outside for you," Ruby said.

Gideon didn't answer as she put Daniel on the floor and gave him a wooden spoon to play with. Then she searched through the cupboards until she found the supplies they had purchased in Millersburg on Thursday. This would be the children's first breakfast in their new home, although Gideon had been living here since they had finished renovating the house last week.

"I hope oat porridge sounds good for breakfast," Ruby said. "I brought cream from home to have with it."

Gideon still didn't answer, and Ruby glanced toward him to find that he was staring at her. He had filled a cup with water from the pump and was drinking it.

Ruby started a fire in the stove. "I know oat porridge isn't a very big breakfast, but I thought I would also fry some of the bacon we bought in town. Should I also cook some eggs to go with it?"

When she looked at him again, he was still staring at her, a frown on his face.

"What is wrong?"

His eyes widened. "Nothing is wrong."

"Why were you staring at me?"

"Was I?" He rubbed his beard and finished his water. "I didn't mean to. I was thinking of something else. Did you know your daed planned to give me a cow?"

Ruby put some larger pieces of wood on the fire. "He never told me anything about it. Which cow is it?"

"The younger one. Bett. He said we had more need of a milk cow than the two of them."

We. The word started a warm feeling that Ruby quickly squelched. He meant the children. His family. The word had nothing to do with her.

"That sounds like Daed. He is always giving away things he doesn't think he and

236

Mamm need anymore."

Gideon sat at the table and pulled Daniel onto his lap. "He said he'd bring her over later today, so this afternoon we'll have our own milk."

"That's good." Ruby's thoughts went to the tasks she would need to add to her work. Straining the milk, making butter, making cheese. She smiled, thinking of how much fun it would be to do the chores along with Roseanna and Sophia. "Do you want me to milk her, or will you?"

"I'll do it. I only have the horses to care for." He frowned again.

"Now what are you thinking about?" Ruby put a pot of water on the stove to heat and poured in the oats she had set out to soak last night after putting the children to bed.

"There are things whirling around in my mind." He glanced at her. "Do you mind if I talk to you about them? That's one thing I miss —"

He shut his eyes, and Ruby waited. She knew the pain of missing Lovinia.

When he opened his eyes again, she said, "I know how valuable it can be to talk about things that are going through your mind, and I'm a good listener."

Gideon tapped the table with one finger until Daniel grabbed it and stuck it in his mouth. He smiled at his son, then looked at Ruby.

"I'm not sure about the condition of the roof." He looked up toward the ceiling. "It seems to be solid, but with rain coming, I'm not sure if we'll stay dry."

"I'll keep a watch out for leaks and let you know."

"I'll still want to replace the roof before winter. Does your daed have a shingle cutter?"

"I think so. You'll have to ask him."

Gideon tapped the table again and sighed. "Another thing. The election for a new minister will be in two weeks. I understand that the church recently lost one?"

Ruby nodded as she stirred the grain. "Since our bishop moved away, Amos has been the only preacher."

"Abraham asked if he could tell the others that I was already a minister and suggested that I could serve as one here."

"That is a good idea. I'm sure you were a wonderful minister in your church in Maryland."

Gideon shook his head. "I wasn't. My flock is scattered, and I'm no longer a minister. I'm not certain I could ever be one again."

"You must be. You are thoughtful and

kind. People listen to you and want to confide in you." She pressed her lips together before she said too much, then changed the direction of her thoughts. "God doesn't withdraw his calling so easily."

"That's the same thing Abraham said."

Ruby put more wood on the fire. The heat was beginning to warm the top of the stove, but it would be several minutes before she would be able to start cooking the bacon, so she sat at the table with Gideon. "Daed is usually right."

He didn't look at her.

"What else?" she asked.

"I can't stop thinking about Morgan's Raiders coming this way."

"We don't know they're headed toward us. We only heard that they are in Ohio."

Gideon rubbed at a rough place on the table. Daniel bounced on his knee, but he didn't seem to notice. "You never know which way they'll go. If they come here —"

Ruby leaned toward him. "You don't know that they will. That trouble is for tomorrow. We only need to worry about today."

"But we need to be prepared. We need to find a place in the woods for you and the children to hide, and we need to be able to hide the stock too. The grain in the fields . . .

well, they'll probably just trample it." His eyes glimmered in the light from the lamp in the center of the table as he looked at Ruby. "I know what these soldiers are capable of. We need to be ready for them."

"Have you talked to Daed about this? Or anyone else?"

"You know they wouldn't understand the need, just like you. You've never lived through it, so you don't know the devastation they leave behind and the violence they're capable of."

Gideon was right, she had never experienced what he described. But soldiers had passed near them before, volunteers on their way east to join the army. They had left the farms alone as they passed by. Then she remembered Jonas's letter and his description of the aftermath of the battle in Pennsylvania. Maybe Gideon was right to be concerned.

Daniel wiggled in Gideon's lap and he turned the baby toward him, making faces to keep the little one amused. Ruby let concerns about the war slide away as the bacon started sizzling. She rose to stir the oatmeal. It wasn't beginning to steam yet, so she moved the bacon to a cooler part of the stove to continue cooking slowly.

When she turned back to the table, Gideon was staring at her.

"What are you thinking about now?"

She pumped water into the coffeepot and poured grounds in. After setting it on the stove, she sat in her chair again, taking Daniel as he reached for her.

Gideon tapped the table again with his finger, frowning as he watched it. "Has Salome Beiler said anything to you about me?"

"Salome rarely speaks to me. I don't think she considers me a good example of an Amish woman. Why?"

"I have noticed her watching me. Watching us when we were standing together a couple weeks ago. She didn't look happy."

Ruby sighed, then went to the stove with Daniel on her hip. The oatmeal was steaming, and she stirred it before turning back to Gideon. "Salome has appointed herself to be the overseer of the women in the church since her husband is the minister. In all the years I've known her, she has never approved of me."

Ruby turned the bacon. Salome's disapproval had heightened when Ruby was a young woman. Could she know about Ned Hamlin? She hitched Daniel higher on her hip. No one knew about him except for Elizabeth, and her sister would never confide in Salome.

"So I should ignore her." Gideon leaned back in his chair.

"If she has a concern about you, she'll take it to Amos first. If he thinks there's something to complain about, he'll let you know." Ruby turned to Gideon. "Breakfast is almost ready. Would you hold Daniel while I call the children?"

"I'll get the children. The smell of the bacon frying is making me hungry, and you still have eggs to cook." He took Daniel from her, then caught her elbow before she could turn back to the stove. "I appreciate you taking the time to talk with me. It helps me clear my thoughts."

His eyes were soft in the lamplight and the pressure of his hand was warm and safe. Not the adrenaline-pulsing rush she had felt during her one week with Ned, but comforting, asking for more. Asking for . . . love?

He squeezed her arm gently, then went up the stairs. Ruby rubbed her elbow, now rapidly cooling. She must have only been imagining it. She didn't deserve anyone's love. She didn't.

10

Abraham brought the cow over that afternoon as he had promised. Gideon had spent the morning making a pen for her in the barn and repairing the fence that formed the boundary of the pasture. When he had first looked at the barn, he hadn't thought it was salvageable, but when he had examined it, he saw that the roof had been sagging because one of the ridgepole's supports had broken. Samuel and Abraham, along with the three Stuckey brothers, worked with him on Saturday, and now the roof was as solid as the day it had been built.

"That old barn looks almost new," Abraham said as he led the cow up the lane from the road. He tugged on his beard. "We've both turned a bit gray, that barn and I, but it looks like we're good for a few more years."

Gideon glanced at the older man. "I'd say more than a few for both of you."

But the memory of the vision of the red bloom on Abraham's white shirt made his palms sweat. He pushed away the thought that it might have been a premonition of his friend's death.

"We missed the children at our house this morning," Abraham said as he put the cow in her pen and unfastened the lead from her rope halter. "With only Lydia and I for breakfast, the house was too quiet."

Gideon leaned on the side of the pen watching the cow. "When we showed up at your door last spring, I didn't have any idea we would be imposing on you for so long." He swallowed. If Lovinia hadn't been ill, he might have driven on the next morning, and then he would have missed Abraham's friendship. The sight of Ruby sitting at the table with him in the early morning with the lamplight making her face glow, reflecting off the tendrils of red hair, jolted him. If they hadn't stayed in Weaver's Creek, he would never have met Ruby.

"We're glad you stayed. And we're also glad you're settling so close. Lydia misses your children so much, you would think you had moved all the way to Millersburg."

Gideon grinned. "They've been gone for less than a day."

"And I passed Ruby on the road just now

as she was taking them down to see Lydia."
Abraham chuckled. "My wife baked some
cookies this morning, hoping she would
have a chance to spoil them today."

"I appreciate all you've done for them.
For us. My children have never known what
it is like to have grandparents, but you and
Lydia have given them that gift."

The cow found the hay Gideon had put
in her manger and pulled some out with a
twist of her head, the strands protruding
from her mouth like whiskers as she
watched them.

"The Good Lord brought you and your
family to us." Abraham leaned his forearms
on the top plank of the pen. "That brings
me to the subject of our church. We need
you as a minister. We need you to fulfill your
calling."

Gideon's head felt light and he took a
deep breath, whooshing it out. How many
times would Abraham bring this up? "That
calling is over. I failed, and the Lord won't
ask me again. Look at King Saul, in the
Bible. He failed, and God removed his
blessing, putting David in his place."

"There are many more examples in the
Bible of God using people who failed to accomplish his purpose. That same King David comes to mind. He sinned against the

245

Lord many times, most notably in the affair with Bathsheba, but the Bible still refers to him as a man after God's own heart."

Gideon didn't answer. How could he? Abraham didn't know how completely he had failed. How he had gone against the teachings of the church and God's Word. Because of him, a man was dead. Because of him, his wife was gone. Because of him, their little church in Maryland had broken up, the members scattered.

"I could list many more," Abraham said. "Paul, Peter —"

"You don't have to name them." Gideon ran a hand over his face. "Maybe I heard God wrong and he never called me to be a minister in the first place."

"You were chosen by lot from among the members of your church?"

Gideon nodded.

"Then you were chosen to shepherd the flock." Abraham stepped closer to him. "What are you afraid of?"

Still leaning on the top board of the cow's pen, Gideon buried his face in his hands. "I lost my flock. I neglected them, and they scattered. I don't deserve that kind of responsibility."

Abraham was silent for a moment. "I have a question for you. Whose church do you serve? Yours, or God's?"

Gideon peered at the other man. What point was he trying to make?

"The church is God's church."

"That's right. And the people of the church are God's people, his sheep. The minister doesn't own them, and he isn't the shepherd. Jesus Christ is the Good Shepherd. The best the minister can be is a faithful hireling. And Christ will never desert either his hired man or his flock."

Gideon closed his eyes again. Abraham was wrong. God had deserted him from the time he had first heard the roll of the drums echoing over the ridge last spring. From that time until now, his life had gone terribly, horribly wrong, and everyone else had suffered for it.

Mein Herr . . .

He massaged the bridge of his nose. "You don't know what I've done. You don't know how wrong everything has gone. I'm not fit to be a minister."

Gideon suppressed a shudder. He didn't even deserve to be a member of the church . . . if Abraham knew, he would send Gideon and his family on their way.

"You've said that before, that you think you're responsible for everything that has happened to you."

247

"I know I am."

Abraham sighed, and Gideon waited. The older man had to see that Gideon was right.

"Imagine you are driving a spring wagon with a spirited team hitched to it. A green, barely trained team of horses."

Gideon turned and leaned his back against the cow pen. He remembered a team like that, the ones he had raised from colts. They had been stolen by the army more than a year ago. Where were they now?

"You're holding on to the reins, in control, even though the horses are fighting against you."

Gideon nodded. What did this little game have to do with him?

"Now imagine that I'm sitting on the seat beside you, and I reach over, put my hands over yours, and try to drive the horses myself."

"That could lead to a crash. The horses wouldn't know who is driving and they would be confused."

"That's right." Abraham leaned into the pen and scratched the cow's face.

Gideon saw Abraham's point. "I'm trying to control my life, but I'm not the driver. God is." A cold stream of ice made its way through his stomach. "But if I let go of the reins . . ." He let his voice trail off. When he

248

thought he controlled his life, it had been a disaster. Memories of the past year flashed through his mind, then lingered on Lovinia's face. "If I let go of the reins the wagon will crash."

Abraham didn't answer.

"I don't know how to do that. I can't do that. I feel like this wagon of mine is careening downhill behind a team of runaway horses. Everything has gone wrong —" His voice hitched.

"Maybe it is time to let go of the reins. Submit to God's will."

Gideon ran his hand over his face again. Perhaps Abraham was right. He longed for the peace he had once known to fill his soul again, but first he had to fix whatever had gone wrong.

On Wednesday morning after breakfast, Ruby was just getting out the flour and butter for the day's baking when William came to the door.

"Did you come over to play?" Ruby asked.

Her seven-year-old nephew shook his head. "Mamm says to go to *Grossmutti*'s today and bring the morning's milking if you can. Daed killed one of our bull calves yesterday, and Mamm says she has rennet."

Roseanna's eyes grew round. "The poor calf!"

Ruby smiled. Anna had told her Samuel's plans yesterday. The calf's stomach lining was needed to make cheese, and Samuel knew the women of the family would want to have a work frolic for the occasion.

"It's all right, Roseanna. The calf was doing poorly, so Samuel decided he could kill it. I wasn't certain when he was going to do it, but now we can make cheese."

"Can I help?" Roseanna asked.

"We're all going to help," William said. "Mamm says to hurry, and while we're waiting for the cheese, we can play."

"Why do we have to wait?" Sophia's face puckered. "I want cheese now."

Ruby cupped the girl's head in her hand. "All good things are worth waiting for. We have to cook the milk, then cut the curds, then press the whey out. We will store the cheese until fall to let it ripen, but we'll be able to eat some fresh cheese today."

Roseanna and William took turns carrying Daniel, and Ruby carried the pail of milk Bett had given them that morning. When they reached the road, Elizabeth was already waiting for them.

"Cheese-making day!" she said. "Are you ready for a frolic?"

"William must have stopped at your house before he came to get us."

Elizabeth took Daniel from William and carried him so William and Roseanna could run down the road toward the stone bridge. "I'm glad he did. My days have been so different since you're here at Gideon's all day."

"I'm not there all day. We went to work in the garden at your cabin yesterday, and on Monday we went to Mamm's for the afternoon."

They walked slowly to keep pace with Ezra and Sophia.

"Anna said she has been saving milk for the cheese making all week, so we'll have plenty to make today."

Ruby laughed. "I thought we had more than enough last year, but Anna and Samuel have four cows now instead of three. What are we going to do with it all?"

"She's planning to trade it at the store in Farmerstown. Mrs. Lawrence said they have plenty of customers who come in asking for good cheese, and you know ours is the best."

"You shouldn't brag like that." Ruby frowned at her, and then laughed. "But it is true, isn't it? I can't wait for fresh cheese."

Elizabeth waited until the children had gone into the house and stopped Ruby in the middle of the bridge. "How are things going with Gideon?"

Ruby felt her face heat but kept her voice light. "What do you mean?"

"Has he said anything about getting married? That is why you're spending your days there, isn't it?"

"We haven't talked about it except to say that neither of us are looking for marriage. It's too soon after Lovinia's passing."

"That might be what he says, but that was more than a month ago, wasn't it?"

Ruby glanced toward the house, but the children had all gone inside. If she knew Mamm, they were all eating cookies before they went outside to play.

"It was a month ago today." Only a month, but it seemed like it had happened only a few days ago.

"Well, that might be Gideon's excuse, but what is yours? You don't have any reason to wait. He needs a wife and you need a husband. There's nothing complicated about that."

"I don't need a husband." Ruby shifted the milk pail to her other hand. "You know that better than anyone."

"You aren't still thinking about Ned Hamlin, are you?"

"Not Ned, but how I acted with him. It was stupid of me, and silly to think he might have actually liked me."

"Ned Hamlin was a pig."

Ruby suppressed a giggle. "You shouldn't speak ill of the dead."

Elizabeth grinned at her and bounced Daniel in her arms. "But it's true, isn't it? He convinced you that he loved you and then took advantage of your kindness." Her grin turned to a frown and the look in her eyes grew distant. "He was a pig, just like —" She pulled her lower lip between her teeth.

Ruby put one arm around her sister's shoulders, pulling her close, and pressed her lips against Elizabeth's ear. "I know. I know. They are both pigs. You don't need to say it."

Ruby's eyes filled. It was her fault that Elizabeth had even met Reuben Kaufman. If it hadn't been for Ruby confiding in Elizabeth about her dalliance with Ned, her sister might be happily married to one of the Stuckey boys, or one of the Lehman brothers. Anyone but Reuben.

Movement at the top of the hill they had just walked down caught Ruby's eyes. "Someone is coming this way. It looks like the Beilers' wagon."

Elizabeth shifted Daniel to her other hip. "I don't want to stay here and risk having a conversation with Salome Beiler. That woman acts as if I don't exist just because I'm not a member of the church."

"Let's go into the house. Mamm and Anna are waiting for us."

But they were too late. Before they reached the porch, the Beilers' spring wagon crossed the bridge and pulled to a halt. Levi was driving and crimped the wheels so his mother could climb down from the seat safely.

"Don't forget to pick me up on your way back," Salome said to Levi. "I don't want to walk home from here."

"Yes, Mother." Levi held the horses still until Salome was on the porch next to Ruby. He briefly met her eyes and shrugged an apology before the horses were off again.

"He is on his way to Farmerstown to see if there are any letters from Jonas, the dear boy. He goes twice a week and then delivers the letters to Katie." She shook her head. "If only that girl would come to her senses and marry my Levi instead of that soldier."

As Salome pushed her way past Ruby and Elizabeth, Ruby exchanged glances with her sister. Salome seemed to have forgotten that "that soldier" was their brother. Or perhaps she hadn't forgotten. Salome could be as kind as anyone when she wanted to be, but her tongue could also cut like a knife.

"Ach, a cheese-making frolic!" Salome was saying as Ruby and Elizabeth went into the kitchen. "Don't mind me. I won't get in your way. I only stopped by to chat for a bit until Levi comes back from Farmerstown."

Mamm smiled as she poured a cup of tea for Salome and set it in front of her. "We're glad you stopped by. Aren't we, girls?"

"You are so blessed to have such a wonderful daughter and daughter-in-law to work with you." Salome untied her bonnet and laid it on the table. "At our house, there are only Millie and I to do the work. But that will change when Levi marries."

"I have two daughters and a daughter-in-law helping today, Salome, and it is a wonderful blessing." Mamm's smile was tight as she hung Salome's bonnet on a hook by the door where it would be out of the way.

The children slipped out of the door one by one, led by William. Sophia, her cookie uneaten in her hand, stared at Salome until Ruby gave her a gentle push toward the door too.

Ruby set her pail of milk on the kitchen shelf, then took Daniel from Elizabeth. He was fussing, ready for a drink of milk and his morning nap.

"Here's some milk for the baby," Mamm said, handing her a cup.

Ruby sat down at the table and Daniel reached for the cup. She helped him guide it to his mouth and take a sip, then used a clean diaper to mop up the drips.

She turned slightly in her seat to make Daniel more comfortable and saw that Salome was watching her with a queer expression on her face.

"You've become quite the expert mother," Salome said. "I noticed the other three children are quite clean and well behaved too. Gideon must be very happy with you."

Ruby glanced at the others, but they were busy. Anna was at the stove, stirring the first batch of milk in a big pot, and Elizabeth was tying a string to the bit of rennet. Mamm was sorting through the cheese hoops Daed had made. None of them were paying attention to Salome's needling remarks.

"I don't know if Gideon is happy or not. We don't talk to each other very often." Unless you counted the cup of coffee they had together each morning after she arrived at the house to make breakfast for the family.

"Has he spoken of marriage? Are you planning to make your arrangement acceptable in the eyes of the church?" Salome crossed her arms and leaned against the back of her chair.

Daniel rubbed his eyes and leaned against her, pushing the empty cup away. Ruby's hand shook as she set the cup on the table. "There is nothing about our arrangement that would be considered unacceptable in the eyes of anyone, including the church."

Salome's mouth curved in a smile that made her look like a snake. Ruby turned Daniel around and he rested his head on her shoulder, sighing deeply as he drifted off to sleep. She didn't look at Salome again as she went into Mamm's bedroom to lay him down for his morning nap.

She shouldn't let the woman's comments bother her, but they did. Salome thought she and Gideon were in a sinful relationship when they had no thought of anything like that. Salome was wrong, but she might not be the only one who assumed the worst.

Friday morning brought visitors to the Beiler farm. Levi straightened up from his work in the wheat field to see who was driving the wagon. It was Abraham Weaver, with Gideon next to him in the seat. He set aside the sheaf of wheat he had just tied and headed toward the house. He could return Gideon's book to him while he was here.

By the time he reached the house, Abraham was seated on the porch with Father, while Gideon stood near them, leaning on the porch rail.

"It's highly irregular," Father said, ignoring Levi's approach.

Levi joined Gideon, leaning against the porch post as he listened.

"What is so irregular?" Abraham asked. "Gideon is already a minister. We would only need to leave it to the congregation to decide if they are willing to accept his transfer from his church in Maryland to our community." Abraham seemed relaxed as he rocked in Mother's chair, but his fingers drummed on the armrest.

"I understand that church in Maryland no longer exists."

Father folded his hands over his stomach, and Gideon flinched slightly at his words.

Abraham looked toward Gideon, his eyebrows raised.

Gideon hesitated, then said, "That is true. Our community had settled along a main road, but the soldiers of both armies have used that road as they moved back and forth. They destroyed our crops, ate our livestock, and stole our horses. The people had no other choice but to move away, and most of them moved north to Pennsylvania where they had family."

Father frowned. "Why didn't you go with them? The community should stay together, shouldn't they?"

Gideon cast a look toward Abraham, who nodded his head. "Most of the community left while I was away."

"Away." Father made a disapproving sound that made Levi wince. "And where did you go when you abandoned your church?"

"My wagon, my team, and I were seized by a company of soldiers. I was forced to use my wagon to haul their supplies and their wounded men."

Abraham leaned forward. "His absence was out of his control. He didn't abandon his church, he was taken from them."

Father stroked his beard. "That's what he says now."

Gideon stood straight, his fists clenched. "You are saying that I have lied to you?"

Father raised his hands in a helpless gesture. "I'm not accusing you of lying. But we have no one to be a witness to your story." He rocked back in his chair, preparing for his next accusation. "There is also the question of your home life. A minister should be above reproach."

Levi stood to protest, but Abraham's soft

voice cut in first.

"You can't think that Gideon's life has anything in it that is sinful, can you?"

"I have heard that your daughter Ruby, your unmarried daughter, is at his house at all hours of the day and night. That is highly improper."

Abraham grunted, a sound that was almost a growl. "There is nothing improper in Ruby caring for Gideon's children while he works. She is at the house while Gideon works with me on the farm, and no longer than is necessary for the care of the family. I don't know where you heard this rumor, but it is false."

"Is it a rumor?" Father gazed at Gideon, whose face was dark red. "A man is still a man, and his wife has been dead for more than a month." He smiled. "No one would be surprised to hear that you gave in to temptation with an available young woman, but that sin is still sin. I can't recommend a man like that to be a minister in our church."

"There is nothing sinful going on between me and Ruby," Gideon said. "But if someone in the church thinks so badly of me, I'm not sure I want to be considered as a minister. I can't serve in a place where folks don't trust me."

Gideon stepped off the porch and stalked toward the wagon. Abraham rose to follow him but turned to Father first.

"At this point, you are the only minister in our congregation, Amos. That is against the *Ordnung* and the tradition of the church. That is too much power for one man, and it can easily be abused."

Father rubbed his hands together, looking at the porch floor as if he was thinking deeply. "You are correct in that, Abraham. That is why I have arranged for the election next week. But I can't agree to inviting Gideon to fill that position without consulting the congregation and without confirmation from the Good Lord. If he is nominated, he will have the same consideration as any other nominee. That should satisfy him, shouldn't it?"

"It isn't Gideon who needs to be satisfied, but God. He is the one who called Gideon to serve him, and that is a permanent calling. It isn't in your hands." Abraham took a step closer to Father. "I had to convince Gideon to come here today. This wasn't his choice. I am ashamed of how you treated him."

"To me, he's an outsider." Father's eyes narrowed. "You may think he is as he ap-

261

pears, but I wonder what his motives really are."

"You are suspicious beyond belief, Amos. Perhaps you should spend some time with him, like Levi has, and like I have."

Abraham followed Gideon to the wagon and they drove off. Father watched them go with a frown on his face.

Mother tipped the screen door open. "What was that all about, Amos?"

"That Gideon Fischer wants to be brought in as a minister in our church."

Stepping out onto the porch, Mother barely glanced at Levi. "You didn't agree, did you?"

"For sure, I didn't." Father shook his head. "We don't want a man who acts the way he does to hold a position of such influence."

"What do you mean?" Levi couldn't keep quiet any longer. "Gideon acts the same as anyone else. That rumor you mentioned is false. It has to be."

Father's eyebrows rose as he turned toward Levi as if he was surprised to see him there. "I hate to mention such a delicate subject around a boy like you, but Gideon and Ruby have been seen conferring closely together, much closer than is proper for an employer and employee."

"And she treats those children as if they were her own," Mother said. "I can only imagine what sinful things go on behind closed doors." She shook her head. "I don't want to see you spending time with that man anymore, Levi. You don't know what he might influence you to do."

"There is nothing wrong with Gideon, and Ruby is only helping him out by caring for the children since his wife died. He's a good man."

As his parents exchanged glances, Levi remembered the conversation he had overheard. How could they suspect Gideon and Ruby of falling into the same sin they had?

Father gestured toward the wheat field. "How far have you gotten in your work today, Levi?"

"Half of the wheat is bundled and shocked." Levi glanced down the road but could no longer see Abraham and Gideon. "I have a book to return to Gideon. I'll do it during the noon hour."

"Don't stop to talk to them," Father said. "You heard what your mother said, and I want that wheat in the shocks by this evening."

"I'll get it done."

Rather than pushing past Father to go into the house through the front door, Levi went around to the back door, stopping to wash his hands before going in. Mother was still on the front porch with Father, but he could smell the appetizing fragrance of dinner in the oven, and a pot of potatoes was boiling on the stove. Never mind. He would rather go without eating than to sit at the dinner table with Father and Mother today. How could they accuse Gideon and Ruby of wrongdoing? They couldn't have witnesses, only suspicions. *Hypocrisy* was a mild word for what he had witnessed on their front porch this morning.

Levi retrieved the book from his room and set out for Gideon's house. He would have to hurry to return home by the end of the noon hour.

No one was in the yard when he arrived at the newly painted house, so he went to the kitchen door and knocked. Gideon opened the door.

"Come in, Levi." He stepped back as he pulled the door open. "You're just in time to join us for dinner."

Past his friend, Levi saw the children sitting at the table. Ruby, holding the baby in one arm, was already setting a clean plate in a spot for him.

"I didn't mean to interrupt your dinner." He held up the book. "I just wanted to return your copy of Menno Simons, and to apologize."

"Come and sit down. We'll talk while we're eating."

Levi set the book on the end of the kitchen shelf, then sat next to Gideon at the table. He bowed his head for a silent prayer while the others waited, then helped himself to the mashed potatoes Ruby passed to him.

"I haven't seen your house before," Levi said. He looked around at the comfortable kitchen and the front room that he could see on the other side of the stairway leading to the loft. Everything looked clean. Homey. He relaxed and dished some chicken and noodles on top of the mashed potatoes.

"You're welcome to stop by any time," Gideon said. "Ruby always cooks more than enough food for our family."

Ruby smiled at Levi. "Mamm taught me to always be prepared in case a friend drops by during mealtime."

A friend. Levi nodded his thanks to Ruby and took a bite of his dinner. He felt more welcome here in this little cabin than he did at the table at home.

Roseanna was watching him. "Where do you live?"

"Roseanna, let Levi eat his dinner," Ruby said, reminding Roseanna of her manners with a slight frown.

"I don't mind," Levi said. "I live with my parents on their farm." He smiled at Roseanna as he put some pickled beets on his plate.

"Do I know them?" Roseanna asked.

"They are Preacher Amos and his wife, Salome," Gideon said, answering for Levi. "You've seen them at Sunday Meeting."

"And Salome came by when we were making cheese this week," Ruby said.

"Oh." Roseanna looked at him again. Levi thought he saw a flash of pity on the little girl's face, but that had to be his imagination.

After dinner, Ruby and the children cleared the table while Gideon took the baby and led the way into the front room. There was a comfortable rocking chair in one corner and a bench along the wall. Gideon sat in the chair, holding the baby against his chest. The little boy's eyes were closed.

"I can't stay long," Levi said, taking a seat on the bench. "Father expects me to finish shocking the wheat before nightfall. I am sorry for the way he acted this morning. He can be obstinate and demanding, but I don't remember him being so rude before."

"Don't worry about it," Gideon said. "Going to see Amos was Abraham's idea, but I'm not sure I'm ready to be a minister again. Shepherding a flock is not an easy calling."

Levi studied the planks of the floor. Not too long ago, he had thought the calling to be a minister was the most important thing a man could do. "How is it hard? Father doesn't seem to think it is."

Gideon rocked the chair. "Perhaps it isn't for some men. But I have always felt the weight of the responsibility. Sometimes, that weight nearly cripples me."

"Shouldn't the minister rely on the Lord to help him bear that weight?"

The rocking chair slowed. "All I can think of is how the people depend on me, but Abraham recently reminded me that the job isn't mine alone."

Levi laced his fingers together and propped his elbows on his knees. "I think that if I were a minister, I wouldn't think of it as my task at all. Something I read once makes me think that the ministers aren't the shepherds of the church, but only the helpers. The hired men. Jesus is the Good Shepherd."

"Abraham said the same thing." Gideon shifted Daniel to his other shoulder. "But your father doesn't seem to believe that."

Gideon's words dug into Levi. His friend was right. Father didn't believe that at all. In fact, Levi wasn't sure what Father believed.

"I hope you are chosen to be our minister," Levi said. "There is no one else I can think of who would make a better one, unless it was Abraham."

"What about yourself?"

Levi gazed at the floor between his feet. "There was a time when I was prideful enough to think that was my calling. But now all I want is to do God's will, whatever it is. I have no ambitions other than his plan."

"Gelassenheit."

Levi smiled at Gideon. "Ja. Gelassenheit."

11

Ruby planned to spend Saturday morning in the woods, looking for the bee tree she had found early last spring. She had cleaned Elizabeth's washtub and had Gideon's milk pail to use. The next stop was Anna's, to borrow another milk pail or two.

Roseanna and Sophia held Ezra's hands as they went up the slope from the road to Samuel and Anna's house. The children ran back and forth between the two houses so often that they were wearing a path. As Ruby struggled up the steep hill to Samuel's house with Daniel in her arms, she tried to imagine how she was going to carry honey out of the woods. Somehow, she would have to find a way to do it.

But once Anna heard her plan, she said, "Leave the children with me today. They can play with William and Dorcas, and you know how much I love taking care of babies."

She took Daniel from Ruby's arms and held him close.

Ruby pressed her knuckles into the small of her back. Daniel was almost a year old and getting heavier every day.

"Denki, Anna. Are you sure? It will be more work for you."

"Just share some of that honey with me, and it will be worth it." She smiled as she showed Ruby a stack of clean milk pails. "Take as many as you need."

Ruby took two of the pails. "I had thought of asking Mamm to take care of Daniel today, but I was concerned about the others. Once I start getting the honey, the bees are going to be quite angry. I would hate for them to be stung."

"Take your time." Anna shifted Daniel to her other hip. "I'll put the children to work weeding the garden, and there is a lot to be done."

Ruby hurried back to Gideon's house with the two pails. Yesterday, she had borrowed some old clothes from Daed, and now she put them on, tucking her skirts into a pair of baggy trousers and covering her arms with Daed's long sleeves. She was just putting on an old hat with cheesecloth sewn to the brim when Gideon walked in the kitchen door.

He stared at her.

"I know I look ridiculous," Ruby said, trying to untangle her fingers from the cheesecloth, "but I don't want to be stung when I get the honey."

"You aren't going alone, are you?"

"Anna wanted to keep the children for the day, so it looks like it will be just me." She tugged at the cheesecloth, smiling at the thought of a few hours to herself.

Gideon stepped forward and unwound the tangled cloth from her hand. "Would you like some company? I can help carry the honey home."

Ruby paused, her vision of an afternoon alone in the woods taking flight. But with Gideon along, she wouldn't have to lug the honey home alone. Besides, he was good company.

"Do you have some old clothes to wear? I have more cheesecloth."

He put the empty milk pails into the washtub along with the hatchet Ruby had borrowed from Daed. "Bees don't bother me. I haven't been stung yet."

"Never?"

Gideon shook his head. "Either I haven't been stung or the stings don't bother me. I don't remember ever having a problem with them."

Ruby narrowed her eyes. "Have you ever gotten honey from a bee tree?"

"Does it matter? You just take the honey out of the tree, don't you?"

"The bees don't like it."

He grinned at her. "So, they don't like it. We'll leave enough for them to eat through the winter, right?"

Ruby gave up and led the way toward the woods on the west end of Daed's fields. The ground rose above the valley as Weaver's Creek turned to the southwest. They followed a small stream that tumbled down the slope toward the larger creek until they reached the top of the ridge. Old growth trees were thick here, even though Daed often harvested firewood from this end of his farm.

"I was here in the early spring with Daed," she said, waiting for Gideon to catch up. "He was selecting dead and dying trees to cut down for next year's firewood, and we found the bee tree then."

"Are you sure you know where you are?" Gideon looked around them at the surrounding trees.

"For sure." Ruby pointed to a couple stumps. "Here's where Daed cut down two of the trees. The bee tree is this way."

She led the way downhill, toward a narrow spot where the rain ran off toward the west, away from the Weaver's Creek valley. In the middle of the gorge, a large tree trunk was wedged between some boulders. From the hollow center of the trunk, the constant hum of bees sounded.

Gideon stopped. "Are you sure we can reach that? It must be six feet off the ground."

"Ja, for sure." Ruby pointed to another fallen tree below the first one. "If we stand on that, we can chop the hive open and get to the honey."

Gideon took the hatchet in his hand and climbed onto the lower trunk while Ruby secured the cheesecloth around her neck. He swatted at a bee.

"Are you sure you don't want some netting around your face?"

He swatted at another bee. "I haven't done anything yet, but they are still trying to drive me away."

"They're only trying to protect their hive." Ruby called to him over the buzzing. "You have to work quickly."

Gideon swung the hatchet once. The blade bit into the wood with a solid thud that brought the bees swarming out of the hive. He jumped to the ground, the bees clouding the air around him.

"Get away from the hive, then roll on the ground," Ruby called. "As long as they think you are a threat to them, they'll come after you."

When the bees had quieted down again, Ruby found Gideon sitting on a log at the top of the hill. His arms were propped on his knees, and he glowered at her when she couldn't stop laughing at the red welts on his cheeks and forehead.

"I should have listened to you when you said they would attack." He probed his swollen forehead gingerly. "Now I know what you meant." He rolled up his sleeve to reveal at least a dozen more stings.

"Do you want my help now?" Ruby asked, holding up the cheesecloth.

He frowned at her but let her swathe his head in the gauze. Then she helped him tie the bottoms of his sleeves and trouser legs with some string.

"I'm ready to tackle the bees again," he said, grinning at her as he settled his hat firmly on his head.

"Remember, they'll start swarming more quickly this time because they're on the alert. You have to work fast."

"I'll break open the hive, and then we'll scoop the honey into the buckets, so be ready."

They went back to the bee tree. The hatchet was still embedded in the wood, and the bees were thick, both in the air and on the trunk.

Gideon pulled on his gloves and climbed up again. He brushed the bees off the hatchet handle and started chopping. In a few blows, he had split the front of the hive off and was ready for the pails. Ruby handed them up to him one by one, emptying the full ones into the washtub until every container was full.

They carried the washtub home between them, leaving the milk pails for a second trip. They set their heavy load on the kitchen table, and Ruby slumped in a chair, breathless.

"I don't know how I would have carried that by myself," she said as she took off Daed's hat and unwound the cheesecloth from her neck.

"You could have asked for help," Gideon said.

"I don't ask for help when I don't need it," Ruby said, but brushing off his remark wasn't easy. It clung as tightly as the bees that were tangled in the gauzy fabric in her hand.

Gideon bent to untie the strings from the bottom of his trouser legs. "I don't know anyone who doesn't need help from time to time. I'm glad I was available today, or you would still be out in the woods, trying to get honey out of that hollow tree."

"You don't think I could have done it?"

"I know you could have. You can do pretty much anything you put your mind to. But I would hate to see you hurt, lying out there in the woods somewhere with a twisted ankle or something."

Ruby started unfastening the shirt she was wearing over her dress. "So now I'm helpless too."

Her frustration made her fingers fumble and she pulled at the shirt in exasperation. The kitchen was hot, and she was sweltering in the extra clothes. She changed tactics and tried to untie the rope she had used to keep Daed's old trousers from falling down, but that knot defeated her too.

One snicker from Gideon caused her temper to boil over.

"What is so funny?" She stood up, pulling at the trousers, but they didn't budge. She stamped her foot on the floor in frustration, an action she regretted when Gideon started laughing harder.

"You. You're so independent that you would rather broil in that silly outfit than ask for my help."

She gave him her best glare. When he didn't notice, she stomped her other foot on the kitchen floor. He only kept laughing. She wiped the sweat from her forehead and tackled the knot again.

"Do you want me to do that?"

Ruby tried to frown at him, but the sight of his face covered in red, blotchy beestings was too much for her. She tried to keep it in, but a giggle escaped and turned into full-blown laughter until she had to sit down again.

"You're just as stubborn as I am," she said, her breath coming in gasps. "Your face is full of welts from the bees." She covered her mouth, trying to control the laughter. "It must hurt terribly."

"Not really." Gideon felt the stings again. "They're beginning to disappear already." He grinned at her, leaning back in his chair. "But you're right. We are some pair, aren't we?"

Ruby dabbed at her eyes with her sleeve. "All right. I give up. I'll let you help me untie this knot."

Gideon knelt in front of her and tugged at the rope, then started picking at the knot. As he worked, she counted the beestings. Two on his left ear, three on his neck, five on his forehead —

"I'm not pulling too hard, am I?"

He looked into her eyes, inches away. Ruby swallowed. His brown eyes were soft, concerned. His eyelashes were long and dark, gentle curls brushing against his cheeks.

She shook her head. "Is it coming loose?"

"I think I'm going to have to cut it. Is that all right?"

Ruby blinked. His face was so close . . . what would he think if she gave in to the urge to push that stray strand of hair off his forehead? She drew back, away from the temptation.

"Ja, ja, ja. Go ahead and cut it."

Once the rope was loose, Ruby kicked off the trousers and pulled the shirt over her head, happy to be free of the hot confines of Daed's old clothes and wearing only her own dress and kapp. Then she went to the sink and splashed her face with cold water, careful not to look in Gideon's direction.

Her cheeks were hot, but it wasn't from the warm day. She could only hope that Gideon hadn't noticed her blushing.

The trip back into the woods to retrieve the rest of the honey was pleasant as Gideon followed Ruby along the trail. The late morning sun was warm, but the trail was in the shade and still cool. They retraced their steps until they reached the spot where they had left the pails by the side of the stream, covered with a length of cheesecloth to keep insects away.

Ruby stopped and pushed some stray curls out of her face. "If you want to walk a little bit farther, I know a place that will give us a good view of the surrounding country. It isn't far from here, and we'll be able to feel the breeze."

Gideon stood with one foot propped on a log and looked around them. "Do you mean up on the ridge?"

"It's on the south end of the ridge. It's called Weaver's Knob, and it's the highest spot in the township."

He looked in the direction she pointed and could make out a taller hill through the trees. "For sure, let's go. We can rest for a bit up there before we head home again."

She grinned at him, meeting his eyes for the first time since they left the house. "It's quite a climb. Are you sure you're up to it?"

He grinned back. "I'll get there long before you do."

Ruby laughed and started out, holding her skirts up to allow her to walk faster. Gideon jogged past her, following a deer trail that led up the ridge.

Something about Ruby brought out a side of him he hadn't seen since he was a boy in school. Participating in foot races or swimming races, he had experienced the joy of competing against the other boys, and he had missed it. Ruby brought out that same competitiveness and seemed to enjoy it as much as he did. He chuckled as he thought of the look that would be on her face when she finally caught up to him at the top of the hill.

It wasn't until the trail topped the ridge and started down the other side that Gideon realized his mistake. He stopped, looking down the trail behind him, but Ruby was nowhere in sight. The knob rose to his left, but the trail he had followed went around the narrow hill rather than up it. He should have known a game trail would take the easier route. He would have to retrace his steps until he found the spot where Ruby had turned off and try to catch up with her again.

But before he did, he took a few steps farther along the game trail. Perhaps it would lead to an open spot where he could climb up. The faint path skirted the edge of the knob, and ahead he could see a limestone outcropping rising twenty feet or so above the trail, the western edge of the knob. Just before he reached it, he stopped short at the edge of a clearing.

Someone had been here recently. Bushes had been broken, a few small trees had been cut down. A ring of stones outlined where a campfire had been, and Gideon saw where horses had been tied. At least five men and horses, possibly more.

He froze, his heart pounding, listening for any sound of their presence. Nothing. They had been here, but now they seemed to be gone. But who were they? Keeping a close watch on the underbrush surrounding the clearing, he looked around the fire circle. The ashes were cold, but they hadn't been rained on. The last rain shower was two days . . . no, three days ago.

Hoofprints covered the ground, leading to a larger trail that went north and west, down the ridge. On the other side of the clearing, a similar trail led south and east, around the base of the knob.

Whoever had been camping here hadn't been gone long, and they could still be in the area.

Ruby.

Gideon looked up at the knob. Everything seemed quiet. He took off at a run, retracing his path until he found where Ruby had turned off the game trail and headed straight up the hill. When he reached the top, panting, she was there, sitting on a rock.

"I thought you said you were going to get here before I did." Her eyes sparkled as she laughed at him.

Gideon dropped to his knees, still trying to regain his breath. "You didn't see anything on your way up here? Did you hear anything?"

Her smile faded. "Only the birds singing. Why? What is wrong?"

"I found a campsite down below. There had been a group of men and horses there not more than two or three days ago."

"They aren't there now?"

He shook his head, still trying to catch his breath.

"They were probably just hunters, or travelers passing through."

Gideon sat on a rock near hers, looking out over the farm fields and woods to the west. He knew, even though he had no evidence, that the men who had camped there weren't peaceful hunters or travelers. "These men didn't want to be seen. This is a remote area. Have you ever seen strangers up here before?"

"I don't come here that often, so I wouldn't notice. Maybe people use that spot to camp in all the time."

Gideon stood and turned in a slow circle, trying to see beyond the trees, trying to spot anything out of place. Where had those men gone?

Ruby sighed. "Why are you so worried? Just enjoy the view."

"I can't stop thinking that there is danger somewhere out there."

"Maybe it is only your imagination." She leaned forward, resting her elbows on her knees. "Your time with the army last spring has made you see danger behind every tree. But we're not in Virginia, we're here on our own land. This is Weaver's Knob, in the middle of Holmes County, Ohio. This is the safest place I know of."

Gideon gave himself a shake, trying to clear his head, then sat on the rock again.

"You're right." He smiled at her. "There is nothing to be worried about." He ignored the relentless dread in the back of his mind.

Ruby turned to look at the view to the west. "Isn't this beautiful?"

Gideon followed her gaze. It was as lovely and peaceful as she claimed. He began to relax.

"I was up here one time at sunset," she said. "It was wonderful, with colors filling the sky as if someone had painted them."

He glanced at her. "You wander around

these woods alone at night?"

She hugged herself, as if she was suddenly chilled. "Not alone." Ruby stood up, turning away from the view. "I guess we should get the rest of the honey back to the house. I need to strain it and then get jars from Mamm and Anna to put it in."

As Gideon followed Ruby back down the faint trail, he watched her. No longer purposeful and confident, she was hesitant, careful. As if she was afraid she would take the wrong step.

He looked back up at the limestone outcropping, wondering what memories that place had brought to her mind. Every moment he spent with Ruby opened a new door, giving him another glimpse into her mind and personality. It would take a lifetime to learn to know her completely.

12

Monday morning was washday, and Ruby took the family's laundry to Elizabeth's to take advantage of the sunny open yard. Gideon's cabin was sheltered by trees, which helped to keep the house cool on hot summer afternoons, but drying the clothes took a long time.

Ruby pulled the little cart Gideon had made on Saturday. The cart was similar to a dog cart, but smaller. It had high sides so that Ruby could haul clothes or wood, or just about anything else. Today, Daniel rode on top of the pile of laundry, holding on to the vertical slats and laughing at every bump.

"I like going to Elizabeth's house," Roseanna said as they pulled the cart together. "But I wish she had children to play with."

Ruby pulled the wagon around a rough spot in the road. How could she tell an eight-year-old that some families were never blessed with little ones?

"Elizabeth enjoys having you come to visit too. She doesn't like being alone so much."

"Doesn't she have a husband?"

"She does . . ." Ruby drew the answer out. Roseanna asked such complicated questions.

"Where is he? Why haven't I ever seen him?"

"He is away, fighting in the war."

Roseanna peered at her. "Isn't he Amish?"

Ruby shook her head. "He isn't Amish."

"But Elizabeth is."

"Elizabeth has never been baptized. She isn't a member of the church." Ruby bit her lip. If Elizabeth hadn't married Reuben, she would have joined the church years ago. But now she couldn't. Not as long as she was still yoked to an unbeliever.

They reached Elizabeth's house before Roseanna could ask another question. Her sister already had a fire burning under the big iron pot and was pouring a bucket of clear water into the rinsing tub.

"It looks like you're ready for us," Ruby called as Elizabeth waved.

"I started as soon as you left for Gideon's this morning. I knew you wouldn't let time go to waste."

Elizabeth lifted Daniel from the cart and

snuggled him close. She longed for a child, but she had confided to Ruby that she was afraid that her little ones would have a hard life with Reuben for a father. So as her longings went unfulfilled, she was torn between sadness and relief. At the same time, she enjoyed her nieces and nephews, and claimed Daniel whenever she could.

As Roseanna and Sophia took Ezra to play in the sandy spot at the edge of the garden, Elizabeth watched as Ruby shaved soap into the warm water in the pot. "How is Gideon this morning?"

"I suppose he is doing well. I was busy getting the laundry together while he ate breakfast with the children."

"You didn't talk this morning?"

"He has been extra busy lately, and we haven't spent time talking like we did last week."

"Busy doing what?"

Ruby glanced at her sister while she stirred the soapy water with the washing bat. "You are very curious this morning."

"I want you to be happy. I want you and Gideon to fall in love, get married, and give me many more nieces and nephews."

Ruby ignored the clutching of her stomach at Elizabeth's words. "We are friends, and I'm sure things will stay that way."

"Didn't you tell me that you promised Lovinia you would marry him?"

"I promised her that I would take care of the children, and that I would consider marrying Gideon. I've considered it, and so has he. This arrangement satisfies my promise to Lovinia, and I'm not looking for anything more."

Elizabeth didn't answer until Ruby looked at her again. Then she stepped around the fire to stand next to her. "Don't tell me you don't think about what it would be like to have Gideon for a husband. He's a handsome man, and gentle. I've never seen a man who is kinder to his children. So you won't convince me that you haven't thought about being his wife."

Ruby picked through the laundry until she found Gideon's white Sunday shirt and put it into the water along with Roseanna's and Sophia's aprons and Ezra's white shirt. She added her own white Sunday apron to the water, then swished the laundry with the bat.

"All right, I do think about it. But that doesn't mean I'm ready to marry him. There is more to consider than my feelings."

Elizabeth looked past her toward the road. "Someone is coming. A man."

Ruby glanced over her shoulder. The man

288

was dressed in black and riding a sorry-looking mule.

"He'll probably just ride past."

"He stopped at Mamm and Daed's. I saw him earlier."

Ruby kept stirring as she watched the man urge his mule off the road and onto the grassy space in front of Elizabeth's house. Then he stopped, took off his shabby hat, and addressed both of them.

"Excuse me, ladies. I'm looking for Miss Elizabeth Kaufman?" The man's voice was soft and his words dripped from his mouth like slow molasses.

Ruby and Elizabeth exchanged glances.

"I'm Elizabeth." Her hands were shaking as she handed Daniel to Ruby and stepped forward. "What is it? Do you have news of my husband?"

"I don't know about a husband, but I do have a message for you." He reached inside his coat and dug into a pocket. When he didn't find what he was looking for, he patted the front of the coat, raising a cloud of dust, then fished in another pocket before pulling out a folded piece of paper. "My name is Cyrus Benson, a minister of the gospel, lately of Vicksburg, Mississippi."

He nodded to both of them, ignoring the paper in his hand. "I had the pleasure of officiating at the wedding of Captain Reuben Kaufman and Miss Emily Parker during the winter past."

"Wedding?" Elizabeth's voice squeaked.

"Yes'm. I see that news has come as a surprise. You see, the wedding had to be rushed, if you understand my meaning, and he didn't want to take the time to send word to his family. And with the war and everything . . ." He lowered his eyes. "We have been under great duress in Vicksburg and have only lately been overrun by the Yankees. It was a terrible thing."

Elizabeth turned to Ruby. "I . . . I need to sit down."

Ruby helped her to the bench in front of the cabin as the man urged his reluctant mule to follow them, still holding the paper.

"The baby was born in the spring, miss, and it was a fine boy. Captain Kaufman was quite proud, as was Mrs. Kaufman."

Elizabeth's face paled.

"But the bad news, Miss Kaufman, is that your brother was killed in the battle." He peered at Elizabeth. "I assume he was your brother?" She didn't respond, so he continued. "When Mrs. Kaufman went through her husband's things, she found your name and where to find you. He had mentioned a family, she said, but never anyone by name.

Since I was coming north to escape . . . Well, I mean, to leave the deplorable conditions around Vicksburg, she asked me to find you and give you this letter from her."

Elizabeth didn't move, so Ruby took the paper from the man's extended hand.

"Thank you," she said. The envelope was worn and smudged with dirt, but Elizabeth's name was written on the front.

"I'll be on my way, then." He nodded to Elizabeth and to Ruby, then turned the mule and headed back to the road.

Ruby sank down to the bench next to Elizabeth and set Daniel on her lap. She held the letter where her sister could see it. "Do you want to read it?"

"He betrayed me." Elizabeth turned toward her. "And now he's dead."

"I'm so sorry," Ruby said, taking her sister's hand. Elizabeth was trembling. "At least now you know."

Elizabeth wiped a tear from her cheek, then hiccupped. She made a strangled sound that was almost a laugh. "It's over. It's finally over."

Ruby wasn't sure she heard her right. "What did you say?"

Elizabeth turned to her, eyes brimming with tears. "I was afraid to ask for this, but God still answered my prayers. He's never

291

coming back. It's over. Even if he hadn't died, he would never have come back, not after . . . He would never leave his son."

"You aren't angry?"

"I'm only thankful." Elizabeth pressed a fist to her mouth as a sob escaped. "I'm so very thankful."

A thunderstorm came on Monday afternoon, but not until after Gideon and the Weavers had shocked the last of the wheat. They had seen the clouds building in the distance, so had hurried to finish before they lost any of the crop. The first drops fell as Gideon ran for his house, and he reached the porch just as the hail started.

Ruby had left both doors open to catch the breeze that came ahead of the storm, and the house was cooling quickly as he stepped in. The children sat at the table eating bread with butter. Ezra grinned at him and waved his bread. Gideon hung his hat on the hook just as the gloom was lit by a flash of lightning. When a crack of thunder crashed directly over the roof, Ezra jumped, startled, then dropped his bread as he reached for Gideon, his face twisted in a frightened cry. Both girls hunched their shoulders and covered their ears.

"It's just thunder," Gideon said, raising

his voice above the noise of the rain and hail hitting the roof.

He picked up Ezra, then reached for the back door. The wind had risen, and rain was blowing in. Just as he closed the door, he saw a figure running through the trees toward the barn. He opened it and looked again. Nothing. He closed the door again.

"Where is Ruby?"

Roseanna uncovered one ear long enough to point to the loft, then cringed as another boom of thunder rolled over them. Ezra buried his face in Gideon's shirt. Ruby came down the stairs, holding a crying Daniel.

Ruby smiled when she saw Gideon and said something, but Gideon couldn't make it out over the noise of the storm. He just shrugged an answer and pointed up, indicating that he couldn't hear her. She nodded her answer and sat at the table between the girls. Gideon joined them, Ezra still clinging to him.

As the thunder moved farther away, Ezra and Daniel both calmed down, but the rain still drove into the roof, making conversation impossible. Gideon settled in to wait for the driving rain to end. Roseanna picked up her slice of bread and took a bite, then grinned at Sophia. His younger daughter slowly removed her hands from her ears, then grinned back at Roseanna when she heard the thunder in the distance.

Ruby sat across the table from him, holding Daniel close. He had laid his head on her shoulder and his eyes drifted shut. Ruby leaned her cheek against the top of his head, then kissed his silky hair, damp with sweat and plastered to his head.

That simple gesture squeezed Gideon's heart. His children were content and cared for. More than that, Ruby gave them the love that Lovinia would have given them. She had stepped into the place in their lives that would have gaped like an empty hole without their mother, but Ruby had filled it with light, love, and common sense. He couldn't imagine what their lives would be like without her presence. Lovinia knew him better than he knew himself.

After Roseanna and Sophia finished eating, they went into the front room where Ruby kept their toys. Ezra slid off Gideon's lap and ran to join them. The rain still pounded on the roof, but it seemed to be lessening. Ruby took the sleeping Daniel back upstairs, and by the time she came back, the rain had let up enough to make conversation possible again.

"That was some storm," she said, clearing

the table of crumbs and empty milk cups. "Did you get all the wheat in?"

Gideon stretched his legs out, crossing his ankles under the table. "All in shocks, safe and sound. We worked quickly for the last hour, though. We could see the storm coming, and it was moving fast."

"We were at Elizabeth's when we saw it coming." Ruby set a glass of water in front of him and sat down in Roseanna's chair with one for herself. "We were able to get the clothes off the line and come home before the wind picked up." She gestured toward the cart, filled with clothes and sitting just inside the door. "The cart made the task so much easier than it could have been. I'm glad you made it."

"I had made one for Lovinia a few years ago, and she talked about how useful it was. She wasn't able to carry the heavy baskets of wet clothes from the house to the clothesline . . ." His voice dropped as a sudden thought struck him. The cart was a convenience for Ruby, but it had been a necessity for Lovinia. She had been ill, even then, and he hadn't realized it.

"I put both boys in it with the clean clothes on the way home, and they enjoyed the ride." She smiled at the memory.

Gideon hadn't noticed how her freckles

had grown numerous over the past few weeks. He remembered seeing a sprinkle of them on her nose, but as the summer progressed, they had spread across her cheeks. Today in the rich sunlight filtering into the kitchen after the storm, they glowed brownish red against her pale skin, nearly the same color as her hair. He grinned when he saw that the curls were even more unruly today, circling her face with a reddish halo.

"What are you smiling about?" she asked. "Did something funny happen out in the wheat field?"

He cleared his throat and sat straight. "Nothing out of the ordinary. Samuel's boys are good workers. He has taught them well."

"I enjoy spending time with all of Samuel and Anna's children." She leaned her elbows on the table and sipped her water as a frown appeared. "We had a visitor at Elizabeth's today."

"What kind of visitor?" Was that who he had seen during the storm? Or had he seen anything at all?

"A minister, he said. A stranger. He said he was from Vicksburg, in Mississippi."

"That's a long way to travel. Why was he here?"

"He had a letter for Elizabeth."

Abraham had told him about Elizabeth

and her marriage to a man outside the church.

"He also brought the news that Reuben had been killed at Vicksburg." She bit her lower lip, not looking at him.

"How did Elizabeth receive the news?"

"Of all things, she was relieved, sad, and angry at the same time. The minister also told her that Reuben had married another woman in the South and had a child with her. He had betrayed her."

Gideon's first thought was that Elizabeth was well rid of a man like that, but then he remembered. Another soul had died, most likely an unrepentant soul, according to Ruby's description.

"I wish she had never married him."

Ruby's voice was quiet, almost as if she was talking to herself as she rubbed her thumb over the condensation beads on the side of her glass. But then she looked up, meeting his gaze. "It's my fault that she had such an unhappy marriage."

A deep thrum sounded somewhere inside Gideon. He recognized that sound . . . that feeling. In the past, he had always supposed that it was God's way of telling him to listen, to minister to the person he was talking to. But not now. It couldn't be. But he still leaned back in his chair, attentive, waiting to listen to what Ruby had to say.

"How is it your fault?" he said, encouraging her.

She watched him, her bottom lip between her teeth. She was hesitant to share with him, like many people were, but Gideon still waited, knowing that if God prompted someone to share what was on their heart, he had a reason.

"It happened so long ago." The skin between Ruby's freckles turned pink. "I was sixteen and Elizabeth was only fourteen, but we thought we were grown women. At least, I did, and I know that influenced Elizabeth."

She paused, crossing her arms as she stared at the table, her eyes unfocused as she went back through the years in her memory. Gideon still waited.

"I had met Ned Hamlin at school, even though he stopped coming when he was still a little boy. I had heard that his mother had died when he was young, and his father had no use for schooling. Ned being Ned —" She stopped and glanced at him. "I forgot, you never met him."

Gideon shook his head.

"Ned and his father lived in the woods south of Daed's farm. They lived by hunting and trapping, and who knows what else." She sighed and rubbed her arms. "I thought Ned had the perfect life. No rules. No Ordnung. He could do whatever he wanted, whenever he wanted. We . . . grew close that summer. I ran into him when I was berry picking by myself one day, and he helped me. It was fun, so we made arrangements to meet the next day."

Ruby twisted her fingers together.

"We spent a lot of time together, meeting at least once a day. One night I met him after everyone else in the family was asleep, and we went up to Weaver's Knob to watch the moon set. By the end of the week, I thought I was in love." She looked at him, trying to laugh at herself. "I suppose you think I was rather stupid and silly."

"Not at all. I was sixteen once."

"Miriam and Rachel, my older sisters, were both married, so there were only Elizabeth and I at home, along with Jonas. At night, I would tell Elizabeth all about my romantic encounters with Ned." She brushed a tear from one cheek. "Then we would giggle about it." She wiped away another tear. "Then Ned introduced Elizabeth to his new friend, Reuben, who had recently come to the area from Germany. He had bought the farm north of Samuel's, so we had seen him around."

Ruby pressed one fist to her mouth, and Gideon waited until she regained her composure.

"Then what happened?" he asked.

"You have to understand, we thought we were so daring and mature, keeping company with men who weren't Amish." She shot a glance at him, then looked away. What had she seen on his face? Not condemnation. Not with the burden of sin he carried.

"The next week, on Wednesday, I went to meet Ned in the woods, near the salt lick where the berries grow best. He said he wanted to show me where to find the best berries, in the middle of the brambles. He had made a path to the center. He said it was his own, private place." She shuddered as she sighed a deep breath. "That's when I found out I had only been playing a game, but Ned was serious. He tried to —" She broke off, glancing into the front room where the children were playing. "I fought him and got away, but I didn't tell anyone. No one."

She turned toward him, her eyes brimming with tears.

"I should have told Elizabeth. Maybe she wouldn't have done what she did if she had only known what kind of men Ned and

Reuben were. We thought they were like the boys we knew from church, but they weren't. They lived by a different set of rules . . . or no rules at all." She wiped her eyes with the hem of her apron. "That weekend, she was gone. Reuben took her to Millersburg, and when they came back a few days later, they were married." Ruby's voice dropped to a whisper. "She was only fourteen, and I had ruined her life."

Gideon leaned forward. "You can't blame yourself for someone else's actions." Anger rose in him against these men he had never met, against Ned and Reuben. "This man used Elizabeth, and he is the one to blame."

"But she encouraged him." Ruby sniffed. "She wanted to be with him and wanted to marry him."

"She was only fourteen. She was a child, and children aren't old enough to make decisions like this by themselves." Gideon took Ruby's hand. "It is over now, and Elizabeth is free to go on with her life, and you are free to stop blaming yourself for what happened to her." He leaned closer. "I know how close you and Elizabeth are, closer than many sisters. She doesn't blame you, either."

Ruby shook her head. "No, she doesn't."

"Then let the blame fall on the men who took advantage of two young girls." He swallowed as a sudden thought tightened his throat. "Reuben was killed, but what happened to Ned? Does he still live in the woods with his father?"

"He died last year. He was in the Confederate army with Reuben, but we had word that he died of an illness." She looked at him. "I have never told anyone about Ned, about what he tried to do. I've never told anyone how Elizabeth met Reuben, either. I've kept those things hidden inside and they have eaten away at me." A slight smile crossed her lips. "You are a good listener, Gideon. There is something about you that makes me feel safe to tell you these things."

Gideon smiled, but his stomach turned, longing for the relief Ruby had found in sharing her secret with him. But he would never have that relief. His secret would stay buried.

Levi opened the door of the general store and post office in Farmerstown, smiling at the familiar tinkle of the bell. After a year of making this weekly trip to the post office, the little building was as welcoming as his own home.

His smile faded. Sometimes the store was even more welcoming. Ever since Levi had overheard his parents' discussion last month, he knew he would never be able to please Father, no matter what he did. So he avoided his parents as much as he could.

"Good morning, Levi," Mr. Lawrence said, coming from behind the counter to shake his hand. "I was just telling Mrs. Lawrence that it didn't seem like Tuesday until we saw you walk in that door. How is your young soldier? Still well, we hope?"

"In his last letters, he said he was working at a field hospital near the Gettysburg battlefield."

"Tsk, tsk, tsk." Mrs. Lawrence shook her head as she sorted through the stack of letters on the post office portion of the counter. "We read about that battle in the newspaper. Such a terrible thing, with so much loss of life. But our boys won and sent the rebels home."

Levi didn't answer. Jonas's letter had described the aftermath of the battle, and from his words, there was nothing to celebrate.

"Here we go." Mrs. Lawrence handed him two letters. "And there is a package for you, Levi. It feels like it might be another book."

Taking the package, Levi grinned. "For sure, it is. I ordered my own copy of *Martyr's Mirror*. It is a history of the faithful followers of Christ who have been martyred through the centuries."

Mrs. Lawrence shuddered. "That sounds like gruesome reading."

"In many ways, it is." Levi fingered the knot of the string tied around the package. "But the stories are quite encouraging. Through them we can see the strength of the faith of those who have gone before us."

"I believe you, but I still don't think it is the kind of book I would want to read." She came out from behind the post office counter, closing the little gate behind her. "Is Katie doing well? She is such a sweet girl, and I miss seeing her. She used to come with you every week."

"Katie is fine. Her mother was ill last winter and still hasn't fully recovered. Katie needs to stay home and care for her." Levi didn't add that since he had tried to convince Katie to marry him, neither of them felt comfortable spending time together without friends or family around.

"Well, give her our best. And tell her we hope to see her Jonas back home soon."

Mr. Lawrence had been sweeping the floor while Mrs. Lawrence talked with Levi, but now he leaned on his broom. "You folks in Weaver's Creek have heard about Morgan's Raiders, haven't you?"

Levi shook his head. "Nothing at all. Who

are they?"

"A group of Confederate renegades. They were making their way through Ohio, bent on destruction, I'm sure, until the Union army caught up with them."

"Was there a battle? Here in Ohio?"

"Down near Pomeroy. Morgan tried to cross the river and escape back to Kentucky with his men, but between the river being flooded and the Union gunboat waiting for them, they didn't have a chance. The newspaper reported more than a thousand of Morgan's men were captured or killed, but Morgan escaped and headed north and east with the Union army behind him."

"So he is still somewhere out there?" Levi's fingers grew cold. "Could he be heading this way?"

"Got word just this morning that Morgan was captured along with his remaining followers over at Salineville two days ago. He's a prisoner now, and he won't be a danger to anyone, at least until this war is over."

"That is good news." Levi whooshed out a breath of relief. "I can't imagine soldiers this far from the battles."

Mr. Lawrence nodded. "We have been safe from the fighting up here, and it looks like we will remain that way, thanks to our boys in blue."

Levi waved to the couple as he left the store. He looked at the letters, one for Katie and one for Abraham and Lydia, then tucked them under his leg as he sat on the wagon seat. Champ started for home. Levi kept his pace at a slow walk while he tore the paper off his new book. He ran his hand over the leather binding and held it to his nose. Fine leather and fresh ink. He couldn't think of a more satisfying fragrance. He opened the cover and flipped through the pages, anticipating hours spent reading his own copy of this book that many Amish families kept in their homes.

When he reached Katie's house, the little cabin that had belonged to her brother Karl and his family until last winter, he didn't even need to get down from the wagon seat. Katie had seen him coming and was waiting on the front porch.

"There was a letter for you," Levi said, handing it to her. "And one for Abraham and Lydia."

"None for you?" Katie smiled, but her gaze was on her letter, not him.

"Not this week. But a book I've been waiting for was there."

"Denki, Levi. I hope it isn't a burden for you to travel all the way to Farmerstown every week."

"I do it for you and for Jonas." And he did it to see the smile on Katie's face. Someday he hoped and prayed that God would bring a girl like her into his life.

His next stop was at the Weavers', then he started for home. As he passed the lane leading to Gideon's cabin, he decided to see if Gideon was home. He was in no hurry to get back to the chores Father had waiting for him.

He found his friend in the barn, clearing out the haymow. Gideon stopped his work and climbed down the ladder.

"Getting ready for the next cutting of hay?" Levi gestured toward the barn loft.

"Abraham said we would be able to start mowing again next week, and his barn is nearly full. So most of this crop will be stored here. I needed to make sure the loft was empty and ready for it."

Levi felt a pull of jealousy but pushed it away. The Good Lord saw fit to give Gideon a pleasant place to raise his family, and it wasn't Levi's place to envy him.

"The election for the new minister is on Sunday," he said as Gideon led the way to the pump in the barnyard. "You haven't changed your mind about letting us nominate you, have you? You know that if your name is called, you have to participate in the drawing of lots."

Gideon splashed the cold water over his face and hair. "I haven't changed my mind. Abraham convinced me that it was the right thing to do. Besides, the final decision is up to the Lord, and I'm content with that."

"That's good." Levi ran a thumb up and down his suspender. "Do you need any help cleaning out the haymow?"

"I'm finished. I was just heading down to Abraham's to see if the scythes need sharpening."

Levi sighed. Sharpening scythes was a one-man job. "I suppose I had better head for home, then."

"You don't sound like you want to."

"I don't. Not really." Levi smiled, trying to make light of his reluctance. "I know Father has a list of chores for me to do, and I'm just putting them off. I went to Farmerstown to pick up the mail, and my copy of *Martyr's Mirror* arrived."

"You didn't need to buy one," Gideon said. "You could have borrowed mine, or your daed's."

"I know, but I wanted my own copy. One that will be part of my own home." If he ever married. "I heard some news while I was there. Mr. Lawrence said there had been a group of Confederate raiders in Ohio."

Gideon's face grew pale and he leaned against a nearby maple tree. "I heard something about that when I was in Millersburg last week." Nearly two weeks ago now. "Where are they? Did he say?"

"He said there was a battle somewhere near the Ohio River, but the leader escaped. He was captured a couple days ago east of here. He had made it nearly all the way to Pennsylvania."

Gideon rubbed his hand on his trouser leg. His face had dried from the splashing he had given it, but now it shone with perspiration.

"Are you all right?" Levi asked. He had never seen Gideon act this way, like he was frightened of something.

"They captured all of them? Are they sure?"

"I only know what Mr. Lawrence told me. Most of the men were captured or killed in the battle, and then the leader was captured. It sounds to me like the whole thing is over."

His friend shook his head. "We can't be sure. We need to keep a lookout for strangers. They are dangerous men."

Levi would have laughed if Gideon's face hadn't been so serious. "I don't think we have anything to worry about, from what Mr. Lawrence told me."

"You never know. Be careful going home."

Levi watched him go into the house without saying anything more. He looked around the quiet farm. The view through the trees gave him a glimpse of the cornfields of Abraham's farm, and to the west, all he could see was trees. Everything was calm and peaceful, without a hint that anything was out of place or threatening. He went back to the wagon. Father was waiting for him to finish cleaning out the barn.

13

By Wednesday morning, Ruby was convinced that something was wrong with Gideon.

He hadn't eaten supper with the children the night before but paced along the length of the porch until after she had put them to bed. Then he had walked with her along the lane to the road, watching her until she reached Elizabeth's house.

All that time, the only thing he said was to watch for strangers and to tell him if she saw any.

When she arrived in the morning, he was sitting in a kitchen chair he had brought out to the porch, his eyes lined and weary in the dim light. It was nearly dawn, but a layer of gray clouds covered the sky.

"Did you sit out here all night?" she asked.

Gideon nodded.

"Why?"

He glanced at her, his hat shadowing his

face. "Watching for varmints."

She nearly laughed, but his serious expression stopped her. "You don't have any chickens yet, and Bett and the horses aren't in danger from foxes or raccoons."

He didn't answer but stared into the trees surrounding the barnyard.

Ruby went past him into the kitchen and laid the basket of eggs from Elizabeth's chickens on the table next to the pail of fresh milk from Bett. Gideon had already done his morning chores. She listened at the bottom of the stairway, but didn't hear the children stirring, so she started making breakfast.

By the time the children had finished their meal, Gideon had still not come inside the house. Ruby poured a cup of coffee and took it out to the porch.

As she handed him the cup, he glanced at her. "Did you see anyone about last night or this morning?"

She shook her head. "No one. What are you worried about?"

"Do you remember the day we went to Millersburg? When we heard about Morgan's Raiders coming through Ohio?"

"For sure, I do. But that was two weeks ago, and nothing has happened." She looked at Gideon's red-rimmed eyes. "Has it?"

"There was a battle south of here last week, along the Ohio River."

"That is more than a hundred miles from here. You can't think we're in danger."

"Some of the raiders escaped from the battle, including their leader, John Morgan. According to the news Levi brought yesterday, Morgan was captured east of here."

"If the leader has been captured, then we don't have anything to worry about."

He rubbed his fingers across his forehead. "I saw something . . . someone on Monday, during the storm. And then I heard something last night. It's possible that some of the raiders escaped capture. Then there is also that fellow you and Elizabeth saw. What was a man from Mississippi doing in Ohio?"

"That minister was delivering a letter, and then he went on his way. Besides, what would any of them be doing here?" Ruby looked around the barnyard. Nothing seemed out of the ordinary.

"If they are hiding out, they would avoid the main roads to keep from being seen. They would sneak around the farms in the area and steal anything they needed before they moved on. But if they are trying to carry out their leader's mission, they would work to create havoc, destroying and burning anything they could."

"Why? I don't understand why someone would do that, especially to people who would never harm them."

Gideon stared into the woods, the leaves dripping from the light rain that had started falling. "I don't understand either, but it is the way of war. The purpose is to strike fear into the heart of your enemy, and what could make the North be more afraid than an act of senseless violence in the middle of Ohio?"

"Whatever is going on, it doesn't look like it's going to happen this morning. You need to get some sleep."

He rose from the chair and drained his cup of coffee. "I told your daed I'd help him start cutting hay, but with this weather, it looks like we'll have to put that off." He looked around the barnyard again, tapping his finger against the side of his cup. "Don't stay here at the house today." He turned to Ruby as he spoke, his eyebrows peaked in concern. "Take the children to your mother's. We're too isolated here, hidden from the road and the neighbors."

"I don't see why I should leave. I have so much work to do around here."

"I need you to, Ruby. I can't take a chance —"

He broke off, looking into the woods past

her shoulder. Ruby turned, but she only saw a deer bounding away, its white tail flashing in the dark underbrush. Gideon shook his head, then grasped her elbow, pulling her close.

"I can't risk losing you too." Gideon's voice was low, nearly a moan. His eyes, so close to her own, were dark in the dim light. "Obey me in this. Please. I won't be able to rest if I don't know that you and the children are safe."

Safe. The word echoed in Ruby's mind. She had always felt safe in Weaver's Creek, but Gideon's experiences had made him wiser to the ways of the world than she was. His actions while they were in Millersburg had shown her that.

She nodded. "For sure, Gideon. I will do whatever you want. Whatever you need me to do."

"Denki." He caressed her arm, then his hand moved to her back and pulled her close, tightening his hold until she was pressed against him, enclosed in his arms. He spoke into her ear, his voice intense. "Stay there until I come for you. Your mother won't mind, will she?"

Ruby shook her head, breathing in Gideon's scent, safe in his arms. "She will enjoy having us stay as long as we need to."

"It won't be long before I join you there later today. But you are right, I need to sleep."

Her breath caught when he tightened his hold on her once more, then she pulled back, looking into his face. His gaze lingered on her eyes, then dropped to her mouth. He paused, cast a glance into her eyes once more, then leaned closer. Ruby stilled, waiting for his kiss, knowing it would be tender and careful, just as he was.

"What are you doing?"

Ruby jumped at the sound of Roseanna's voice. She tried to pull away from Gideon, but he didn't release her.

"I'm hugging Ruby and enjoying it very much."

Roseanna's eyes narrowed. "You never hug me like that."

Gideon finally let go of Ruby and turned to his daughter. "That's because you are my daughter. When I hug you, I kiss you here —" He kissed the top of her head. "And I kiss you here." He kissed her cheek. "And sometimes I kiss you like this." He buried his face in her neck and blew raspberries until she pushed away, laughing.

"Daed!" Sophia came running out of the house. "Kiss me silly too!"

He grabbed Sophia and kissed both girls,

tickling them until they were breathless.

"Now you've both been kissed, so go get ready. Ruby is taking you to Lydia's house today."

They ran into the house and up the stairs, still laughing.

Gideon turned to Ruby, his grin at the girls' joy fading as he looked at her. "I . . . I don't know why I held you like that. I didn't mean to do it, I guess I . . ."

"You aren't thinking clearly." Ruby finished for him, her back and shoulders turning ice cold after the heat from his touch. "You haven't slept. I understand."

He took a step closer. "I don't know what to think about you, Ruby. You came into our lives just when we needed you the most, and you continue to bring happiness to my children." He stroked his beard, his eyes searching the woods again. "Lovinia has been gone for more than a month, but it seems like we buried her yesterday. And with the possibility of danger, I can't help thinking about what happened last spring, like I'm reliving a nightmare."

"That nightmare is in the past. It won't happen again."

"Won't it? You don't know that, and neither do I. We're in the midst of a war, and none of us are safe from its devastation." He scanned the woods again. "You'll take the children to your mother's then?"

"For sure, I will. As soon as we're ready."

He followed her into the house, then with a final squeeze of her hand, he went into his bedroom and closed the door. Ruby peered out of the window over the sink into the thick trees. Nothing was moving. He must be imagining things, but she would still do as he wished. Anything to erase the haunted look she had seen in his eyes.

Gideon woke feeling sluggish and weary. The clouds had moved on, and the noonday sun shone brightly. He sat on the edge of his bed, listening. Even though he was alone in the house, the old building creaked as a gust of wind shook the leaves outside his window, showering drops of water as it passed.

Rubbing his face, Gideon tried to bring himself to full wakefulness. His imagination had been playing tricks on him, making him see raiders who weren't there. What must Ruby think of him? What had she told Lydia and Abraham?

He got dressed and went out to the kitchen. Ruby usually left the coffeepot at the back of the stove so they could enjoy a second cup partway through the morning, but as he headed toward it, something on the floor made him freeze. He looked closer. It was a leaf. A wet leaf.

Breaking into a cold sweat, he looked around. The loaf of bread Ruby had made yesterday wasn't on the counter where she had left it, and the coffeepot was sitting on the table. He lifted it. Empty. He stared at the leaf.

Gideon shook himself. His imagination had carried him away again. For sure, Ruby had emptied the coffeepot before she left, and she had taken the loaf of bread to her mother's. The leaf? It had blown in the door when Ruby and the children went out on their way to Lydia's.

"Gideon?"

Levi's voice called to him from outside. Gideon shook his head to clear it of the lingering thoughts and stepped out the door.

"It's good to see you," Gideon said.

Levi came jogging toward him. "Have you seen Champ?" He was breathless by the time he reached Gideon and leaned his hands on his knees.

"Your horse? Did he get loose? We can check the barn and pasture to see if he found his way over here."

"I don't know how he got out. I know I fastened the stable securely last night. I checked it twice."

Gideon halted halfway to the barn door. "You're sure?"

Levi nodded. His normally pink face was red with exertion. "Father blames me for being careless, but I don't see how he could have gotten away."

"Was anything else missing or out of place?"

"I don't think so." Levi frowned as he thought. "Mother did make a comment that the chickens hadn't given as many eggs this morning."

"Have you seen any strangers around?" Gideon's hands shook. He clasped them behind his back, trying to appear relaxed.

"You mean like those raiders we were talking about yesterday? No one like that."

"But strangers?"

"A man came to the door yesterday evening. He was looking for a handout, and Mother gave him a plate of food."

"What kind of man?"

"Old, I guess. He wore a black suit that was worn at the elbows and knees." Levi looked at him. "He didn't look like he could be a soldier. He said he was a minister, on his way west. But he couldn't have taken Champ."

"Why?"

"He left long before I checked the barn for the night. I saw him riding his mule along the road toward Millersburg soon after supper."

Gideon continued toward the barn, Levi hurrying to keep up with him. He had to make sure nothing had happened to Bett and his team.

"You think that old man is a thief?" Levi asked as Gideon opened the barn door.

The horses and the cow were grazing in the pasture on the other side of the barn. Gideon whooshed out a breath of relief.

"I don't know if he is or not. But he sounds like the same man that stopped by Elizabeth's house on Monday. Ruby said he was on his way west then, so why was he still in the neighborhood yesterday?"

Something heavy fell in the haymow above their heads. Levi's eyes grew wide as he stared at Gideon. Gideon put one finger to his lips in a warning for Levi to remain silent. He went to the horses' stalls and called them in from the pasture.

"As long as you're here, Levi, you can help me harness Samson and Delilah. I was getting ready to take them down to Abraham's when you stopped by."

He put halters on both horses and tied them.

Levi glanced up at the floor of the mow. "For sure." He took Delilah's harness off its hooks and started toward Samson.

"Wait —" Gideon's voice broke and he cleared his throat. "This is Samson's harness." He took the other harness into Samson's stall. "You have Delilah's." He worked to keep his voice steady, but it was higher pitched than normal. He cleared his throat again and harnessed the horse, not bothering to brush him first.

Levi didn't say anything but worked until Delilah was ready.

"I'll drive the horses along the road. Meanwhile, would you open the back gate for the cow? She can graze in the woods this afternoon."

The younger man glanced upward again. "I'll meet you at Abraham's then?"

"Ja, for sure, at Abraham's. We'll see if he's ready to cut hay now that the sun has come out. The fields might be dry enough."

Gideon gathered the reins and drove the team out of the barn and along the lane toward the road, walking behind them. His back itched, but he resisted the urge to look behind him. That noise he and Levi had heard might have been a rat, but only a man could knock over an object that large.

Levi caught up to him just as he turned

the team off the road and toward Abraham's barn. The children were playing by the barn and waved when they saw him.

"What was in your barn?" Levi said, his breath coming in puffs. "Was it that minister?"

"It could have just been an animal." Gideon risked a look back toward his house, but it was obscured by the trees at this distance. "Or it could have been a man. I don't think it was the man you saw last night, though, because we didn't see his mule."

Abraham came out of the barn as they approached. "I didn't expect you to come by today, Gideon. Ruby told us you had been up all night."

"Let's go in the barn to talk," Gideon said, looking up the road again. "Someone might be watching us."

As they unharnessed Samson and Delilah, Abraham asked, "What is going on?"

Gideon related the story of Morgan's Raiders and the danger they might be in.

"Our driving horse, Champ, is missing, and Gideon and I heard someone in his barn," Levi said. "That's why we brought his team down here."

Levi sounded more frightened than he was. Gideon laid a hand on the younger man's arm to calm him.

"We don't know if it was a man in the barn, but something was there. And with the Beilers' horse missing, I didn't want to take a chance leaving the team at home."

Abraham scratched at his chest under his beard. "But the horse might have wandered off. And you might have heard a raccoon in your barn loft."

Levi glanced at Gideon. "I was sure I had fastened Champ's stall door securely."

"Haven't you had problems with that horse before?"

"You don't believe me," Gideon said. His arms ached, and he rubbed his elbows. He didn't know if his suspicions were correct or not. But he couldn't shake the feeling that something was terribly wrong.

"I believe that you heard something, and I believe you might have a reason to be worried. But we've had drifters travel through here before, and things have gone missing from our farms. There's no reason to think these raiders might be involved. It might be serious, or it might be nothing to worry about. Let's go talk to Amos and see what he thinks."

By the time they reached the Beilers' farm, Gideon was feeling embarrassed. Abraham's supposition that there could be drifters in the area was reasonable, and they had seen no signs of strangers in the area during the three-mile drive. If a company of soldiers was nearby, surely he would see signs of their camp, or they would hear men moving about. At the very least, a wagon with three men would be stopped and questioned, but the road was quiet. The late summer insects droned in the grass along the road.

Amos was on the porch as they drove up. "Did you find that horse, Levi?"

Levi jumped down from the wagon seat. "Ne, Father. He just disappeared."

The minister's face was as red as his son's as he faced them. "You should check the woods." He pointed around the side of the house, where a large stand of trees covered a hilltop. A thin thread of smoke hung in the air above the treetops. "Someone is back there, and they might be the ones who took my horse."

Levi gave Gideon a panicked look, and Gideon knew how he felt. He was not going into those woods to confront anyone.

"You should come too, Amos." Abraham tied the reins to the brake handle and climbed down from the wagon. "Whoever is back there is on your property. We should welcome them, and if you don't like where they're camping, we can suggest a better place."

Gideon's head roared. If those two men walked into a rebel camp, they might not survive.

"Let me go," he said, his mouth dry. "I won't let them see me. I'll just find out who they are and if they're any threat to us."

Amos turned to go back inside his house. "See if they have Champ too. I paid too much money for that horse to lose him to a bunch of thieves."

"Do you want me to go with you?" Levi's face was pale.

Gideon shook his head. "This is something done best by one man." He judged the distance to the edge of the woods to be a quarter of a mile. "I should be back in an hour. I'll let you know what I find out."

Abraham patted his shoulder as he left the Beilers' barnyard. The long, lonely walk across the fields awaited him, and he would be exposed to anyone who was watching.

Supper in Mamm's kitchen was crowded. Ruby had already forgotten how much room Gideon's family took up at the kitchen table, but Mamm didn't seem to mind. She gave the three older children tasks to do to help put the meal on the table while Ruby held Daniel. He was fussy this evening and wasn't happy sitting in the tall chair Mamm kept for her grandchildren.

"He might be getting a new tooth," Mamm said as she sliced the cold ham she had brought in from the springhouse.

Ruby tried to open Daniel's mouth to look, but he buried his face in her dress.

"I've tried everything I know to soothe him," Ruby said, rocking him in her arms.

"Try this." Mamm sorted through her drawer of cooking tools until she pulled out a thick wooden ring. "You used this when you were a baby, and it helped."

Ruby turned Daniel around. He reached for the ring and pulled it to his mouth. His crying stopped as he chewed on the toy.

Roseanna patted her brother on the back. "That is better, isn't it, Danny?" Her voice crooned soothingly.

"You're going to be a good mother someday, Roseanna," Ruby said, holding a clean diaper handy to catch the drool dripping from Daniel's mouth.

Hugging her brother, Roseanna said, "I like babies. Except when they're crying."

Ruby noticed Sophia watching them. "What about you, Sophia? Do you like babies?"

The six-year-old shook her head. "They

stink too much. I like grown-up boys like Ezra."

Mamm laughed as she put the sliced ham on a plate. Ruby put Daniel in his chair and tied him securely with a length of cloth, then took the loaf of bread from the bread box.

"I should have brought the loaf I had at Gideon's house. We could have had that with our supper."

"It will be there when you take the children home. How long did Gideon want them to stay?"

"He didn't say. He is very worried about the possibility of —" Ruby broke off, remembering that the children were listening. "He is worried that the roof might leak in the rain and the children could get wet during the night. So I know we'll stay here for tonight, at least."

"Where did the men go this afternoon? Your daed took the spring wagon, and Gideon and Levi were with him. They were gone most of the afternoon."

"I don't know, but I'm sure they'll tell us about it at supper tonight." Ruby took the lid off a pot of boiling water. "It's time to put the corn in."

"Roseanna, will you go ring the bell?" Mamm put the plate of cold ham on the table, out of Daniel's reach. "Supper will be ready as soon as the corn is cooked."

Gideon was silent during supper, not eating much, and even Daed only gave short answers to Mamm's questions.

Finally he said, "We'll talk later," with a slight nod toward the children.

So Ruby and Mamm talked about the quilt they planned to make.

"Who will it be for?" Ruby asked.

"I thought it might be good to give it to Elizabeth. I was surprised when she didn't come with you today."

"I think she was feeling lonely after hearing about Reuben. This morning she said she would spend the day with Katie, and possibly all night. Katie has been begging her to come for a long visit."

"That's too bad about Reuben. Such a sad end, and Elizabeth has already been alone for so long," Mamm said.

Daed took a piece of bread and spread butter on it. "We can't help Reuben, but we can make sure Elizabeth is no longer alone."

"She has talked about joining the church," Ruby said, then stopped, biting her lip. "I'm sorry, I shouldn't have said anything. Elizabeth has talked to me about it, but I should leave it to her to tell you."

"It's all right," Mamm said. "She already

329

talked with us. At least something good will come out of the last several years."

Ruby glanced at Gideon, wondering what he thought of their conversation, but he seemed to be paying no attention.

Finally, when it was time for the children to go to bed, Daed sat in the front room with Mamm. Gideon was already in a chair when Ruby came downstairs to join them.

"Are you finally going to tell us what you did this afternoon?" Mamm asked. "You are being very mysterious."

"We didn't want the children to hear." Daed leaned his forearms on his knees, his head bent. "We discussed whether we should tell anyone, but Gideon thought folks should be aware."

"Of what?" Mamm looked from Daed to Gideon.

Ruby glanced at Gideon. He leaned on his knees like Daed, his head in his hands.

"What happened?" Ruby whispered, knowing their voices could carry up the stairs. "Is it the raiders like you feared?"

"They have a camp in the Beilers' woods," Gideon said. "I counted five of them, but there may be more. They had ten horses, including the Beilers' driving horse."

"How could they be so close without any of us noticing them?" Mamm asked.

"They work at night, stealing food, livestock, money. Whatever they can find." Gideon lifted his head, glancing at Ruby, then looking at Daed. "They won't hesitate to kill anyone who opposes them."

"We wouldn't get in their way," Mamm said. "They are welcome to anything we have —"

"They don't know that," Gideon broke in. "They assume everyone is just like they are and will fight to keep what is theirs."

"What did Amos say?" Mamm turned to Daed.

"He said we should give them what they want and wait for them to move on."

"That sounds sensible to me." Mamm sat back in her chair.

"But they won't do that." Gideon sat up, frustration in his voice. "They will stay here until they get what they want or destroy everything. I don't know how they escaped being captured at the same time as their leader, but I heard them talking about where they were going to meet him. What they don't know is that he won't be there."

Ruby leaned forward. "What can we do? We won't fight against them, but it seems like that is all they understand."

"Amos says we should go about our usual business." Daed brought the tips of his

331

fingers together in a peak. "If they steal our food, we will grow more. If they steal our animals, we will buy more. And we wait for them to move on."

Gideon rubbed his open palm on his knee. "You know I don't agree with that. Those men will take everything we have until our children are starving and we have nothing left. They'll destroy the crops in the fields so we won't have any food for next year, either." His hands closed into fists. "If we sit and do nothing, evil will win."

"You have forgotten one thing, Gideon." Daed bowed his head again. "Obeying our Lord is the most important thing we can do. Amos is right. We cannot fight them or resist them. We are called to turn the other cheek."

Gideon's fists clenched and unclenched, then he got up and walked out of the room and out into the barnyard. Daed started to follow him, but Mamm stopped him with a hand on his arm.

"Let him go. He's talked to you enough today. He needs to sort through this on his own."

Ruby slipped out of her chair and followed Gideon. When she reached the porch, she saw him leaning on the pasture fence, silhouetted against the rising moon that was nearly full. Other than Gideon, the barnyard was empty, even though she almost expected to see soldiers creeping from the shadows. She shivered, then ran to Gideon.

"Are you going to try to convince me to see your daed's point of view?" He moved over to give her space to lean on the top board of the fence next to him.

"I don't know what to think." She stood close enough to Gideon that she could feel the warmth of his arm through her dress sleeve. "Lovinia and you both have told me how terrible it was for you in Maryland. You've lived through it, and you're afraid of the same thing happening to us here."

Gideon turned to face her. "Abraham and Amos want to follow the teachings of the church. Teachings have been tested time and time again in the last two hundred years."

"The martyrs died for their faith." Ruby's fingers grew cold. Would the Good Lord call them to be martyrs at this time? To sacrifice their homes, and possibly their lives? "When our ancestors' faith was tested, do you think they questioned whether or not they should follow Christ's teaching?"

"I wonder if they were as torn as I am." Gideon's quiet voice echoed in Ruby's ears.

"They must have been. I don't understand, though. We try to live in peace. We try to treat others the way we want to be treated. And yet, time and again the world is against us. We're not supposed to fight, and we're not supposed to resist, but it seems like we're fighting a battle all the time."

" 'For we wrestle not against flesh and blood, but against principalities, against powers, against the rulers of the darkness of this world, against spiritual wickedness in high places.' " Gideon rubbed the side of his nose. "Paul wrote that in the letter to the Ephesians. We are fighting a battle, a spiritual one. But sometimes flesh and blood gets in the way."

"Then what do we do?"

Gideon looked across the pasture, silver in the moonlight. "We obey God, and we trust him. Your father is right." His shoulders slumped. "But I fear that the children will suffer even more than they already have." He put his arm around Ruby and drew her close. "And I worry about you. Your family. The community. What will happen to us tomorrow, or the next day?" His hand on her shoulder squeezed tight. "Most of all I fear that I will fail. That I won't be strong enough."

Ruby covered his hand with her own. "But the Good Lord is strong enough. Depend on him."

"I'll try." He smiled at her. "That's all I can do."

14

Sunday morning worship was at Abraham and Lydia's home. The house was hot and close with the entire community in the big open room. The benches were crowded together, and Gideon was wedged between Abraham and Samuel. His children were sitting with Ruby and Lydia, like usual, and he was glad to be able to concentrate on the worship today.

His mind was still in turmoil. Saturday had been a quiet day. He had mowed hay from sun up to suppertime and had seen no sign of rebel soldiers anywhere. If he hadn't seen their camp last week, he wouldn't have believed they were in the area. His conversation with Ruby the other night hadn't solved anything, and his questions still hung in the air. Was he strong enough to face the rebel soldiers without fighting? Could he stand by and do nothing if they came to his house? If they harmed his children?

Mein Herr . . .

His prayer died away before he could form words to say. How should a man pray in times like this?

The hymn ended, and Harm Bontreger called the number for the next hymn, *das Loblied,* the hymn of praise sung in every Sunday morning service. That was followed by a sermon from Amos.

Since he was the only minister in attendance until after the election that afternoon, his sermon went on for much longer than normal. The Scriptures for this Sunday were from Luke 12 and 13, a section of the Bible filled with illustrations appropriate for this time of the summer when the farmers were bringing in the hay, but Amos went to the end of chapter 13 for his text. As he preached on the narrow door that leads to salvation, Gideon had a hard time following his points, until he realized that Amos was talking about someone specific.

Even though he didn't name this person, the more he talked, the more Gideon understood that Amos was talking about him. He twisted the Scripture to make it sound like Gideon was the man who came to the gate and who the Lord did not recognize. A stranger. An evildoer. Then he wandered from the text, accusing him of all kinds of sins, including being a false prophet and a fornicator, taking advantage of the innocent people of the valley.

Gideon nearly walked out, but then saw that no one was looking at him. No one else had identified the unnamed man in the sermon as him.

Then Amos drew to the end of his sermon. His face was red, and his hand shook as he pointed into the congregation.

"The sinner is here among us. He and his woman of Babylon. They are in our midst and will bring destruction on us all if we don't cast them out into the darkness!"

As soon as Amos started toward his seat, folks on both sides of the center aisle erupted in conversation. Gideon was certain they had never heard a sermon like the one Amos had just delivered. He certainly hadn't.

Abraham went to the front to address the congregation. It was customary for other ministers and men of the church to bring up their own points concerning the sermon text or to question the preacher. He waited until silence had descended again, then cleared his throat.

"Your sermon was very vivid in its descriptions, Preacher Amos," he said. "But it sounded as if you had someone specific in mind. I am sure you did not mean to accuse anyone directly, but perhaps you meant your tone to be an illustration of what could happen within our midst." He scanned the congregation. "Any of us can fall victim to the wiles of sin, and we must all be on our guard."

Amos shook his head, but Abraham smiled and went on, speaking on the same passage Amos had focused on, but using the parable to encourage them all.

"Strive to be humble and pure, always seeking the good of your fellow man," he concluded. "Be content to linger behind, letting others go before you, knowing that in our Lord's kingdom, the first shall be last and the last shall be first."

After Abraham sat down again, another man rose to speak, focusing on an earlier parable in the same chapter of Luke. Amos sat in his seat on the front bench, his back hunched and his head bowed. Gideon knew Amos had meant to accuse him of something, but Ruby couldn't be the "woman of Babylon" he had mentioned. He wasn't even sure what Amos had meant by that.

The service concluded without another mention of Amos's sermon, and the women started preparing for the fellowship meal. Gideon helped to convert the benches to tables, then went out to the porch to wait for his turn to eat. He leaned against one of the posts, looking up the hill toward the Beilers' farm. No hint of woodsmoke hung in the air above the trees, and he didn't hear any sounds that didn't belong to a peaceful Sunday afternoon.

Levi came out of the house and stood next to him. "I'd like to apologize for Father. He was out of line in his sermon. I don't think he meant to say everything he said."

"I'm not sure what he meant to do." Gideon looked past Levi's shoulder into the house where Amos was talking with Simeon Keck. "If he thinks I should be under the discipline of the church, he went about it the wrong way."

Levi turned to look into the house, then stepped closer to him. "I think he was trying to make an illustration, like Abraham said. You might not be the one he was talking about. There are some folks in the community who are hiding sins from the past."

Gideon's fingers grew cold. No one knew what he worked so hard to keep in the past, did they? He had never mentioned it to anyone, not even to Lovinia.

"Do you know this for certain?"

Levi's perspiring face turned pale. "Ja, I know this for certain, but I can't talk about

340

it. Not yet. It is something I overheard."

Relaxing, Gideon moved away from the porch steps as a couple younger boys ran out of the house, intent on their own plans for the afternoon. "Perhaps you are mistaken. Perhaps the one you overheard was talking about something else."

He nodded slowly. "Perhaps, but I don't think so."

"Is it something serious? Something that would affect the church?"

Levi glanced into the house again. "I'm not sure. Do you think that all sin has to be exposed? Especially if it is something that happened long ago?"

Gideon's mind flashed to the dying boy at his feet, and he closed his eyes. He just wanted to forget his sin but covering it up wasn't working. It was still there, haunting him, drying up his spirit. What did the psalmist say? *For day and night thy hand was heavy upon me . . .*

"When we hide sin, it affects us. It should be exposed and confessed, at least to our Lord if no one else. In one of the psalms, David wrote about keeping silent about his sin, and how God's hand was heavy upon him. But when he confessed to the Lord, his sins were forgiven."

He couldn't look into Levi's eyes. His own

341

words mocked him. He had taken his sin to God time after time, but he still carried its weight like an anchor around his neck. He had seen God's forgiveness in other people's lives and he believed in God's grace and mercy, but not for himself. He could counsel others, but he was still dying inside.

"What if the person doesn't acknowledge it as sin?" Levi wiped the sweat off his nose. "What if they live their lives thinking that hiding the sin is enough?"

Gideon opened his hand, showing Levi a splinter embedded in his palm. "I got this splinter while I was cutting hay yesterday. If I ignored it and left it there, it would either fester and cause me a lot of pain, or the skin would grow over it. It could remain there for years, always a bit sore. I could continue to ignore it, but it would still be there." He rubbed at the splinter, but it was too deep for him to work it out on his own. "When we try to cover up sin, it is the same. We become calloused, thinking it doesn't affect us. We might even think it is gone. But that unconfessed sin is still there."

"What do I do?" Levi looked miserable. "I can't talk to this person. They have no idea that I know."

"Pray that God will prompt them to confess or pray that he will show you the right time to expose what you know."

"You're saying I should leave it to God."

"I'm saying that you need to listen to God's prompting. Be ready to act if needed, but wait for him."

Levi nodded. "Yield my worries to him rather than take the matter into my own hands."

Gideon patted Levi on the shoulder as Amos called the people to prayer before the fellowship meal. "Ja, for sure. Gelassenheit."

Levi looked at the plate he had filled for his Sunday dinner. Cold ham, slices of cheese, and bread smeared with apple butter had looked appetizing, but suddenly he wasn't hungry. His talk with Gideon before the meal gave him much to think about, but other worries intruded. Was it nerves about the coming election this afternoon? Or concern about the encampment of soldiers in the woods behind their house?

Mother hadn't slept well since Gideon had told them who was camped back there, but Father chose to ignore them, saying they would go on their way soon, that drifters always did. Levi's head pounded like a drumbeat, pulsing in the summer heat. Father was good at ignoring unpleasant things. He pushed his plate toward Caleb

Lehman, who was sitting between him and Millie's new beau, Wilmer.

After talking with Wilmer and getting to know him a little bit, Levi approved of him. He didn't seem to follow the change-minded teachings of the folks up in Oak Grove and was interested in moving to Weaver's Creek. He was a good, solid Amishman, although Levi would wait to tell Millie what he thought. If he told her that he liked Wilmer while she was in the rebellious mood she had been in lately, she might just throw the poor fellow off in a show of independence.

Meanwhile, he chatted with Wilmer and Caleb, waiting for the meal to be over so they could finish the day's business. After talking with Abraham and a few other men from the congregation, Father had agreed to elect two new ministers this afternoon. A community needed more than one or two men to lead it, Abraham had argued, and Levi agreed. Father held too much power as the only minister, and that power needed to be divided among all the ministers. The church also needed a bishop, a role Father had taken on by default. They would select their new bishop from among the ministers when they met again in two weeks.

When the fellowship meal was finished,

the members of the church met back inside the Weavers' house for the election. Levi chose a seat in the back of the room with Caleb, Henry, and Wilmer, where he could observe the proceedings. Father had wanted him to sit in front, but he preferred to stay in the background today. His head still throbbed, and the heat was oppressive. The sounds of the children playing in the yard drifted in through the open windows and doors, and every once in a while, a little breeze did too.

As the only minister present, Father went into the bedroom next to the kitchen alone.

"Another minister should be with him," Levi said in a whisper.

Caleb looked at him. "Why?"

"There should be more than one man to hear the nominations. We should have asked a bishop from another community to oversee the election."

"It's too late now," Caleb answered.

Levi nodded. It was too late. He should have thought of it earlier. But it wasn't until this moment that he realized how Father was in the perfect position to sway the election to the result he wanted. All he had to do was to claim that the names he wrote down were the ones who had been nominated, no matter which names had been whispered to him by the people.

The folks filed to the door one by one. They had been instructed to nominate two men, so the process took longer than usual. When Levi reached the door, he whispered Gideon's name and Abraham's name. Father made no sign that either name surprised him, or that he even recognized that Levi was there.

Afterward, Father emerged from the bedroom with a list in his hand. Every man who had received two or more nominations would be the ones called to the front.

"Abraham Weaver," Father read, and waited for Abraham to make his way to the front. "Simeon Keck." Another pause. "Johan Lehman."

Father stopped, then glanced at Mother. He looked at the paper again.

"Gideon Fischer."

Mother stood. "I object to that nomination."

Wilhelm Stuckey stood up on the men's side. "You can't object to a nomination. They were given in due order, and we must accept them."

"But that man doesn't meet the requirements. He is a sinner."

Wilhelm looked at the folks sitting on the benches. "And who among us isn't a sinner

346

who has been forgiven by the grace of our Lord?"

Mother looked furious. "I meant, he is living in unrepentant sin right now."

Abraham took a step forward from the line of nominees standing at the front of the room. "What sin do you accuse him of, Salome?"

"He is carrying on with your daughter, Ruby." Mother pointed at Ruby, standing in the back of the room with Daniel in her arms. "And they are doing it right under your nose, in the house you provided for them."

Mother looked at the women sitting around her, waiting for them to join in her protest, but even though the people of the congregation talked among themselves, no one stood up to join in Salome's accusation.

Finally, Lydia stood, waiting for everyone's attention. When the room was quiet, she said, "I have known Gideon since he brought his family to Weaver's Creek. I knew his wife, and I know his children. Most of all, I know my daughter, Ruby. I have seen no evidence of the truth of Salome's accusation in all that time."

Mother frowned. "You must have seen how close they are and how much time they spend together."

Lydia nodded her agreement. "Talking together, ja. Ruby promised Gideon's wife that she would care for the children after the poor woman passed on, and she is doing an admirable job. She and Gideon often confer on how to handle issues that come up."

Mother looked around again. "I've seen her go to his house early in the morning, much earlier than is suitable for a normal caller."

Millie tugged at Mother's skirt, her face red with embarrassment. "Mother, sit down. You just heard that Ruby isn't doing anything more than caring for the children. She would need to be at the house early to make their breakfast."

Mother cast a glance at Father, but he wasn't looking at her. He studied the paper in his hand. Mother sat down on her bench with a thump.

"The next names on the list are Wilhelm Stuckey and Karl Stuckey."

Levi nodded to himself. Either one of Katie's brothers would be a good minister.

Father brought six copies of the Ausbund from the bedroom and laid them on the table in the front of the room.

"As you know," he said, "we are selecting

two ministers today, so two of these books have the lots hidden inside. We will now have a time of silent prayer before the candidates select their books."

During the prayer time, Levi couldn't focus. He felt a twinge of disappointment that his name hadn't been on the list of nominees. At one time, he would have been in despair, knowing that years could pass before the church needed to select another minister, but not today. He searched his mind, his heart . . . but he only found contentment and relief. The Good Lord knew he wasn't ready for such a task. A thought passed through his mind that the preparation the Lord had for him might be unpleasant, or even sorrowful. Gideon had been through such trials, and it had made him wise and compassionate. Levi sighed.

Whatever it takes, Lord, make me more like you.

He shuddered slightly. What if the Lord answered his prayer?

Father cleared his throat and the selections began. The men chose their books in the order their names had been called.

Abraham was first. He leafed through the thick hymnbook, but no slip of paper appeared.

Simeon Keck was next. Levi knew God's

will must be done, but he couldn't help hoping that Simeon would not be one of the new ministers. In Levi's opinion, he was too sympathetic to the change-minded part of the church. But there was no slip in his book, either.

The same for Johan Lehman, and then it was Gideon's turn.

Gideon was hesitant, reaching for one book, then changed his mind and took a different one. As soon as he started turning the pages, a slip of paper fluttered to the table. Gideon stopped, his head bowed, but murmurs of approval went through the congregation.

Wilhelm also hesitated. There were only two books left. He finally took the one Gideon had almost chosen, and the second slip appeared. Wilhelm held it between two fingers as if in disbelief. Karl put his arm around his brother and held him in a tight hug.

Father cleared his throat again. "Gideon and Wilhelm are our new ministers. The other nominees may take their seats, and we will have a time of prayer for the men God has selected for us."

As Father started to pray, Levi was surprised to hear humility in his voice rather than his usual droning tone. He looked at him, standing in front of the people, his hands on the shoulders of the two men who had just been chosen to lead the community alongside him. His tone might be humble, but his stance was just as unyielding as ever. Levi looked toward Mother. She sat next to Millie, but her head was not bowed. She was staring at Father with a look Levi could only describe as disappointment.

Perhaps he could stay at Gideon's house tonight. He didn't want to be at home while Mother and Father discussed today's events.

Amos's prayer had just started when Gideon heard a sound from outside the house that left his mouth dry.

It was the roll of hoofbeats drumming on packed earth. The sound grew louder and distracted the congregation. Abraham left the meeting, heading toward the kitchen door, and Gideon followed, walking down the aisle between the two rows of benches.

Gideon passed the kitchen table, hurrying to stop Abraham before he opened the back door, but he was too late. The screen door moved slowly, swinging out as Gideon looked past it to see mounted men lined up at the edge of the porch. Beyond them Gideon saw the children in the barnyard. The older girls who had been watching them had gathered them together in the center of the yard, exposed and vulnerable.

"What can we do for you?" Abraham asked. His voice didn't quaver as he took a step onto the porch.

"We're here to make an example."

The leader, a captain, raised his pistol, pointing it at Abraham. The man's finger tightened on the trigger, bright in the morning sunlight. The trigger slid back —

"No!"

Gideon leaped forward as the gun exploded in black powder, smoke, and sound.

He grasped Abraham's shoulders as the older man fell back into his arms, a bloom of red on the front of his white shirt. Abraham's legs crumpled and they both fell to the floor in the doorway.

"Are you ready for the same?" the rebel asked as he raised his gun again.

Trapped under Abraham's limp body, Gideon stared at the man's finger, still on the trigger. But he was wedged in the doorframe, unable to scramble to his feet.

The other raiders laughed. One of their voices squeaked shrill, then deep. Gideon focused his gaze on the boy until his laughter stopped. The boy licked his lips, then cast a nervous glance at the captain.

Behind him, Gideon heard folks in the

congregation whispering, and someone sobbed. Out in the barnyard, the children had disappeared. Gideon could only hope that the girls had hidden them somewhere far away. Gideon gave up trying to stand and clutched Abraham closer.

"I've heard of you Amish," the captain said as he spit tobacco juice into the grass at the edge of the porch. "You won't fight to save your own lives." He lifted the gun and gestured toward Gideon. "You stay right there, and my boys will take what we need. We're after horses and feed today, and I'm sure there are plenty of both in yonder barn."

He turned toward his men. "Corporal, take as much feed as you can carry, and the best of the horses. If we need more, we know where to find it."

The captain spit again, this time the brown juice hitting Abraham's shoe. "We'll see y'all again. This is a friendly neighborhood, and we like it here." His eyes narrowed. "Just don't get any ideas about calling in help. We'll be watching the roads in and out of here. One of you leaves, that's the one who'll get it next."

His men came riding out of the barn, leading the horses by their halters. Gideon was sick as he saw Samson and Delilah run across the stone bridge behind the soldiers, and then Abraham's team. Well trained and hard workers, all the horses strained at their lead ropes.

Then they were gone. Gideon waited until the last soldier was out of sight up the hill, then tore off his coat and pressed the wadded fabric into Abraham's wound.

"Help me get him inside," he called to the group behind him. "If he hasn't lost too much blood, we can still save his life."

Levi and Caleb helped pull Abraham into the kitchen, then Gideon knelt beside the wounded man in the middle of the kitchen floor. He pressed his coat, now red and sticky, into Abraham's shoulder. He felt heat increase behind him as someone lit the stove, then Lydia was kneeling beside him.

"What do we need to do?" she asked, her voice and face calm. She was ready to face this trial.

"The first thing to do is to slow the bleeding, then we'll need to examine the wound. The bullet is in there somewhere, and we need to get it out."

"I'll get the doctor from Berlin," someone said.

"Wait. No one can leave without being killed, remember?" Gideon's hands shook. He took a deep breath and let it out slowly.

"We'll have to take care of him ourselves."

"Have you ever —" Lydia's voice broke, then strengthened again. "Have you ever removed a bullet?"

"I've seen it done."

Gideon took another deep breath. He had to do this. He didn't have any other choice if Abraham was going to survive. He looked away from Abraham for the first time, searching the crowd around him. Where was Ruby? Where were his children?

Abraham groaned as he began to regain consciousness.

"Lydia, we will need some laudanum if you have any."

"We're already heating up some water," Levi said from behind him. "What else do we need?"

"Strips of clean cloth for bandages, and we should get him off the floor."

Lydia stood, taking charge. "There are some sheets in the cupboard under the stairs," she said. "We'll use one for a stretcher to carry him into the bedroom. Some of you girls can cut another one into strips. Anna, you know where I keep the laudanum."

As the crowd shifted, some going outside, some to follow Lydia's instructions, Gideon lifted his bloody coat from Abraham's shoulder. The bleeding had slowed, but still oozed into the gaping wound. Just before the blood filled the cavity, he glimpsed the bullet lodged next to a bone. The wound looked clean, with no bullet or bone fragments to worry about. He pressed the cloth against the wound again.

"What happened to the children? Where are they?" he asked, but no one heard him.

He searched the room and finally found Ruby. She sat on one of the church benches, Daniel in one arm, with Ezra and the girls leaning close to her. Her face was splotchy under her freckles and her eyes were puffy, as if she was holding in her tears. He tried to give her a reassuring smile and saw the corners of her mouth turn up a bit.

Abraham came to full consciousness and reached his right hand toward his wounded shoulder.

"Abraham," Gideon said, and waited until the man's eyes focused on his. "You've been wounded, and we need to take the bullet out."

"Lydia? Is she all right?"

"I'm fine," Lydia said as she knelt next to them again. The bottle of laudanum and a spoon were in her hands. "No one else is hurt, and the soldiers are gone."

"The children —" Abraham grunted as he

struggled to sit up. "The children were in the barnyard . . ." He lay back, exhausted.

"The children are safe." Lydia poured some of the brown liquid into the spoon. "You need to take this. It will make you more comfortable."

"It will put me to sleep," Abraham said, frowning.

Gideon caught his hand as Abraham tried to push the spoon away. "You will want to be asleep. Moving you is going to hurt awfully bad."

Abraham let Lydia spoon the laudanum into his mouth, then relaxed, grimacing.

"Does it hurt?" Lydia asked.

"It tastes . . . terrible . . ."

Abraham's eyes closed, and Gideon gave Ruby a nod. She smiled then and spoke to the children.

Someone brought a sheet and they worked to lift Abraham onto it. Gideon released the pressure on the wound as the men carried Abraham into the bedroom, then he sat next to him and examined his shoulder, using the clean strips from the sheet to sponge away the blood as it seeped in. The bullet wasn't too far in. It looked like he could reach in with a thumb and finger and pluck it out, but the doctor he had observed one time in Virginia had used the point of a knife.

Gideon sat back, leaving the cloth on the wound.

Mein Herr . . . He licked his lips, his mouth suddenly dry. *Give me strength.*

15

Ruby longed to be with Mamm as the men carried Daed into the bedroom, but her first thoughts were for the children.

Roseanna and Sophia stood by her side, leaning close as she held Daniel in one arm and Ezra on her lap.

"Is Abraham going to die?" Roseanna asked, her eyes wide as she gazed at the bedroom door.

Ruby swallowed. "I don't know. We have to wait and see."

"He got shot," Sophia said, taking her thumb out of her mouth. "When folks get shot, they die."

"Have you seen someone shot before?" Ruby asked.

Roseanna shook her head. "Soldiers came, and they were hurt. Mamm said they had been shot in the war. One of them died and they buried him in our woods."

Sophia nodded. "He died. He was a soldier. He was a bad man."

Ruby looked at their faces. Both girls were calm. Resigned. They had witnessed much more of the results of war than she had thought. "Who told you he was a bad man?"

Roseanna shrugged her shoulders. "The soldiers killed Bessie and ate her. They killed the pig, too, and all the little pigs. When they left, they took all of our food. That's what bad men do."

Ruby didn't answer right away. Who was she to judge which men were bad and which ones weren't? Although the soldiers who had ridden into their farmyard this afternoon certainly seemed like they were bad. Violent. Ruthless. But did they deserve Sophia's and Roseanna's calm pronouncement? Were they any worse than she was?

Her stomach turned. They were enemies, and the Good Book was clear on how they were to treat their enemies.

"We must forgive those men," she said.

She spoke quietly, more to herself than to the girls, but Roseanna heard her.

"But they're bad."

Ruby nodded. "Jesus said we must love our enemies and pray for them." She hugged Ezra as he laid his head down on her shoulder. Did she really believe what she was saying?

She looked up to see Mamm take a seat on the bench in front of her.

"You are right. We must forgive those men and pray for those who persecute us." She took Sophia onto her lap and looked around at the people who were still in the room. "Wilhelm, I don't see Amos anywhere. Would you lead us all in prayer for forgiveness of these men?"

Wilhelm glanced at the closed bedroom door. "And we will pray for Gideon, as he seeks to remove the bullet from Abraham's shoulder." He cleared his throat. "Will you all join me in prayer?"

Ruby barely heard the words of Wilhelm's prayer as her mind swirled with accusations. Her actions so many years ago had been a worse sin than that of the soldiers today. They had a reason for what they did, even if it was wrong, and they served a government. She had betrayed her conscience when she had spent those days with Ned, and she had betrayed her sister when she made her believe there was nothing wrong in seeing men who weren't part of their church. She was the older one, and she should have been the wiser one, but she had led her sister astray.

The soldier who shot Daed had sinned against him and his family, but she had sinned against God. She could see no forgiveness for her actions.

After Wilhelm ended his prayer, the folks who stayed in the house settled into the time of waiting while Mamm went into the bedroom where Gideon was working to remove the bullet from Daed's shoulder.

Most of the families had gone to their homes, some of them fearful that they would find their own livestock stolen. Ruby heard Amos's name mentioned several times.

"Where did he go?" Margaretta Stuckey asked. "He is our minister and should be here with us at this time."

Katie came to sit on the bench across from Ruby, bringing her mother with her. "I don't know where Amos is, but Wilhelm is still here, and Gideon. They're both ministers now."

Ruby hadn't noticed when Amos left, but she agreed with Margaretta. Amos should be with them during this time.

Evening was coming, so Ruby found something for the children to eat, then took them upstairs. She sat with them until they were all asleep. Even Roseanna was tired after the day's events. By the time Ruby came downstairs again, the sun was sinking below the western horizon. The Sabbath was nearly over.

Finally, the bedroom door opened. Gideon leaned against the doorway, his face more tired than Ruby had ever seen it. His undershirt was stained with blood, and his suspenders hung from his waist.

"The bullet is out, and we have cleaned the wound and closed it as well as we could. Abraham seems to be comfortable. We will need to wait for morning to see how he feels then."

He walked into the kitchen to wash up, and Ruby slipped into the bedroom to fetch a clean shirt of Daed's for him to wear. Mamm sat at the bedside, holding Daed's hand.

"How is he?" Ruby whispered.

"He's sleeping," Mamm said.

Ruby gave her a hug. "I'll be in the other room if you need anything. The children are asleep upstairs, and the rest of the people are going home."

"Denki, Ruby. I'll leave everything in your hands."

Gideon was in the kitchen with Levi, stripped to the waist, his bloody shirt on the floor. Ruby averted her eyes as she handed the clean clothes to Levi and was startled to see the blood that had seeped into the wooden floor where Daed had lain

363

this afternoon. She must clean those stains . . . erase them before Mamm saw them.

"Did your parents go home?" Gideon asked Levi.

"Several hours ago. It has been a long day, and Father was quite shaken by the events."

"Where is Wilhelm?"

"He left just a few minutes ago. He waited until everyone else had gone to their homes. Lena had taken their children home earlier in the afternoon, and he wanted to be with them."

"You will stay here tonight, won't you?" Ruby asked Levi as she pumped water into Mamm's scrub pail. "It's getting dark, and you can't walk all the way home. It might be dangerous."

Levi nodded. "I was going to ask if I could. Or Gideon and I could stay at his house."

Gideon tucked Daed's clean shirt into his trousers. "I want to stay here with Abraham, so I won't be going home."

"You can sleep upstairs, Levi," Ruby said. "Jonas's room is available. I don't think I'll sleep tonight either. Mamm may need me."

As she lifted the bucket from the sink, Levi took it from her and put it on the floor next to the bloodstain.

"I'll go out to the barn and do the chores, then." Levi started toward the door. "Those soldiers only took the horses. The cow still needs to be milked."

"Two cows," Gideon said, taking a seat at the kitchen table. "Bett made her way down here after we let her into the woods the other day."

Ruby fetched Mamm's scrub brush and the box of salt. She sprinkled the salt onto the floor, then dipped the brush in the water and started scrubbing. The stain had soaked deep into the wood. She glanced once at Gideon, but he had laid his head on the table and was sound asleep. She didn't disturb him as she sprinkled more salt on the wood.

By the time Levi returned from the barn, Ruby had to give up. She had cleaned most of the stain, but a residue still remained, like a shadow on the wooden floor.

"That might be the best you can do," Levi said as he sat at the table.

"I hate for Mamm to see this reminder every day." Ruby bit her lip. She hadn't heard a sound from the bedroom.

Levi took her pail outside while she took the brush to rinse off in the sink. As she pumped the water, Gideon stirred, then sat up.

"I didn't mean to fall asleep. Is everything all right?"

"Mamm hasn't come out of the room, so I think that means Daed is sleeping."

Levi came back and sat at the table next to Gideon. He looked as tired as Ruby felt. She served the leftover cold meat and cheese for supper, then cut slices of the pie Mamm had made for tonight's Singing. Another reminder of how this day's routine plans had changed with one senseless act.

After they ate, Gideon went in to check on Daed while Levi went upstairs to bed. It was full dark outside, and the waning gibbous moon was just rising. Ruby watched it through the kitchen window as she washed the dishes. She took the lamp into the front room. Someone had put the house in order during the afternoon. Most likely Samuel. She had a vague memory of his boys carrying the church benches out to the wagon in the yard.

Ruby sat in Mamm's comfortable chair, weariness pulling her into a drowsy yawn. Gideon came out of the bedroom, closing the door quietly behind him. He slumped into Daed's chair.

"Abraham is sleeping well, and your mamm is going to sit up with him."

"I don't know what we would have done

366

today without you."

"I only did what I saw a surgeon do one time, but I'm lost from here on. I won't know what to do if the wound doesn't heal right." He ran his hand through his hair. "And what if I did something wrong? What if Abraham loses the use of his shoulder? What if I destroyed something when I was trying to get the bullet out?"

Ruby leaned forward. "You saved his life. Don't unsettle yourself by worrying that you did something wrong. Leave that in God's hands."

Gideon also leaned forward, his elbows on his knees. "At least this time God used me to save a life."

"What do you mean?"

He shook his head. "Never mind." He reached for her hand. "Are you doing all right? You seemed to be so strong earlier. You took care of the children and made sure Levi and I had something to eat, but you look exhausted."

"So do you." She smiled. "I think I'm fine, or I will be when Daed wakes up and is recovered."

"Tomorrow will be another long day. You should sleep while you can."

Ruby's eyes burned. He was right, she should sleep. "I don't think I can. What if

Daed wakes up and I miss it?" She sat up, suddenly remembering. "Has anyone sent word to Elizabeth? She would want to be here too."

Gideon squeezed her hand. "Samuel told Elizabeth. She's staying with them tonight and will be here in the morning, along with your other sisters."

Sleep pulled at Ruby's mind and her thoughts swirled. Maybe she would just close her eyes for a minute. She leaned back in the chair, pulling her hand from Gideon's grasp.

He stood, leaning over her. "Give your worries to the Lord, Ruby. He will give you rest."

Then she felt his lips, soft and tender, kissing her forehead, but she was too close to sleep to respond.

"I should have stopped them," Gideon said, his head bowed. "When I saw their camp last week, I should have done something."

"What could you do?"

Abraham reclined against the pillows in his bed on Tuesday morning. He had no fever or sign of infection but was weak from losing so much blood. He had spoken of seeing to his chores that morning, but Lydia wouldn't hear of it. Gideon was glad the older man had agreed to stay in bed for another day or two.

"I don't know. I should have gone to Millersburg to tell someone they were here. Or I could have . . . ." Gideon shifted his feet, then stood and paced the length of the bed. "Maybe I could have stolen their guns during the night, or their horses. Something to make them leave."

"You are one man, Gideon. You did what you thought was right at the time, so don't condemn yourself for not acting differently. Everything has worked out well."

Gideon stopped his pacing. "You can't mean to consider that things have turned out well when you're lying in bed recovering from a gunshot wound."

Abraham started to shrug, then winced as he rubbed his left arm. "I am alive. That is more than I hoped for when I saw that pistol raised."

"I still think I'm to blame. If I had only —"

"Stop." Abraham raised his hand to halt Gideon's train of thought. "We've talked about this before. You are not to blame. You didn't hold that pistol and fire it, did you?"

"I saw him lift it and point it at you. I could have pulled you out of the way or jumped in front of you."

Abraham raised his eyebrows. "And then who would be wounded, or possibly dead?" He shook his head. "You know there was no time to do anything but what we did."

Gideon paced up and down the bed again until Abraham pointed to the chair. "Sit down, son. You're wearing me out."

He sat on the chair, his head in his hands. This guilt had been tearing at him ever since he had heard the jingle of harnesses and the drumming roll of hoofbeats when the raiders rode into the Weavers' barnyard on Sunday. If Abraham had died . . .

Mein Herr . . .

"Why does this bother you so much?" Abraham waited, but Gideon couldn't answer. "What is it that is putting you through this turmoil?"

Gideon was back in Virginia, in a dell tucked under the ridge. He held Samson and Delilah's reins, waiting until the battle was over. Waiting . . .

For day and night thy hand was heavy upon me . . .

He had meant to confess his sin to the Lord on Sunday, but then the raiders had come. Had he waited too long? Time passed so quickly. Had he lost the opportunity?

"Tell me, Gideon. If something is causing you distress, bring it out into the open.

370

Don't hide it until it festers."

Gideon opened his palm. The place where the splinter had embedded itself was red and swollen. He had nearly forgotten about it, but he would never forget that day in the early spring.

"We were in northern Virginia, on a ridge in the mountains. The company I was with had found a small camp of the enemy. I mean, their enemy."

He glanced at Abraham. The older man nodded, waiting for him to go on.

"I was well away from the battle, holding my team and wagon, waiting for the skirmish to end so we could go on. By that time, I had been with the soldiers for more than a month. My mind was numb. I only did what they ordered me to do and no more. I only did what I was ordered to do."

He buried his face in his hands, trying to blot out the sights, the sounds, the acrid odor of gunpowder.

"Then the battle moved closer to me. I could hear the roll of the drums beating in cadence, and I saw soldiers on the ridge above me. The gunfire was constant, with the balls whining over my head. Cannons fired too. One cannonball hit a tree near me, cutting it in two. Then the boy landed at my feet."

Gideon's mind wanted to block out the memory, but he wrestled with his will. He had gone this far in slicing open the festering wound, and he wouldn't turn back.

"He was . . . he was still alive, but I don't know how. His body . . . was torn to pieces. His eyes shone with tears and his mouth gaped. He begged me, pleaded with me to shoot him, to end his misery. Then one of the officers saw me and the boy and thrust his pistol at me. The fighting was coming over the ridge. We would be in the middle of it soon. The officer told me to shoot the boy. To end his suffering."

"Gideon . . ." Abraham stared at him, suffering in his eyes. Suffering for him.

Gideon shook his head. "I couldn't do it. I couldn't obey that order. The officer shoved me aside and raised his pistol. He called me a coward for letting the boy suffer. His agony was so horrible, and he was as good as dead already. Then the officer's finger tightened on the trigger and the gun flashed."

Gideon swallowed. The boy's expression didn't change after he was shot, but his eyes . . . they lost focus . . . as if a light behind them had gone out. He rubbed his hand over his face.

"Everything after that is vague. I know I

tried to get the horses back, away from the fighting. The officer went down when a man from the other side thrust a bayonet through him." He closed his eyes. "Then it was over. The other side had won. They took the surviving soldiers as prisoners, but they let me go. I led my team out of there and started for home."

He dropped his hands and looked at Abraham.

"Where is my peace? How can I rid myself of this guilt? I stood there and watched while that officer shot the boy. He took his life and I did nothing. There were men killing men all around me, and I did nothing. Nothing."

Mein Herr, help me . . .

Abraham's soft voice broke through. "You have asked the Lord for forgiveness?"

Gideon's heart wrenched. "Time and again, but I still can't rid myself of this pain."

"You need to accept his forgiveness. You don't rid yourself of the burden of your guilt, Jesus Christ has already taken it on himself. But you need to believe that. Accept it. Have faith that Christ's sacrifice was sufficient even for this."

Opening his hand, Gideon stared at the red blister that had formed over the splinter.

He had rubbed at it over the past few days, trying to work it out, but it remained there. He would need to ask Ruby to help with it. He swallowed. He had been doing the same thing with his sin. Trying to work out his own forgiveness instead of going to the only one who could help him.

He left Abraham to rest. The older man's eyes were already closed, and his breathing was deep and even.

Ruby was in the kitchen, slicing tomatoes, preparing dinner.

"Could you help me?" Gideon asked. "Do you have time?"

"For sure. What do you need?"

"I have a splinter that I can't get out."

Ruby smiled at him as she rinsed and dried her hands. "Mamm keeps a needle here in the kitchen for an emergency like this."

She found the cork in the cupboard with a needle stuck in it, then she sat next to him, holding his hand still.

"That is getting infected." She looked at him, concern in her eyes. "Are you certain you want me to do this? It's going to hurt."

"For sure. Get it out of there before it gets worse."

Ruby bent over his hand, poking at the splinter with the needle. It hurt, but Gideon concentrated on watching her loose curls wave at the edge of her kapp as she worked. He felt her squeeze the skin, then work with the needle, rubbing along the skin to remove the splinter. In a minute, she was done.

"There." She held the tiny piece of wood up. "I can't believe you didn't ask me to remove this earlier. It must have been bothering you for days."

"It has been." He took it from her and threw it in the stove. "But now it will be better."

She cleaned off the needle and stuck it back in the cork, then stood to put it away. She picked up her knife and started slicing the tomatoes again, her back to him as she stood at the kitchen shelf. "Dinner will be ready in a short while. Will you ring the bell?"

"For sure."

But Gideon didn't move right away. He had the urge to walk up behind her and clasp her in his arms. He wanted to kiss her, right where red curls shone against the nape of her neck. Would he betray Lovinia's memory by doing that?

He went out to the back porch to ring the bell. Somehow, he didn't think Lovinia would mind at all.

Over the next several days, Ruby and the children fell back into the routine they had followed before Gideon had moved into his house, except that she stayed with Mamm and Daed. Elizabeth remained at Samuel's house. The raiders were still camped in the Beilers' woods, and no one felt safe with them in the area.

By Saturday, nearly a week after the raiders had attacked them, Daed was spending time out of bed, sitting in the front room or eating with the family at the kitchen table. Even though he was still weak, his wound was healing so well that even Mamm was happy with it.

"We still need to get that hay in," Daed said at the noon meal.

Gideon stopped in the middle of buttering a slice of bread. "You aren't going to cut any more hay this summer, Abraham. Your shoulder won't take that kind of work until it has more time to heal."

"Don't worry." Daed winked at Sophia. "Between you, Samuel, and his boys, we should be able to get it all in without much delay. Will we still be able to store it in your barn?"

"For sure," Gideon said. "The haymow is cleaned out and ready. Your barn here is full, but I think Samuel has some room in his."

Sophia's thumb was in her mouth as she stared at Daed.

"You need to eat," Ruby reminded her. "Your corn is going to get cold."

"She's waiting for Abraham to die," Roseanna said. "I told her he wasn't, but she said he was."

"I'm not going to die today, so eat your dinner." Daed smiled at her again. "I'm tougher than I seem."

"But the soldiers shot you. When you get shot, you die." Sophia crowded close to Ruby on the bench, still watching Daed.

"Not everyone who is shot ends up dying," Gideon said. "You can see that Abraham is getting better every day."

Mamm passed the plate of ham to Abraham. "What are you going to do about horses? Is there any possibility of getting yours back from the raiders?"

Ruby looked at Gideon and he met her gaze. He shook his head slightly, then took another bite of his bread.

"I hope to get them back," Daed said, "but I don't expect to. We'll have to borrow Samuel's team until I can find another pair."

"Harvesttime is coming," Gideon said. "Will Samuel's team be able to handle all the work? Or should we try to get more horses before then?"

Ruby smiled to herself as she cut a slice of ham into bites for Ezra. Gideon was talking like he was part of the family rather than an outsider, and from Daed's expression, he had noticed the change too.

"We might ask around, once we're able to leave the valley again."

"Do you mean you believe that the raiders are going to continue to keep us captive here?" Mamm asked.

Gideon nodded. "I think we should take them seriously. Until they move on, we need to stay in the valley."

Ruby watched Gideon's face as he talked. Instead of the haunted, frightened look she had seen before the raiders came, he seemed calm. Peaceful. Even though the threat was more real now than before, he was ready to meet the challenge. Something had changed.

After dinner, Ruby put Daniel and Ezra down for their naps. Mamm had started teaching Roseanna and Sophia to sew, and they were working on quilt blocks. When Ruby came downstairs, only Gideon was still in the kitchen.

"Come for a walk with me," he said. "It is a nice afternoon, and cooler than it has been lately. We can go out and check on the corn for your daed."

He held out his hand in an invitation, and Ruby was tempted.

"I thought I might make a cake while the oven is still hot."

"There are still cookies left from yesterday. You can make a cake another day."

Ruby looked around the kitchen. She didn't want to go off and have fun if there was work waiting to be done.

"The work is done," Gideon said, as if he could tell what she was thinking. "Come with me."

He wiggled his fingers, his hand still extended toward her. She grinned and took his hand.

"Just for a little while."

"Maybe for a little while." He led her toward the cornfields to the west of the house. "Or maybe longer."

"What if the boys wake up from their naps?"

"Lydia is there. She'll take care of them until you get back." He helped her as she slipped between two boards in the fence. "How long has it been since you've gone out to the fields?"

"I used to all the time when I was a little girl. I'd take lunch out to Daed or help him with the hay."

They walked along the path that followed the creek.

"Not since then?"

"I think the last time I helped Daed was when I was twelve or fourteen. Then Jonas was old enough to start doing a man's work, and I stayed at the house."

"So you haven't been out here in almost twenty years?"

Ruby stopped just before he led her across the board bridge. "How old do you think I am?"

He tugged her across the bridge after him. "I don't know. Maybe thirty years old?"

She laughed. "Why that guess?"

"Because I'm thirty, and we must be close to the same age."

"I'm only twenty-eight." She took a deep breath. "An old maid, for sure."

She glanced at him to see his reaction to her confession, but her age didn't seem to bother him.

"Lovinia was the same age." He smiled at her. "No wonder the two of you became good friends so quickly."

"We talked about that. Our birthdays are even in the same month, so we said we were twin sisters."

Gideon pulled her hand into the crook of his elbow. Ruby leaned into his arm, enjoying the pleasure of being close. They walked in silence until they reached the end of the fields, where the creek came out of the woods in a narrow spot of rushing water. It bubbled over the rocks in a gorge. To their right, Weaver's Knob rose above the trees, but Ruby remembered that if they kept following the creek, they would find a small waterfall. She let go of Gideon's arm and led the way as the trail climbed. When they reached the spot where the water tumbled over a pile of rocks in a gorge, Ruby found a log to sit on, and Gideon sat beside her.

"Look at that," he said.

Below them, the farm spread through the wide valley with the creek running through the center. Fields on both sides were lush and green with corn and oats. The wheat field held the newly harvested shocks, the grain drying until threshing time. The house and barn stood nearly a mile away, the white of the buildings shining against the deep green of the fields and the woods behind them.

"God has truly blessed your family," Gideon said. "This is a beautiful place."

"Daed always says that God blessed us

with land, but our faith and a family are more important than dirt and buildings. He always reminds us that our ancestors left their homes in Europe to come here where they could be free to worship God as they were led. We need to remember that they didn't consider Switzerland to be their home any more than we consider this valley to be our home. We are only temporary lodgers here, he says. Our true home is with our Lord."

"It makes our problems seem very small when you consider it that way." Gideon held her hand in both of his.

"Even the problem of the raiders?"

"Even that."

Ruby leaned against his arm, as if she couldn't get close enough to him. She missed their talks over coffee in the mornings when it was only the two of them alone in the kitchen.

"Something has changed," she said after a few moments. "You used to be so worried about soldiers coming into our valley."

He opened his right hand and rubbed the place where she had removed the splinter. "See that? It is already healing. The swelling is going down and you can barely see where the splinter was."

She nodded, and he went on.

"I had been carrying a burden of guilt around with me, and it was festering like that splinter. Talking to Abraham a few days ago, I told him . . . confessed my guilt to him. He helped me see that I needed to give that burden to my Lord. It wasn't mine to carry." He rubbed his palm again. "Ever since then, I haven't been afraid of what the soldiers might do to us. I have a feeling that this isn't done, that they will continue to steal from us, and they might even try to destroy us. But I have confidence that the Lord will take care of us. We can trust in him, no matter what happens."

Trust in the Lord? Ruby sat up, moving slightly away from Gideon. She had been the one saying those words to Gideon not so long ago, but that was before she had witnessed the raiders' violent attack.

"It's hard to trust him when so many terrible things have happened. How do we know everything will turn out the right way?"

"We don't. At least, we don't know if things will turn out the way we want them to. I am certain, though, that things will always turn out the way God intends for them to."

"When Lovinia died? Did God intend for that to happen? And when the raiders stole the horses? Was that what he intended too?"

Gideon leaned on his knees, looking out over the valley.

"I can't answer those questions, but I do know that whatever has happened that we consider to be evil, God can use for good. Something good will come from the horses being stolen, even though we may never know what that might be."

"And Lovinia? Can something good come out of her death?"

Gideon sighed, then turned toward her and took both of her hands in his. "The best good that came from her death is that I'm certain she is with our Lord, living without the pain and weakness that plagued her for so long. She is no longer ill and suffering."

Ruby pulled her lip between her teeth. Gideon was right. She mourned for Lovinia and missed her. But would she want her friend to suffer longer just because she missed her? Not at all.

"Another good thing is that Lovinia gave us a gift before she passed on." He tightened his hold on her hands. "She gave us each other. She knew we would need to lean on each other and rely on each other as we cared for the children. I think she also knew that we would come to love each other, eventually."

She risked looking at Gideon. He was watching her, waiting for her reaction.

"Do you think we are learning to love each other?" she asked.

"I think we have become friends. Very good friends. I can't imagine my life without you in it."

His gaze moved from her eyes, to her lips, then to their hands, still clasped together.

"Perhaps we should walk back to the house." Ruby stood, ignoring the breathless feeling that overwhelmed her. "The boys are surely up from their naps by now."

"Before we go, I want to do one thing."

He stood and pulled her up next to him. Then he moved closer, or perhaps she leaned toward him. He lifted her chin with one hand and guided her lips toward his. A gentle brush, then a tentative touch of his mouth on hers. A kiss that was tender, questioning. He pulled away, but he kept his eyes locked on hers.

He released his hold on her and looked into her face. "I hope you enjoyed that as much as I did, because I intend to do it again."

Ruby's face burned as she stared at the placket of his shirt. His kiss had been nothing like the bruising, demanding kisses Ned had given her. "I enjoyed it."

"Will you let me do it again? I feel like a man who has been starving . . ."

Her breath caught as he raised her chin again. She put her arms around his neck and he lowered his mouth to hers. This kiss was also tender, but self-assured. He held her close, pulling her into his arms and resting his chin on her kapp.

"I meant what I said, Ruby. I can't imagine my life without you in it. Do you think you could learn to love me?"

Ruby breathed in his scent and closed her eyes, thinking of the time they had spent together. Thinking of how completely safe she felt in his arms.

"For sure, I think I could."

16

The week had passed slowly for Levi as he stayed with the Weavers, helping with the chores and cutting hay. When he went back home the next Monday afternoon, Millie was the only one who mentioned that he hadn't been home.

"Father has been doing your chores for you," she said, standing on the bottom board of the pasture fence as he brought the cow in for milking.

"Did he ask where I was?"

"He thought you were off visiting friends or something. He complained a lot."

Levi tied the cow to the fence rail and grabbed the milking stool and pail he had put by the fence before going out to find the cow.

"I stayed at the Weavers'. Between Abraham recovering and Gideon busy with the farm, I thought they might need help with their chores. That family has been through quite a bit."

"Gideon isn't part of their family." Millie leaned over the fence. "Unless he and Ruby get married. Mother says —"

"Mother is wrong." Levi didn't like to interrupt, but he couldn't listen to the rumor about Gideon and Ruby again. "There is nothing going on between the two of them. If they get married someday, it won't be because they're trying to cover up a sin the way Mother and Father did."

Too late, Levi realized what he said.

"Millie, look, that's a secret that we're not supposed to know. Don't tell anyone, especially Mother and Father."

"What makes you think I didn't already know? Mother tells me much more than she ever tells you."

Levi grasped the top of the fence, opposite Millie. "How long have you known?"

"Since I started going to Singings. Mother wanted me to know how boys — how men are. She didn't want me to be unaware of what some boys try to get girls to do when they're alone after dark."

He hesitated. "Did she say I was to blame for them getting married?"

"Not exactly. She did say things worked out well for them, but it isn't always that way."

Levi went back to his stool and started milking. "Are you still seeing Wilmer?"

"Umm-hmm."

"You must like him."

"I do. But you won't tell him, will you?"

"Why not? I'm sure he would want to know."

"You don't understand how courting works, do you?" She sighed, exasperated. "If a girl is too quick to let a boy know she likes him, then he doesn't get to pursue her. It's better if a boy thinks he has won something in the end. If a girl gives in too easily, he'll think too much of himself."

Levi snorted. "Who told you that?"

"Everyone knows it." Millie leaned over the fence and knocked his hat off, a grin on her face. "Except you. Maybe that's why you don't have a girl."

He grabbed his hat off the ground and frowned at her as she turned her back on him and went into the house. She didn't know anything about why he didn't have a girl. The cow turned and looked at him as she chewed her cud.

"You don't know anything about it either," he said, and finished the milking.

Over the next few days, Levi kept track of the smoky haze above the trees in their woodlot. It looked like the raiders were still camped there, but Levi hadn't seen any sign of them in the community. On Tuesday, he walked to Katie's house to apologize for not making his regular trip to Farmerstown to get the mail. He stopped by the Weavers' on that trip, then again on Thursday. Abraham seemed to be recovering well.

But in his visits, and when he met a couple other men from the community on the road, Levi began to understand that the folks were unhappy with Father's actions on Sunday.

"Someone needs to talk to him," Wilhelm Stuckey had said. "Someone needs to find out what he did after Abraham was shot. No one seems to know, and rumors are ugly."

On Saturday, nearly two weeks after the raiders' attack, Levi finally gathered enough courage to ask Father what he had done on the previous Sunday afternoon. Levi had looked for him during the confusion afterward, while Gideon was examining his wound, but Father and Mother were nowhere in the house.

He knocked on Father's study door.

"Come." As Levi opened the door, Father swiveled his chair around. "I trust the chores have been done?"

"I finished the chores, and everything is

locked up tight."

Father turned back to his desk. "I'll check after supper. We don't want to lose any more of our livestock."

Levi had expected that. Father had never trusted him to do a job the correct way. "Folks have been talking. I heard them at the Weavers' house on Sunday and when I stopped by the Stuckeys' on Tuesday."

"Hmm?" Father didn't turn around. "What are they talking about?"

"They are wondering where you went after Abraham was shot. No one saw you after that, and they thought you should have been there."

"I came home to check on our place. Who knows how much livestock those ruffians had stolen before they reached the Weavers'?"

Levi stepped into the room. "Father, I heard someone say that you left because you were sympathetic to the raiders. That you colluded with them and told them we would all be at Abraham's place."

Father's chair swiveled around again. "Who said that? You know that isn't true."

"I know. But this is how rumors get started. It doesn't help that you have stayed home all week. You haven't even gone to see how Abraham is doing."

"You heard those raiders. They threatened to shoot anyone who was out and about."

"Only if we tried to leave the community to get help."

"They don't know where we're going when we leave here. Besides, someone would tell me if Abraham passed away."

"That isn't the point. Folks think you don't care." Levi stepped farther into the room. "This isn't how a minister should act."

Father pressed his lips together. "And you think you can do better."

"I know I can't. But I do know it's important for you to do something to show the people that you are part of the community."

Father closed the book he had been writing notes in and put the cork in the mouth of his inkwell. "If the community thinks I don't care, that I didn't do anything to prevent this tragedy, then I suppose the only thing I can do is to rectify the situation."

"That isn't what I said."

"But it is what you meant." Father moved him aside and took his coat and hat from the hook on the back of the door. "I will go and talk to the raiders and convince them to return the horses they have stolen."

Levi grabbed his arm. "You can't do that.

They'll shoot you just like they shot Abraham."

Father jerked his elbow out of Levi's grasp. "You would like that, wouldn't you, Levi? You've been planning to take my place for months. Don't think I haven't noticed all the times when you borrowed my books. And when Gideon Fischer came to the area, you and he became awfully close."

"That isn't what I'm doing. I just want . . ." Levi faltered. What did he want? "Father, I only want you to be proud of me. I'm not good at farming or working with my hands. But I enjoy reading and studying." He waved his hand, taking in Father's desk and shelves of books. "I only wanted . . . to be like you."

Levi didn't wait for Father to laugh at him. He didn't wait for the sickeningly condescending tone when Father derided him. He strode out of the room and out of the house. He would stay with Gideon again tonight, or perhaps with Samuel. Someplace where he wouldn't have to face his father again.

On Monday morning, Ruby was helping Mamm fix breakfast when Gideon came back to the house. Mamm had just put ham in a skillet to fry when the screen door slammed shut behind him as he strode into the kitchen.

"The horses are back in their stalls!"

Daed put his cup of coffee down on the table with a thump that made the hot liquid slosh from the cup. "They're back? Are they all right?"

"I didn't look closely, but I think so."

Daed rose from his chair. "I have to go look. I want to see them."

As Ruby picked Daniel up from his chair, Mamm moved the frying pan off the heat, and they all went out to the barn. Roseanna and Sophia ran ahead until Gideon called to them.

"Stay close, girls. Let Abraham go into the barn first."

Gideon had left the big doors open to the morning air, but inside, the barn was dim. Ruby stopped to let her eyes get used to the light, holding on to Ezra's hand. She took a deep breath of fresh hay and horses. She loved visiting the barn.

"There they are," Roseanna said. "Daed was right. The horses are back."

Mamm stroked Nell's nose while Daed opened the stall door and walked in to look at Boss.

"He looks in fine shape," he said, patting the horse's side. "And Samson and Delilah are here too."

Ruby asked. "Did the raiders bring them back?"

"I don't know why they would do that," Gideon said, patting Boss's neck.

Daed ran his hand down the horse's back as if he couldn't believe he was really there, then leaned on Gideon's arm as they left the stall. The trip to the barn had taxed his strength.

He sat on a bench he kept near the horses. "Another question is how they got here. If the raiders didn't return them, then who did?"

"I brought them." Amos had come into the barn behind them, and his sudden appearance startled Ruby. "I went up to the camp and took them back."

"That was dangerous," Gideon said. He stepped closer to Amos. "How did you do it without them seeing you?"

"I was quiet and careful. They didn't even know I was there."

"I'm thankful to get them back," Daed said. "Did you find your own horse too?"

"For sure, I did." Amos stood with his thumbs hooked in his suspenders. "He's in his own barn, safe and sound."

"Why did you take such a risk?" Daed asked.

"I knew you needed them back." Amos's face grew red. "And I had heard the rumors. Some folks thought I was to blame for the raiders being here, since they're camped on my land. I thought if I returned them, that would prove that I had nothing to do with what happened."

Daed pushed himself to his feet, and Amos took his arm to help him up.

"You didn't need to risk your life for a few horses," Daed said. "But I'm glad you're safe."

He put his good arm around Amos's shoulders, and they walked toward the house together.

Mamm followed the men. Ruby knew Amos would stay for a cup of coffee, if not for breakfast. She lingered, waiting for Gideon. He stood in the middle of the barn floor, frowning.

"Can we go to the playhouse?" Roseanna asked.

"For a little while. Until breakfast is ready."

Roseanna and Sophia each took one of Ezra's hands, and they ran out of the barn together as Ruby stepped closer to Gideon.

"You're worried, aren't you?"

He glanced at her, then looked at the horses. "Something about Amos's story just doesn't add up. How was he able to sneak into the raiders' camp and take the horses without them noticing him?"

"You don't believe him?"

"I believe he did what he said he did, but I can't figure out why they would let him get away with it."

"Do you think the raiders will come again and take the horses back?"

His eyebrows puckered. That worried look was back, but without the haunting fear that had once ruled him. "I wonder what their plan is. All I can think is that they let Amos get away in order to retaliate somehow."

"Why haven't we seen them in the past week?"

"They know the Union soldiers are hunting for them, and they might even know that Morgan has been captured. They probably feel safe here in Weaver's Creek, but if they move around the area too much, the soldiers may spot them. I think they are laying low until they can either move east into Pennsylvania or south into Kentucky."

Gideon put his arm around Ruby, drawing her as close as he could with Daniel in her arms.

"Don't be afraid," he said. He kissed the top of her head.

The children's voices drifted into the

barn, happy and carefree in their play.

"I can't help it." Ruby looked into his face. "I hate not knowing where those men are or what they might do. What if someone else gets hurt? What if they hurt you?"

He tucked one finger under her chin. "If anything happens to me, I want you to raise the children here in Weaver's Creek."

"Don't say that. I don't want to think about it."

"We don't know what the future holds. But I want to know that no matter what, my children will be with you, safe and loved."

Gideon gazed into her eyes, then kissed the tip of her nose. He might have continued kissing her, but Daniel tangled his fingers in Gideon's beard and pulled.

"Ouch." He gently removed Daniel's fingers from his beard, then he looked at Ruby. "I love you. There's no other name for what I feel for you, but it seems like such a small word for a grand, wonderful feeling."

Ruby's eyes filled with tears as she laid her hand on Gideon's cheek. "I must love you too. I've never felt this way, but you have become the center of my life. Don't take any risks. Please. I don't want to lose you. We need you, the children and I."

"I don't know what the next few days or weeks will bring, but I can face whatever comes with you here." He took Daniel from her. "Is there someplace where you can take the children if the raiders come again? Someplace you can keep out of sight?"

"There is the cellar under the house."

"The entrance is on the opposite side of the house from the barn, isn't it? If you see them coming, go there as quickly as you can without them seeing you."

"What will you do?"

"I pray that the Good Lord will protect all of us."

He held her close once more, then they walked toward the house, calling the children to come in with them.

Inside the house, Amos and Daed were deep in a discussion about nonresistance and what the church should do about the situation they found themselves in. Gideon poured a cup of coffee for himself and joined them while Ruby helped Mamm finish fixing breakfast.

Daed's face was pale. As soon as breakfast was done, Ruby hoped he would go back to bed.

"I can't believe they will bother us anymore," Amos said. "They have to move on sometime, don't they? If we just stay quiet, they will leave us alone."

"We can hope and pray for that," Gideon said. "But we can't count on it."

"Meanwhile," Daed said, "we have our crops and farms to care for. We're in the middle of cutting hay, and so are the others. The raiders can steal from any farm they choose, or worse, with all the men in the fields."

"We should organize the men of the community," Gideon said. "We can work together on each other's farms and get the crops in. Amos, you can join with the Lehmans and the Kecks. Harm Bontreger lives near you too, doesn't he?" At Amos's nod, he continued. "Then the Stuckeys can work with us, and the folks on the east end of the district can work together."

"How will that help?" Amos asked. "Even working together, the men are all in the fields while the women and children are in the houses."

"Someone from each group will need to stay at the house to warn the others if something goes wrong."

Mamm turned to the men. "I agree that having folks together is a good thing. But you wouldn't need to leave any men at the house. We can sound the alert on the dinner bell if we see the raiders coming."

"Then what would we do if we did see them?" Daed said. "We won't fight them."

Gideon shook his head. "But we can hide our valuables and our families. Each farm should have a plan. In Maryland, there was a cave on the neighbor's land where we all went when the soldiers came by. It kept us safe, even though we lost all of our food and livestock." He glanced at Ruby. "I've already mentioned to Ruby that she should take the children to the cellar if the raiders come here."

Amos drained his cup of coffee. "I'll visit each of the families in the community today and learn what they think about the situation, and we can discuss what to do." He rose from his chair.

"Won't you stay for breakfast, Amos?" Mamm asked. "It will be ready as soon as the eggs are done."

Amos shook his head. "I need to get home so we can start planning. Tomorrow we'll join together to support each other in this time of trial." He looked from Daed to Gideon. "I hope this makes up for what I said at the church election. I listened too closely to my wife and I let her sway my feelings as I prepared for my sermon. I was wrong, and I hope you'll forgive me."

Gideon stood and took his hand. "There

is nothing to make up for. I understand your concern for the well-being of the community."

As Amos left, Mamm set the platter of ham on the table while Ruby took up the scrambled eggs from the pan.

"I never thought I'd see the day when Amos apologized for something," Mamm said as she sat down.

Daed took a sip of his coffee. "The Lord convicts us all of our sins in his own way and his own time. Next week it will be me asking his forgiveness for something I've done."

Mamm smiled at him. "I still say it's been a long time coming."

Late that night Gideon woke, the smell of smoke strong in the bedroom at Abraham and Lydia's house. He jumped to his feet and looked out the window. The barn roof was ablaze, sending flames shooting into the night sky.

He grabbed his pants, pulling them on as he went out to the landing.

"Abraham!" he shouted down the stairs. "Fire!"

Sitting on the top step, he pulled on his boots and laced them tight. He got to the bottom of the stairs just as Lydia emerged from the bedroom.

"What is it? Did you say fire?"

"The barn is on fire." Gideon grabbed his hat from the peg by the door. "I'm going to get the animals out of the barn."

Abraham came out of the bedroom, carrying his shoes.

"Lydia, ring the bell. That might raise Samuel."

"You can't go out there," she said. "You're still recovering from your wound."

"I will be careful, but I can't stay in the house waiting to see what will happen."

As Gideon ran toward the barn, he heard Lydia ringing the big dinner bell. Its peal could be heard all over the farm, and he could only hope it would wake Samuel, and possibly the Stuckeys too.

The barn roof was completely engulfed, and smoke poured out of the big doors hanging open to the night. Horses neighed in fright, and all he could think of was getting them out of the burning barn before the roof collapsed. But someone grabbed him just as he reached the circle of firelight.

"Hold on there."

Gideon pushed away from the hands holding him. It was a stranger, one of the raiders.

"We have to get the horses out of there."

403

He shouted over the roar of the flames.

"My boys have already done that."

Then Gideon saw that the horses were in the pasture, crowded at the end farthest from the barn, neighing and pushing against each other in the effort to get even farther from the flames.

Samuel and his older boys came running from their house, followed by Ruby and Elizabeth. The flames roared higher and hotter and they all took a step back, away from the heat.

Gideon looked into the stranger's face. It was the officer who had shot Abraham. His men stood behind him, their faces reflecting the red light of the flames.

The man's teeth shone in the firelight. "You Amish thought you could steal from us, so this is what you get in return. Your horses are ours, your barns are ours, your crops are ours. If we want to burn a barn, we burn a barn."

Fury seethed in Gideon. Fury at the injustice and the callousness of the man in front of him.

"This is cruelty. Madness. What can you hope to gain?" His body shook as his fists clenched.

The man laughed and gestured toward the barn. "We don't need to gain anything. This is war, you coward. War."

Two of the other raiders passed a bottle, sharing the drink as they watched the barn. Behind him, he heard voices as Abraham joined Samuel. He turned to look at them and saw the flames reflected on their faces. Beyond them, Ruby and Elizabeth were going into the house. His gaze traveled up and saw sparks flying toward the house, landing in the summer-dry grass that surrounded it. Panic set in as Gideon imagined what would happen if the wind strengthened.

"The house," he shouted at Samuel. "We need to get water on the roof and around the building. Get everyone out of there!"

The raider grabbed Gideon's arm. "No one is going anywhere."

As Gideon turned back to his captor, he saw the barn behind the man, heat dancing in waves before it as the wall above the big double doors shifted, single boards falling through the opening. The entire wall would come down soon. The gaps revealed the haymow, once full of sweet, dry hay, but now a glowing ball of pulsing heat, seething dark red and black. The open bay beneath the mow seemed to be empty, but then something moved. A figure ran, doubled over, toward the gaping opening, then fell headlong.

"There is someone in there!"

He pointed and tried to run toward the body lying on the ground just outside the door. It was a man, one of the raiders.

But the officer still had a grip on his arm. "No one is in there."

Gideon turned on the man. "It's one of your soldiers. I saw him fall. He might still be alive. Someone has to save him."

The man's face hardened. "If anyone was in that barn, he's dead already. It's no use risking your own life."

In Gideon's mind, he heard the same words from another man at another time. He was dead already, the soldier had said, and Gideon watched as the soldier ended the boy's life. The pistol shot echoed in his head over the sounds of the flames and the burning barn.

Gideon's eyes stung. "I have to try. I can't stand by and do nothing. He's one of your men."

The man's face shone in the firelight, grimy sweat pouring down his face. He scanned the other raiders standing on either side of him.

"Where is Tad?" The officer looked again, whipping his head from one side to the other. His voice rose. "Where's my boy?"

His eyes grew wide as he stared at the

figure by the barn, and his grip loosened.

Gideon pulled his arm free and ran toward the wall of fire. The heat seared his eyes and he buried his head in the crook of his arm, watching the ground beneath his feet. At the edge of his vision, he saw the boy's hand outstretched toward him. He reached for it just as a cracking noise sounded from inside the barn and the haymow fell with a whoosh of flame and sparks and a deafening crash.

He grabbed the hand and tugged at it, turning away from the flames as he headed back, panic giving his legs the strength he needed to take step after step, the weight at the end of his arm threatening to pull him into the burning pit. The boy's hand slipped in his grasp, but he tightened his hold, dragging him until he met Samuel and some of the raiders. They carried the boy outside the circle of firelight and Gideon collapsed on the grass in the blessed darkness, fighting for breath against the heat, smoke, and pain.

17

In the days after the fire, Ruby and Elizabeth moved back to Elizabeth's cabin. Her sister was quiet. Maybe too quiet, and Ruby watched her closely. When Ruby asked if Elizabeth would rather join her in caring for the children, she shook her head.

"I need time to think, and to pray." The corners of her mouth turned up, but her eyes were serious. "My life isn't what I thought it was a few weeks ago, and I need to think what the Good Lord wants me to do now."

Since Elizabeth seemed content, Ruby ran down the hill to help Mamm each morning. Besides the children, there were sick men to care for.

The soldiers had left the area the morning after the fire, while the sky was still a pale gray. Thaddeus Brown, the captain of the group, stayed behind. His son had been injured badly, even though Gideon had pulled him away from the fire. After two days, the boy passed away, having never regained consciousness. They buried him in the family cemetery on the hill south of the pasture.

Thaddeus still stayed on the farm, though. He set up his tent by the fence at the edge of the pasture and ate his meals with the family, but he had lost the threatening bravado he maintained before the fire.

"I don't understand," Thaddeus said to Daed at the noon meal on Saturday, nearly a week after the fire. "I am your enemy, and yet you've welcomed me into your home. I tried to kill you, and yet you still treat me like a friend. You even grieved with me over my son's death." The man stared at his plate while he regained his composure. "I don't deserve to be treated so well. I should be in a prisoner-of-war camp or shot as a spy."

"We have only acted as our Lord has commanded us," Daed said. He was recovering from his wound but still carried his arm in a sling. "The world tells us to fight and worry, but Christ has taught us to accept what he has ordained, to respond with love, and to create friendship where there is animosity. You have lost much in this war and we grieve with you."

"What will you do now?" Gideon asked.

His voice still held the hoarseness of breathing in the smoke and heat of the fire, but it was better than it had been a few days ago. Ruby had been worried about him, but now he was breathing easier too. He was healing from his injuries.

He swallowed some water, then continued. "Will you rejoin the war?"

Ruby rose to fetch the coffeepot. Thaddeus had changed since his son passed away, but would he go back to the fighting that had cost him so much?

"One thing I know is that I can't go home." Thaddeus stared at his plate. "I've deserted my commission, my farm is destroyed, and my family is gone." He glanced around the table. "And as much as you've welcomed me, I can't stay here in Yankee territory. You may be able to forgive, but I can't. The North has destroyed everything I hold dear. Every part of my life has been taken from me, leaving me empty and worn out. I can't just turn my back on that." He leaned his elbows on the table, pressing his fists against each other. "The only thing I have left is hate. I have carried hatred for the Yankees in my heart for so many years that I can't live any other way, and I don't want to. So, I'll be leaving soon. Maybe this afternoon, maybe tomorrow morning."

"You won't reconsider?" Daed asked. His face held the sorrow that Ruby felt.

Thaddeus shook his head. "There is no place for a man like me among civilized folks."

"We'll send some food with you, enough to carry you through for a while."

The raider nodded his thanks, his face worn and his eyes shadowed.

After they had finished eating, the prayer time was longer than usual. Daed prayed for Thaddeus, asking for God's protection over him as he left Weaver's Creek. Silently, Ruby prayed that he would find peace wherever he was going.

Gideon took the children outside while Ruby and Mamm cleared up after the meal, and Daed went into the front room with Thaddeus.

"Do you think there is anything Daed can say that will make a difference in that man's life?" Ruby asked as she and Mamm washed the dishes.

"If anyone can break through his hatred, Daed can. But only our Lord can change his heart and his mind." Mamm sighed. "The world is very evil, and meeting a man like him reminds me of how that evil destroys lives. I don't know what will become of him."

Mamm went to rest once the kitchen was clean, and Ruby joined Gideon on the back porch. He sat on the step with Daniel, watching the children play under the tree. The playhouse had burned during the fire, but the children had adapted, using sticks laid in the grass for walls and leaves for dishes.

"You are feeling better today, I think," Ruby said.

Daniel sat on his father's lap, his head pillowed on Gideon's chest.

"Every day I feel a bit stronger. I was just thinking about the barn and when we should plan to rebuild it."

"We should do it soon."

Daniel reached for Ruby and she set him on her lap. He yawned and rubbed his eyes.

"You're right, and not only for the good of the farm. The community is unsettled. Folks are worried, and some are even frightened that more raiders could come. They no longer feel safe."

"Is that what you ministers were discussing yesterday when Amos and Wilhelm stopped by?"

Gideon nodded. "They have driven to every home in the area, talking with folks and assuring them that we will recover from this."

Ruby held Daniel close. "I never thought we would be fighting the war here in Weaver's Creek."

"You heard Thaddeus, and he isn't the only one who feels that way. The country is divided with wounds on both sides that may never heal. And hatred has no borders. It spills into every community like a plague. We were foolish to think we were immune to its effects."

"What will happen now?"

Gideon smiled. "We'll have a barn raising. There isn't anything we can do that would heal our church better than working together. Amos is going to announce it tomorrow at next week's Sunday meeting, and we'll plan on having it next Saturday."

"A barn raising! That will be so much fun." She leaned against Gideon's shoulder as he put his arm around her. "I can't remember the last time we had a frolic."

"I thought I might ask Amos to make another announcement." Gideon cleared his throat.

"What would that be?"

"I've had a lot of time to think and pray during the last week as I've been recovering from the fire." He pulled her closer. "I want to keep my promise to Lovinia."

Ruby tried to keep from smiling. "I should

413

probably keep my promise too."

"I knew Lovinia wouldn't want me to marry someone I didn't get along with. Someone I didn't love. But she knew you would be the one for me and for the children."

Daniel's eyes were closed, and Ruby shifted him so that he was lying in her arms.

Gideon brushed the baby's hair off his forehead. "My love for you has grown every day. You are not only beautiful, loving, and wise, but you know me. You understand the grief I still wrestle with and you understand what I have lost. I never thought I would find another woman who I would want to share my life with — every part of my life — but then you came along."

Ruby pulled away from him to gaze into his face. "You don't want someone better? Someone more like my mother?"

He smiled. "You are more like your mother than you think, Ruby Weaver. And I couldn't find a better wife than you if I spent the rest of my life searching. Will you marry me?"

Daniel stretched, screwed his face up as if he was going to cry, then opened his eyes. He grinned, then reached up with one hand and touched Ruby's cheek.

"Mamma, Mamma."

Ruby's eyes filled. "It looks like Daniel has made my decision for me." She looked at Gideon. "How could I refuse him when he asks so sweetly?" She took the baby's hand and kissed it. "I will marry you, Gideon."

"As soon as possible?" His eyebrows peaked as he asked the question, waiting for her answer.

She covered her mouth, trying not to laugh with the joy that coursed through her. "As soon as possible."

With the threat of the raiders gone, the Weaver's Creek community settled back into a peaceful routine. Gideon moved back to his house with the children, and he and Ruby began their practice of having coffee together each morning. And every morning, he felt that their wedding couldn't come soon enough.

The fall harvest was just beginning, and Gideon felt his strength returning as he worked with Samuel and his sons in the fields. The oats were ripe and ready to be shocked, but first, Abraham needed a new barn.

Amos had made the announcement about the barn raising at Sunday's meeting, the day Thaddeus left, and the next Saturday the entire community met at the Weavers' to share in the work. Abraham had contacted Mr. Stevenson, the owner of the nearby sawmill, and traded standing trees from the west end of his land in exchange for lumber. The loads of sawn boards were delivered on Friday.

Saturday morning dawned clear and warm, holding the promise of a hot day ahead. After Gideon did his chores, he carried the pail of milk into the kitchen. Ruby had arrived while he was in the barn and had started a pot of coffee. The tantalizing fragrance drew him in. He looked forward to these quiet moments with her each morning.

"When will you go down to your mamm's?"

Ruby had already poured the coffee and was sitting at the table, waiting for him. Ham sizzled in a pan on the stove.

"Right after breakfast." She smiled at him, ignoring her coffee. "We did the baking and prepared as much as we could yesterday, but we still need to get the chickens ready to roast."

"Other women will bring food too?" Gideon sipped his hot coffee.

"For sure. There will be plenty to feed you hungry men." She sat back in her chair,

416

smiling at him.

"What is it?"

"I was just thinking that in less than two weeks, we'll be doing the same thing, but for a completely different reason."

Gideon settled back in his own chair. Sunlight coming through the kitchen window shone in her hair, and her face was animated with excitement. Her joy in life was contagious.

"Not such a different reason," he said. "Today we're building a barn, set on a solid foundation. On our wedding day, we'll be starting to build our lives together."

"You don't think our marriage will be like a barn, do you?"

He laughed. "Not exactly like a barn, but we'll use loving care in our marriage just as we will with the barn today. And both will be built on an existing foundation. The barn on the packed earth and stone walls that Samuel and I have been repairing this week, and our marriage on the solid foundation of our faith."

Ruby sat up and took his hand in hers. "And remembering those who have given us an example to live by."

He looked into her eyes. "You aren't sorry you agreed to marry me, are you? It isn't too late to back out."

She squeezed his hand. "Oh, I think it is much too late to change my mind." She grinned at him as she went to the stove to turn the ham in the frying pan. "After all, we've already told the children. We can't turn back now, and I certainly don't want to."

She came back to him and placed her hands on his shoulders, and he pulled her down to sit on his lap.

Gideon wrapped his arms around her. "Sometimes I think even the short time we need to wait is too long."

He held her close until they both smelled the ham burning.

Breakfast was a quick meal of ham, eggs, and biscuits, then Ruby filled her little cart with the food and other things she was taking. Gideon carried Daniel down the road to the Weavers' farm while the other children walked ahead of them, pulling the cart. A few wagons had arrived already, and Elizabeth caught up with them just as they crossed the stone bridge.

"Bishop Amos said I can do it," she said, taking Daniel from Gideon.

"I thought he would," Gideon said. He and Wilhelm had put no barriers between Elizabeth and joining the church, but Wilhelm hadn't been sure about Amos's thoughts. The older man had been elected bishop, and he took his now official role seriously. Elizabeth had planned to meet with him on Friday evening.

"I'm glad he did. He said you or Wilhelm can give me instruction for baptism, and then I can join at the fall council meeting in November."

While Ruby and Elizabeth took the children to the house, Gideon walked over to the building site.

"It's a fine morning, isn't it?" Abraham said, shaking his hand.

Samuel and Bram were putting sawhorses together while Peter Lehman walked among the stacks of lumber, jotting notes on a paper in his hand.

"Is Peter the foreman?"

Abraham nodded. "He has a knack for knowing which boards should be used and in which places. He spent last Tuesday at the sawmill, ordering the right length and widths of the lumber, and then he was here before dawn this morning, checking them off his list."

Gideon walked over to the big ridgepoles, lying on the ground next to the smaller poles that would form the frame of the barn. Beyond them were stacks of boards, all sorted by lengths and widths. They would be building a large barn today, a duplicate of the one that had burned nearly two weeks ago.

The rest of the families arrived, and the work started. Gideon strapped his leather tool belt around his waist and joined the team that was framing one of the end walls. Abraham, still recovering from his gunshot wound and loss of blood, pitched in where he could, but left most of the heavy work to the other men.

Halfway through the morning, Gideon straightened from his work and looked around. After all that this community had been through, he was glad to see Amos and Abraham working together to build a window frame, and Levi working next to Samuel. Wilmer Keck worked alongside Caleb Lehman. The young man from Wayne County had told Gideon of his intention to buy a farm in the Weaver's Creek area. His goal was to marry Millie Beiler, and Gideon wished him well.

By the side of the house, the children played together. Roseanna seemed to be in charge of the game of Blind Man's Bluff, but William was helping her with the younger boys. Shrieks of happy laughter drifted on the summer air in between the constant pop of hammers on wood.

Mercy and grace. The Good Lord had extended both to the community in abundance. And with them, peace.

By noon, the walls were all up. Peter laid the ridgepoles himself, fastening the heavy oak beams to the rafters with mortise joints and wooden pins. Supports ran the width of the barn at the roofline, and the frame was done.

The women had been cooking in the Weavers' big kitchen all morning, and now the tables in the yard were laden with roast chicken, mashed potatoes, gravy, sliced tomatoes, and loaves of fresh-baked bread. Another table was filled with pies.

Gideon sat with Levi and Samuel in the shade of the trees that sheltered the house from the summer sun on the south side.

Samuel nudged Gideon's foot with his toe. "Are you ready for the next event in the church?"

Levi leaned toward him. "Your wedding day will be here soon." He grinned at Samuel. "You're sure you want to do this?"

Gideon looked across the grassy space to the tables filled with food. Ruby was in line with Elizabeth and Lydia, filling plates for the children and herself. Sophia tagged along behind her, holding on to her skirt with one hand, while Roseanna kept Ezra busy away from the table. Daniel was content in Elizabeth's arms. As he watched, Ruby bent down to say something to Sophia, putting her free arm around his daughter's shoulders.

He could see Sophia's face, pink from the summer sun and heat of the day, her fine blonde hair plastered to her damp forehead where it had escaped her kapp. She smiled up at Ruby, her eyes shining with happiness and love, and Ruby gave her a quick kiss before turning back to the table. His heart filled.

"Don't worry, Levi." His voice caught, and he cleared his throat. "I have no second thoughts. I'm looking forward to spending the rest of my days here in Weaver's Creek with Ruby by my side."

ACKNOWLEDGMENTS

As each book travels the road from my imagination to the copy you hold in your hands, I must point the way to the true geniuses behind the finished product.

Thank you to the editors and staff at Revell and Baker Publishing Group for the work they do in editing, marketing, typesetting, proofreading . . . the list of tasks they accomplish is staggering. I love working with you all!

I also need to thank my dear husband who suffers through my deadlines as much as I do. I spend more time at my computer than with him sometimes, but we will take that hike in the hills soon . . .

And the biggest thank-you goes to my lord. Without him, I would be less than nothing. A clanging cymbal in a world of chaos. He brings order to my thoughts and my words, for my everlasting good and his own glory.

ABOUT THE AUTHOR

Jan Drexler brings a unique understanding of Amish traditions and beliefs to her writing. Her ancestors were among the first Amish, Mennonite, and Brethren immigrants to Pennsylvania in the 1700s, and their experiences are the inspiration for her stories. Jan lives in the Black Hills of South Dakota with her husband, where she enjoys hiking and spending time with her expanding family. She is the author of several Love Inspired historical novels, as well as *Hannah's Choice, Mattie's Pledge* (a 2017 Holt Medallion finalist), and *Naomi's Hope.*

The employees of Thorndike Press hope you have enjoyed this Large Print book. All our Thorndike, Wheeler, and Kennebec Large Print titles are designed for easy reading, and all our books are made to last. Other Thorndike Press Large Print books are available at your library, through selected bookstores, or directly from us.

For information about titles, please call:
(800) 223-1244

or visit our website at:
gale.com/thorndike

To share your comments, please write:

Publisher
Thorndike Press
10 Water St., Suite 310
Waterville, ME 04901